THE PRICE OF PASSION

Angie Bayliss

Cover design by: Canva

To all my girls...you know who you are!
Especially you Paula!

CONTENTS

CHAPTER ONE

Discovering her boyfriend in bed with another woman was the perfect excuse for Kate Newman to go out and get completely plastered. Emptying the entire contents of her stomach into the toilet however, wasn't exactly the way she'd planned to end the evening, especially seeing as that toilet was located in the Ladies Room of Coco's, one of the trendiest nightclubs in town.

She'd been heaving her guts up now for the last ten minutes. Wrapped around the toilet bowl, hygiene wasn't uppermost in her mind and she clung on for dear life as she brought up the remains of the chicken fajita she'd eaten for dinner four long hours ago.

"You alright in there?" yelled a voice from the other side of the cubicle door.

Clare, her older sister by three years, was equally as pissed but ten times more capable of holding her drink and was expressing concern that quite frankly was a little too much, a little too late. She'd been plying Kate with one drink after another all night; if she hadn't wanted her to get so drunk, she should've made her drink lemonade. As it was, they'd worked their way through the entire cocktail menu and chased each drink with a shot of Sambuca. Not the most sensible of choices but who cared about that when they were drowning their sorrows?

Kate flushed the lever and watched as the mixture of red peppers and chicken was sucked into the vortex of swirling water and disappeared forever.

"I'm good, I'm just coming out."

The image that greeted her when she peered into the mirror made her wince. If the fashion police were on duty she'd be arrested, tossed in a cell and the key thrown away forever. Her face was a mess of smudged mascara and watery eyes and she was in desperate need of a comb, not that there was much point now. She'd never considered herself to be a girlie girl and at ten past one in the morning, nothing short of a miracle was going to make her look any better. She stuck her head under the faucet and rinsed her mouth out then pushed her fingers through her long, unruly curly hair.

There, she thought with a shrug, that would just have to do.

Groups of drunken people were huddled together making it near on impossible to get to the bar but Megan, Kate's best friend and co-conspirator in the evenings shenanigans, was an expert navigator and weaved them in and out of the mass of sweaty bodies until they finally arrived at the bar unscathed and none the worse for wear.

"Three Jäger bombs please Billy," said Meg shamelessly to the bartender, throwing him a sexy wink and a pout of her lips which had just been newly smothered in hot pink lipstick.

Billy rolled his eyes; it was a bad idea. Knowing that he should refuse to serve them but not relishing the mouthful he'd get from his boss, he dutifully prepared the drinks and placed them on the bar. He mentally added the cost to the exorbitant bill the girls had run up already tonight then watched as one by one, they necked them back. All except for Kate, who missed her mouth completely and tipped the deadly concoction of Red Bull and Jägermeister down the front of her dress.

"Oi, Oi," jeered the man standing next to her, openly admiring the way the liquid was dripping down onto her cleavage. "Come here sweetheart, let me help you."

Kate slapped his hand away playfully but secretly she loved the attention. After the trauma of discovering Mark in bed with another woman any interest was welcome, even if that interest was coming from a man who was clearly as drunk as she was.

"I've seen you in here before haven't I?" The man draped his arm casually around her shoulder and spoke directly to her tits which were ultra-enhanced by the push up bra she was wearing. Kate thought that maybe she recognised him too but everything was happening in a blur and she was too drunk to tell.

"It's Kelly isn't it?"

"Kate," she giggled.

"That's right. Kate." He bent his head to hers and their foreheads touched. "What d'ya say you and me get out of here?"

"Hands off, dipshit," boomed a loud voice from out of nowhere. Jason Wright, the club's owner and Clare's fiancé, removed the offending arm from around Kate's shoulder and shoved it, and the body attached to it, into a group of men who jeered and cursed at the physical interruption. One of the men, a salubrious looking type in a white shirt and tie, turned angrily, fully intending to give Jason a piece of his mind but the minute he clocked his stocky rugby player physique and the 'don't fuck with me' expression on his face he quickly changed his mind. Kate however wasn't as easily deterred.

"What did you do that for you idiot? I was well in there."

"Oh don't make me laugh," grunted Jason with a bemused grin. "Even you can't be that desperate."

He was severely protective of the woman who was going to become his sister-in-law in a few months' time and wasn't about to let her be taken advantage of by some dickhead who was too pissed to stand up properly. Looking at the three drunken women before him he shook his head sadly.

"Jesus, look at the state of you lot. What have you been drinking?" He held up his hand. "Second thoughts, don't answer that, I'm not sure I want to know. I'm gonna have to review the free drinks rule if you're going to keep abusing it like this. You do realise you've got vomit in your hair?" he said to Kate. "I think it's time to call it a night, love."

Kate felt her stomach churn. She burped and held her hand to her head. "I think I'm going to be sick."

Jason turned to Clare and gave her a peck on the cheek. "Take her home and for fuck's sake, make sure she doesn't throw up all over my carpet."

Jason secured the nights' takings in the safe in his office. It was almost half past two in the morning and the last of the revellers had finally left, having been not so gently persuaded to leave by the club's security staff. It had been a good night. The tills were overflowing with cash and he knew it would be the same tomorrow night. The club attracted the right kind of clientele and it was situated alongside several bars, all of which conveniently closed at eleven so all Jason had to do was sit back and watch the crowds (and the cash) roll in.

With all the lights switched on the place looked as if it had been hit by a bomb. Glasses, bottles and chairs were strewn everywhere and tables were littered with rubbish and empty bottles. Not that Jason was worried; he knew the cleaners would have it looking spotless again before opening time that night. He wiped over an area of the bar and produced two clean glasses which he filled with whiskey and passed one to the man sitting patiently on the bar-stool in front of him.

Charlie Mortimer was Jason's oldest friend. They had grown up together on the same council estate in London and had known each other for almost all of their thirty-seven years. Taller than Jason by at least two inches and outweighing him by at least a stone, most of which was muscle, Charlie was blatantly flouting the no-smoking rule and was leisurely puffing on a large Cuban cigar. He was expensively dressed; his made to measure Armani jacket fitted perfectly over his broad shoulders and the sloping tapered edges of his white shirt created a cinching effect, emphasising his muscular physique. He had dark hair, brown eyes and was sporting an inch of designer stubble. The only imperfection on an otherwise perfect face was a slightly crooked nose, broken three years earlier in a pub brawl and not reset due to Charlie's aversion of hospitals.

"It's so good to see you mate," said Jason as he raised his glass in salute. "What the bloody hell are you doing back in rainy old England?"

"I fancied a break, you know how it is."

Charlie's deep voice still held the faint trace of a London accent which had never left him despite not having lived there for some years. Relocating to Spain two years ago he had opened a trendy music bar in Marbella which was where he now spent most of his time, only returning to England when business commitments forced him to.

"I thought your life was one permanent break."

"It is," he said with a smile. "But this place is still fucking wicked."

"It's a lot of work mate but then you already know that."

Charlie did know. He'd put up half the money when the previous owner had dropped dead of a heart attack at the tender age of thirty-five. Not wanting the club to fall into the hands of a stranger, he and Jason had jointly invested their cash and spent a few years running it together. These days however, Charlie was more of a silent partner and left the overseeing of the club to Jason, an arrangement that suited them both.

"So when are you coming out to visit me then? The renovation work on the villa's all finished now, you should see it."

"I'd love to," answered Jason truthfully. "There's nothing more I could do with right now than a holiday."

"Then what's stopping you? We could spend a few days relaxing on the beach, hit the bars, pull a few birds. It'd be just like the old days."

Jason pulled a face. "Do you really think Clare's going to let me loose on the Med with you? You forget how well she knows you. Besides I'm getting too old for all of that and so are you mate."

"Tell me about it," agreed Charlie with a nod of the head. "I can't remember where I am half the time or whose bed I'm waking up in."

"Still shagging anything with a pulse then?"

"You know me, not so young but definitely still free and single. Speaking of which, are you and Clare still planning on tying the knot?"

"You're not trying to get out of being my Best Man, are you?"

"Wouldn't miss it for the world mate. Although you know my thoughts on the subject. Being tied down for the rest of your life with one woman, I couldn't think of anything worse."

"Are you seriously telling me that no one's brought you to your knees yet?"

"Not a chance mate and to be honest, I can do without the hassle. I've got enough to deal with as it is. I'm having trouble with Mickey."

Jason wasn't in the least surprised. Mickey had always been a fucking liability. "I don't know why you're still putting up with him."

"You know why," said Charlie in a tone that suggested he didn't want to talk about it. Fleeing to Marbella after serving a three-year sentence for assault, Mickey's failure to check in with his Parole Officer had resulted in a warrant being issued for his arrest. Not that Mickey gave a flying fuck. Cocooned in sunny Spain being bankrolled by Charlie was the perfect life for a loser like him. And Charlie, bound by some blinding sense of loyalty that Jason would never understand, was allowing himself to be well and truly mugged off.

"Come on then," said Jason, not wanting to know but feeling the need to ask anyway. "What's he got himself into now?"

"He's using again," Charlie admitted with a sigh. "He spends most of the time doing smack and kicking the shit out of people. You know me mate, I don't do drugs, I never have. Seen too many people go down that road and it never leads to paradise."

"Well you always knew he was a fucking headcase, why d'you think they locked him up in the first place?" Jason topped up both of their drinks. "But that's enough about that fucker, tell me what you've been up to. You still robbing armoured trucks?"

Charlie shrugged; he made no apologies for the life he led and wasn't about to start now. He'd had a rough childhood but in the part of London where he'd grown up that was the norm. Events had come to a head on the night of his seventeenth birthday when his father, returning from an all-day bender at the pub, had knocked ten barrels of shit out of his mother in a vicious unprovoked attack, one of the many that had been witnessed by Charlie and his two brothers over the years. Being the eldest and regarding himself as the real man of the house, Charlie had taken a breadknife and stabbed his old man in the stomach. The bastard deserved it, not that the police saw it that way. The Mortimer boys were the bane of the local constabulary's life. They'd been running wild on the estate for years causing them no end of grief, especially Charlie who always seemed to be at the centre of any trouble. Deciding it was time for a lesson to be taught, the incident resulted in him being awarded a two-year stint in a Young Offenders institution.

Charlie didn't dwell on it, he wasn't the type, but his sentence didn't have the effect the authorities hoped it might. Whilst serving his time Charlie be-friended the cocky son of a man who ran a protec-tion racket up north and upon his release relocated to Manchester and became the newest enforcer for the Harris family; a notorious group of uncles, cousins and brothers who provided protection for a string of bars and private businesses.

Physically Charlie fitted the bill; he was a big man and wasn't afraid of a fight. His sheer physical presence was deterrent enough to persuade most people to part with their money but when he was ordered to break the legs of a barmaid for not handing over three hundred pounds, Charlie seriously began to question his career choice.

"My days of running around with a sawn-off and scaring the shit out of people are long gone. Who needs to risk being shot at when you can just use this," he said tapping his head, "and these?" He held up his hands and wiggled his fingers. "I've got Jack on the payroll now and he's a computer fucking genius. He can wreak more havoc with the touch of a few buttons than I ever could with a shooter. It's the perfect set-up. He infiltrates these multi-million-pound companies, finds a back door into their systems and all they have to do is pay a very reasonable fee to regain control."

"Cyber ransom you mean? Jesus mate, I hope you know what you're doing. They come down really hard on that stuff you know. If you get caught you'll get a longer stretch than you would for murder."

Charlie gave Jason an aloof smile. "I'm not planning on getting caught. Besides, I've got a job coming up that could see me out of the game for good. What do you remember about Declan Connors?"

"That mad Irish bastard? What the hell do you want to get hooked up with him for?"

"He's planning a job on a security depot in Brighton. The return's enough for me to retire for good. And with the money I can pay Mickey off once and for all."

"You sure that's wise? Won't he just take the money and stuff it up his nose?"

"Well that's up to him but at least I'll have paid my dues. I won't feel responsible for him any longer."

"You never were anyway, it's only your warped sense of loyalty that's kept him hanging around for so long. Anyone else would've seen him off years ago. But it seems you've got it all figured out."

"If only." Charlie took a gulp of his drink. "There's just one small problem. Declan's now married to the delightful Francesca."

"Francesca?" Jason's glass froze in his hand. "As in your ex-wife Francesca?"

"The one and only."

Jason whistled. "Shit Charlie, that sounds like a whole lot of trouble to me."

"Tell me about it. Declan's a jealous fucker and doesn't want me anywhere near her. Says he doesn't trust me around her, I mean come on, it's bloody ridiculous. We were married for five minutes and it was a total disaster. Plus, it was years ago. But he's got it into his head that there's still something between us."

"And is there?"

"No way. The minute I slipped the ring on her finger I knew I'd made the biggest mistake of my life."

"So how are you going to get around that then?"

"Dunno mate, but the job's worth too much money to pass up. You haven't got any ideas have you, I'm all out?"

Always a fast thinker, Jason considered the problem and had a solution in less than a minute. It wasn't perfect by any means but it might help. "What you need is a wife of your own," he stated matter-of-factly. "That way Declan wouldn't have anything to be jealous about, would he?"

"Being married once was enough for me thanks, I'm never doing that again."

"You're missing the point. You wouldn't actually *have* to get married; it'd be a business arrangement. Find someone to pretend to be your wife, pay her a shedload of cash and move her into your villa. Act the part, convince Declan you're not interested in Francesca which seeing as you aren't shouldn't be a problem. Then, when the deal's done, your wife moves out and you tell everyone you've filed for a quickie divorce."

Charlie shook his head. "Nah mate, that'd never work."

"Course it would and if this job's worth as much money as you say it is, then it's got to be worth a try." Yes, it was a bit extreme but Jason could see that Charlie was considering it.

"I like the idea, I really do, but here's the problem. I know a lot of women and they're alright for a quick shag but as for actually living with one? I'm not sure

I could do it."

"You make it sound like a death sentence."

"Not for you maybe but for me, definitely."

"For fuck's sake Charlie, it'd only be for a few weeks. All you'd need to do is keep up appearances and convince everyone you're a pair of newly-weds. Surely even you could manage that? The word would get back to Declan soon enough."

"Alright then, so let's say that I could, who would I get to do it? Finding someone to keep a secret is a massive problem. There isn't a bird in a ten-mile radius that can keep her legs closed, let alone her mouth. Besides, everybody knows me anyway so it'd have to be some random unknown."

"Well like I said," said Jason, swigging back his drink. "It's something for you to think about. Look mate I hate to break up the party but I need to make tracks. It's been a busy night and I promised Clare I wouldn't be too late."

Charlie downed the last of his drink. "Sure mate, no problem."

"Hey," said Jason, his eyes wide as another idea sprang to mind. "Maybe she knows someone who'd be up for some cash and a few week's holiday in the sun."

"Come off it, you know she hates my guts. She won't want me corrupting any of her friends, will she?"

"She doesn't hate you. It's only *what* you do that she disapproves of."

They both stood and Charlie stubbed his cigar into

his empty glass. "Well it's been great mate," he said, pulling on his jacket. "I'll think about it, okay? And don't forget, you only need to call if you want to come out."

"I know and I'll try, I promise. When are you leaving to go back?"

"Another week yet. Got some family stuff to take care of before I go."

They said their goodbyes and Jason waved as Charlie jumped in a taxi and disappeared into the night. He locked the doors and activated the alarm system and satisfied that the place was secure, he exited through the rear entrance.

Finding Kate snoring like a pig on his sofa when he arrived home, his brain went into overdrive. He reached into his pocket and pulled out his phone, a wicked smile forming across his face.

Maybe, just maybe, he might have the solution to all of their problems.

CHAPTER TWO

Kate was still feeling the sickening effects of the alcohol she'd drunk on Saturday night. Two or even three-day hangovers were a usual occurrence for her and despite knowing that the most sensible thing to do would be to give up drinking altogether, she just couldn't do it.

Even if the effects seemed to be more profound on her than they were on anybody else.

She glanced at her watch and realised that there were still seven more hours to go until she could go home and crawl into bed. It was her first day back at work in over a week and she was only here because the company's stringent rules dictated she could self-certify sickness for just seven days. Unfortunately the powers that be didn't recognise the medical phenomenon known as being cheated on by one's boyfriend so she'd had no option but to return to work or risk losing her pay.

To add to her trauma her cheating boyfriend was the Finance Director, her direct boss and he was due in the office at any moment. Not for the first time she cursed her complete stupidity in getting involved with somebody at work but Mark's baby blue eyes and cute dimpled smile had bowled her over the moment she'd met him. They'd had an instant connection that quickly developed into more than just a fling and within a year they'd bought a house together. There had been absolutely no doubt in Kate's mind that one day they'd get married and start a family.

And then Mark had gone and fucked it all up.

Her mind drifted back to the image that she feared would be imprinted on her brain forever. Lying in the super king-size bed that had cost her almost a month's wages, Mark had been straddled by a busty blonde who was riding him with an enthusiasm that rivalled that of a prize-winning jockey powering his horse on to become the next Grand National winner. It had been a sobering experience, one she was sure she would never forget. And no matter how much grovelling and apologising he'd done since, one that she would never forgive him for either.

She took her frustration out on the piece of paper in front of her and scrunched it up into a ball before launching it headlong into the bin. It was hard to concentrate on anything now that she had that picture in her head. Her nerves at seeing Mark again were making her stomach churn and she actually thought she was going to be sick.

And that was when she saw him.

Trailing the intoxicating scent of Paco Rabanne in

his wake, Mark blew through the office like a tornado. His dark grey suit coupled with the pink Ralph Lauren shirt she'd brought him for his birthday made him look both powerful and handsome and their eyes locked over her desk partition just long enough for her to feel as though she'd been sucker punched. Kate looked away first, the exchange unbearable, and tried to stop her hands from shaking. She mentally kicked herself; being at work with him was going to make everything so much harder. Why hadn't she returned at least one of his phone calls and spared herself the embarrassing ordeal of having to face him here?

Several of her colleagues guessed that a drama was about to unfold and she braced herself, aware that she was going to become the subject of whispered voices and prying eyes. She supposed she'd do the same if she was in their position. After all, nothing set the rumour mill alight like an office scandal.

Reluctantly she rose from her seat; she needed to get this over with and the sooner the better. She set off on the walk of shame to Mark's office. It was just as well her feet knew the way because her head was all over the place. She could feel the intense heat of probing eyes and knew for certain that every step she took was being scrutinised. Her relationship with Mark had never been a secret but people just loved to gossip and a spectacular showdown between the Finance Director and the member of staff he was shagging was about to provide them with the most exciting Monday morning they'd ever had.

A small crowd had gathered at the photocopier so Kate did an impromptu U-turn and took an alternative route. It wasn't the most direct way but she was trying to be as inconspicuous as possible. When she reached his office she took a deep breath in, summoning a strength she wasn't sure she had. Then with shaking hands she turned the handle and proceeded inside.

The sun was streaming in through blinds that weren't fully closed and cast strobes of light across the room, causing her to blink rapidly as her eyes focused. Sitting in an executive leather chair behind a shiny walnut desk was Mark. Holding a Starbucks coffee cup in one hand and a manilla folder in the other he glanced up, momentarily startled by the interruption. When he realised who was standing in front of him, he immediately tossed the folder down onto the desk and jumped to his feet.

"I don't think we should do this here. This is neither the time or the place." He hurried to the door to ensure it was closed, clearly not wanting anyone to overhear their conversation.

Kate tilted her head to one side. "You think I've come to tell you what an arsehole you are? Don't worry Mark I think we've established that already."

He pointed to the empty chair in front of his desk. "You'd better sit down then."

Kate didn't want to sit down. She wanted to take the chair and throw it at him. When she didn't move he ran a frustrated hand through his hair. "I don't know what you're expecting me to say. It's been over a week and I've tried to contact you a hundred times. Why haven't you been answering my calls? I've been going out of my mind here."

"*You've* been going out of your mind? Don't make me laugh."

"Look Kate, I've made a terrible mistake. Don't you think I know that? What I've done is unforgivable but that doesn't mean it has to be over between us. I want to put it all in the past and move forward and I know you want to do the same. People make mistakes Kate, it's human nature. We need to put it behind us and move on so just tell me what you want me to do."

"It's too late for that."

"Of course it isn't. Lots of relationships go through something like this and come out alright in the end."

Kate shook her head in disbelief. He just didn't get it. There was no way forward, no way out of the mess he had created and if he thought there was, then he was an idiot. "Relationships are built on love and trust Mark. One can't exist without the other. When the trust is gone there's nothing left. I just wish I knew why you did it," she added, more for her own benefit than for his. "I thought we were happy."

"We *were* happy and we can be again."

"Are you in love with her?"

Mark looked genuinely surprised by the question. "No of course not, don't be ridiculous. I'm in love with you. It was just sex, that's all."

Kate wanted to laugh; men had such a funny idea

of love and sex. She was certain that sex education for boys consisted of one very simple lesson at school; shag whoever you like and don't worry about the consequences. Maybe she should have been a man, it would certainly make things a lot less complicated.

"So if it was just sex and it didn't mean anything why did you do it?"

"I don't know why, I guess I was just flattered."

"Oh poor you," she said with a roll of her eyes. "Wasn't I paying you enough attention?"

He dragged an exasperated hand through his hair, clearly uncomfortable with this line of questioning but she had only just started. There was one more question on her mind and she wasn't leaving until she got an answer.

"Who was she Mark?"

A tiny bead of perspiration formed on his forehead and he wiped it away with the back of his hand.

"I don't see what difference that makes. It doesn't matter who she was."

Kate tried to hold herself together, despite wanting to claw his eyes out. "It matters to me."

Mark was uncomfortable and it showed. His eyes darted around the room and he began to get fidgety. And when he spoke she had to strain her ears to hear him.

"If you must know, it was Tina."

"Tina!" shrieked Kate, her remaining restraint finally evaporating. It was the ultimate betrayal. Mark had been seeing Tina when they'd first met and he had broken off their relationship to be with Kate. She knew she shouldn't have been surprised, after all, once a cheater always a cheater but it still hurt nonetheless. She shook her head in despair. "I don't believe this." She went to leave the room but Mark grabbed her arm and held her back.

"Kate, wait."

"Take your hands off me!" She pulled her arm free and slapped him across the face. "How could you?"

"Ow, that hurt," he groaned as he rubbed his cheek. "And for crying out loud, keep your bloody voice down. You're going to make a complete fool of yourself in front of everyone."

"You've already done that for me," she said, choking back a tear she refused point blank to shed. Two of her colleagues were hovering outside the office door and as she opened it they scampered away. She knew they'd heard every single word of their conversation but she was now past the point of caring. She turned back to Mark who was gaping at her, his mouth wide open.

"I can't believe I was stupid enough to get involved with you," she shouted, just loud enough to ensure that everybody could hear. "You're a lying cheating bastard and you make me sick. In fact, I never want to see you again so why don't you take your job and shove it up your arse."

There was a collaborative sigh as every person in the vicinity stopped working and stared at her. Her cheeks flushed red but she didn't care; it wasn't the first time she'd been the subject of office gossip since her relationship with Mark had gone public.

"Oh, and one last thing," she shouted as she turned on her heels. "You were a totally crap shag."

After a week of moping around, Kate knew she ought to try and pull herself together but it was hard; she'd wasted eighteen months of her life with Mark and the humiliation of being cheated on was still burning a red-hot hole right through her. He'd tried several times to call her and in the end, she'd stopped listening to his messages. They were all the same; he was sorry, he loved her and he wanted her to come home. It was boring.

Dealing with Mark's betrayal was only one of the problems she now faced. Her impulsive outburst meant she had to find another job. Living with Clare and Jason suited her for now but it was only a temporary measure. She was desperate to find a place of her own, especially as they were getting married soon and would need their own space. But all of her money was tied up in the house she'd purchased with Mark and it would be months before he either bought her out or the property was sold. She was stuck in a rut. She had no money and no job and at twenty-nine years old, it wasn't exactly where she'd expected her life to be.

Clare tried several times to persuade her to work some shifts at Coco's; they were always in need of bar staff but Kate wasn't that keen. Late nights and long hours on her feet was too much of a change from spending eight hours a day lounging in an executive, reclining ergonomic office chair but in the end she relented. She needed the cash. But when she wasn't working at the club she searched the internet for jobs. There wasn't a lot available unless she considered a career change but being employed as a delivery driver for a supermarket chain or delivering takeaways on a moped wasn't exactly a step up the corporate ladder.

As a thank you for letting her move in with them, Kate decided that she would cook Sunday lunch. Jason and Clare had a rare day off work together and she wanted to impress them with her culinary skills. She was pretty good, even if she did say so herself. She set about preparing the meat and vegetables, ensuring that the beef was cooked on low following instructions she'd downloaded from a Google recipe when Mark's parents had come for dinner last year. She'd perfected the marinade and was certain it would turn out just as delicious as it had been then.

She'd just drizzled the potatoes with goose fat and popped them into the oven when she decided to take a quick shower. She hadn't bothered getting dressed (what was the point when she wasn't going anywhere?) and was still wearing the pyjama bottoms she'd slept in. A quick soaping of her body took only a few minutes and after drying herself she pulled on the only clothes she could find that didn't require ironing. She wondered into the living room wearing an old denim skirt and a pale pink tee shirt. Her hair was pinned up on the top of her head in a messy bun and her face was devoid of any make-up. A decision she seriously regretted when she caught sight of the man sitting on the sofa.

Dangerously gorgeous, he had jet black hair, a close-cropped beard and deep, dark brown eyes that almost made her hyperventilate. His skin was heavily tanned and when he smiled, he revealed a set of teeth so white, they had to have been featured in their own toothpaste ad. She spotted the Rolex on his wrist as he stood up and held out a hand as big as a shovel.

"You must be Kate," he said in a deep sexy voice that matched his looks perfectly. They shook hands; he had a firm grip and didn't seem to be in any hurry to let go. "I'm Charlie. Thanks for inviting me to dinner."

Kate didn't know she had. And nobody had mentioned that they were expecting company either. She checked out his arms and the hulking muscles that clung to the tight-fitted white tee shirt he wore and tried not to be too impressed. But he was so fit and tanned he looked like Adonis.

"I'm going home tomorrow," he continued, their hands still connected. "And this is my last chance to catch up with Jason."

If it wasn't for his London accent, Kate could have sworn that home was LA or some glamorous paradise island like the Bahamas. Curiosity got the better of her and she casually asked, "Where's home?"

"Marbella," he said with a smile. "I have a bar there."

Well that explains everything, thought Kate disappointedly. She pulled her hand away sharply; the man standing before her was nothing more than a smooth talking, designer wearing, gorgeous looking playboy who cavorted on the sandy shores of the Mediterranean entertaining the bored but glamourous housewives of the Costa Del Sol.

"Oh good, you two have met at last." Jason walked into the room holding two beers. Kate, keen to escape the confines of their good-looking dinner guest, made a hasty retreat to the kitchen. She caught Clare lifting the lid of one of the boiling saucepans and swiped her on the arm with a tea towel.

"Hands off, I'm cooking remember? And who the hell is Charlie and why didn't you tell me he was coming for dinner?"

Clare looked a little cagey. "You remember Charlie, don't you? He owns the club with Jason."

Kate shook her head; she would definitely have remembered *him*.

"Well he's here for dinner and he's one of Jason's oldest friends so be nice."

"I'm always nice," said Kate feeling mildly offended. "I just wish you'd have told me. There's not going to be enough food now."

"Course there is, have you seen how much you've done? We could invite the whole street for dinner and there'd still be plenty to go round."

Charlie put his knife and fork down onto his empty

plate with a crash. "That was great," he said enthusiastically. "I can't remember the last time I tasted food like this."

Kate, oblivious to the compliment, had just spent the last hour listening to him bragging about his bar and the notorious Marbella clientele that drank there and quite honestly, she'd had enough. He'd done nothing but annoy the hell out of her and was, in fact, getting right on her nerves. Just because Jason and Clare wanted to listen to his exaggerated stories didn't mean she wanted to hear them too. His overinflated ego needed deflating and she was in the right mood to do it.

"Don't they have food in Marbella then?" she asked tartly, determined to make him aware of her feelings but if he picked up on her sarcasm, he didn't say so. Instead he raised his beer and gave her a smile.

"Some of the best Michelin Star restaurants around actually but you can't beat a proper home cooked roast. Bloody lovely."

"So, what are you doing here then? If it's all so bloody wonderful in Marbella, why have you come back?" She ignored the kick to her shin that Clare gave her under the table and took a large slug of red wine.

"I'm only back for a holiday. Had a few things I needed to sort out, family stuff mainly." Whether he was being vague or not she wasn't sure but he was clearly an expert at changing the subject because in his next breath, he asked her what she did for a living.

"Fuck all at the moment," quipped Jason before she had the chance to answer for herself. "She got the sack last week."

"Really?" said Charlie, appearing genuinely intrigued. "Why was that, then?"

"She was shagging the boss."

Charlie roared with laughter. "Well you obviously weren't very good at it."

Clare and Jason laughed too. Kate didn't think it was very funny and was really starting to get pissed off. Irritated by his cheap joke she got to her feet; she had to leave the table before she stabbed him with her fork.

"Not that it's any of your business but if you must know, I wasn't sacked, I quit."

"Okay darlin', whatever you say."

Kate stomped off to the kitchen. It was a mess; there wasn't a surface anywhere that wasn't covered in saucepans or dirty dishes. Surveying the carnage, she realised she must've used every utensil in the house. Retrieving another bottle of red from the wine rack she knew she'd have the hangover from hell tomorrow. Not that she cared, but just as she popped the cork Clare came up behind her.

"What the hell's got into you?" she hissed, holding a stack of empty dinner plates in her hands. "You're being really rude."

"I don't like him," said Kate simply.

"Because he's rich and gorgeous?"

"No, because he's a man and they're all wankers. He's been banging on about how wonderful he is all day."

"Give him a break Kate, he's just trying to be nice. Seriously, you need to lighten up, I've never known you like this before. He's a lovely guy, you should get to know him."

"No thank you, I'm not interested."

"Well you'd better behave yourself," warned Clare. "He's Jason's oldest friend and he's going to be Best Man at our wedding."

Great, thought Kate with a sigh. Can't wait for that.

The moment the men were alone Charlie turned to Jason with a bemused expression on his face. "What's her problem then? Is she always so fucking hostile?"

Jason laughed. "It could be that she just doesn't like you which knowing you as I do I completely understand or it could be that she wants to shag you. Either way you're screwed mate."

"You're definitely not wrong there. From the looks she's been throwing my way I think she wants to murder me. I'm just waiting for the knife to come out."

"Take no notice mate, she's been in a mood since she caught her boyfriend screwing his ex." Jason leant in close to ensure he wasn't overheard. "Between you and me he was a fucking tosser anyway. Still, I was this close to giving him a slap." He held his thumb and forefinger an inch apart in an effort to visualise his point. "You don't fancy going round there and giving him a thump, do you?"

"I don't do that anymore, remember? But seeing as it's you, I'd be happy to oblige."

Kate returned to the room and they both stopped talking. She was carrying a chocolate mousse and Charlie was relieved when she placed it down onto the table. For one awful moment, he thought she was going to throw it at him. As she sat back down he allowed himself the liberty of checking her out. Behind the shit attitude she was actually very pretty. She had smooth pale skin and huge green eyes and of course there were those gorgeous tits. He was an expert and could see that they were real, not an ounce of silicone holding them up. She wasn't bad at all really; he'd definitely shagged a lot worse.

She dolloped a spoonful of chocolate mousse into a bowl and thrust it at him. Accustomed to women falling at his feet, her hostility towards him was quite amusing. In fact, the more he sensed her disapproval of him, the more he felt the urge to play along. And he knew exactly how to wind her up.

"Jason tells me you've been working at the club." He leant back in his chair, not taking his eyes off her. "You do realise that it's my club too right so technically that makes me your boss. And just so we're clear, you won't get sacked for shagging me."

Her face was a picture. In fact he'd never seen anyone go so red. A deep beetroot colour crept up from her neck all the way to her cheeks and her mouth was poised in the open position.

"Relax," he laughed, barely able to control himself. "I'm only messing with you." Besides, he wanted to eat the rest of his chocolate mousse. It was really thick and creamy, he'd never tasted anything like it. "Did you make this?" he asked, brandishing his spoon at her. "It's incredible."

"Try not to choke on it."

After dessert the table was cleared and Jason opened a bottle of brandy. Charlie was relieved when Kate disappeared into the kitchen, he'd spent far too much time staring at her tits.

"Thanks for inviting me over mate, it was just what I needed." He took a sip of brandy and savoured the burn as it trickled down his throat. He was a heavy drinker, it went with the territory of owning a bar. The downside was that he had to work out a lot to keep himself in shape, not that that was a problem now his gym was up and running in the basement of his villa. Equipped with weights, a rowing machine, treadmill and bench press he knew he was definitely going to have to put in some time when he got home.

He and Jason chatted easily, their voices rising steadily to compensate for the loud clanging in the kitchen; it sounded like all hell was breaking loose. They exchanged glances when a loud "fuck" reverberated through the walls and both men braced themselves as something crashed loudly onto the floor.

"Christ mate," laughed Charlie. "It's like a fucking war zone. We're gonna have to take cover in a minute."

Kate followed Clare into the dining room and poured herself another drink. She was already feeling fuzzy but needed the alcohol in her system to tolerate the smartass comments from their very annoying dinner guest. She couldn't put her finger on it but something about him rubbed her up the wrong way. It must be because she was anti-men at the moment she figured and hated them all.

Even the hot, gorgeous ones.

"So Charlie," said Clare taking her place next to Kate at the table. "Jason tells me you're looking for a wife."

Kate almost spat out her wine. "You're getting married?" What woman in her right mind would put up with him?

"Not a real wife, idiot," said Jason, looking at her as if she was stupid. "Just somebody to pretend to be his wife."

Suddenly Charlie slapped his forehead with the palm of his hand. "I don't believe it! That's what this is all about, isn't it? How can I be so bloody stupid?" He looked at Kate and shook his head. "I appreciate the gesture mate I really do, but I don't think it's going to work."

"Course it will," insisted Jason. "It's perfect."

Charlie placed one long leg over the other, his ankle now resting on his knee. "You sly bastard. You had this all planned out, didn't you?"

"Had what planned out?" asked Kate, completely confused. She turned to Clare for clarification but her sister suddenly developed an in-depth interest in her wine glass and wasn't saying anything.

"Will someone please tell me what's going on?"

"Charlie's setting up a new business venture and needs a wife as part of the deal," announced Jason as though it was the most natural thing in the world.

"What kind of business venture requires a wife?" asked Kate sceptically. "Sounds well dodgy to me. Good luck, I hope you find someone who'll put up with you!"

"And that's exactly where you come in," said Jason, leaning back into his chair and folding his arms across his chest.

Reality suddenly dawning on her, the glass of wine she was holding almost slipped through her fingers. "You've got to be joking?"

"It's a really good idea, Kate," insisted Jason. "You need a job and he'll pay you loads of money."

"Huh!" she snorted. "I'm not that desperate!"

"Neither am I, darlin'," agreed Charlie, a bit too quickly for Kate's liking.

"Oh come on you two," said Jason. "This is an absolute brilliant idea."

"It's a stupid idea," scoffed Kate sourly.

Charlie downed his brandy and held out his glass for a refill. Jason topped him up and he drank half of that too. "You're right," he agreed. "It's a stupid idea. It'd never work anyway."

Kate was angered beyond belief. If anyone was going to dismiss the idea it was going to be her, not Mr Good Looking and Annoying here. "Oh I get it.

You don't think I'm good enough for you?"

"I don't even think you like me."

"You're right, I don't, but how much money are we talking about?"

Charlie shrugged. "How much do you want?"

"Well that depends. I'm very expensive."

His eyes fell to her creased tee-shirt and he smirked. "I can see that darlin'."

"I didn't get home until half past two this morning after working all night in *your* bloody club," she snapped defensively. "If you must know, I'm knackered."

"Yeah? It shows."

If he was trying to dissuade her from accepting Jason's so-called brilliant idea he was going the wrong way about it. Because what he didn't realise was that the more he wound her up, the angrier she became and in turn, the more inclined she was to piss him off. And right now she knew that nothing would piss him off more than her agreeing to be his wife.

"Well do you need a fucking wife or not? Or have you got some other poor girl lined up to take the job?"

"You won't be able to handle it darlin'," said Charlie in return. "For a start you'd have to move to Marbella with me. And you'd have to be convincing."

"I wouldn't have to sleep with you, would I?" The words came out of her mouth without being filtered by her brain and she realised too late that the wine was doing the talking.

"Not unless you want to," said Charlie, raising an eyebrow suggestively. "Relax, I'm only joking," he grinned as she opened her mouth to yell at him. "We'd sleep in separate bedrooms and I'll even put an extra lock on your door if that would make you happy."

"Would I get to spend all of your money?"

"As much as you want, darlin'."

"And would you stop calling me darlin', darling?"

"You agree to do it, I'll call you whatever you want."

"How long will it be for?"

"A few weeks, a month tops. I promise I'd take very good care of you."

"I can look after myself thank you very much."

"You do realise it's the Costa Del Crime out there," interrupted Clare seriously. "Full of ex-pats on the run from the police."

"It's not that bad," said Charlie in mock outrage. "And there wouldn't be any trouble, I swear."

"You've got to admit it's better than moping around here all day," urged Jason excitedly.

If Kate didn't know better she'd swear he was trying to get rid of her. She supposed she couldn't blame him. She'd turned up unannounced on his doorstep over a week ago with a suitcase in one hand and a box of tissues in the other. Clare and Jason were planning a wedding; they didn't need a pathetic crying mess bringing them down.

"I'll tell you what," said Charlie getting to his feet. "Why don't you think it over? My flight's not until eight tomorrow night so just give me a call, Jason's got my number. Thanks for a great day but I'm going to leave you all in peace now."

Jason walked Charlie out but Kate overheard them as they hovered by the door.

"Don't worry mate, I know she'll say yes."

She could hear Charlie's deep sigh halfway down the hallway. "That's exactly what I'm worried about."

CHAPTER THREE

Waking up the next morning with a banging headache Kate wondered if it had all been a dream. Agreeing to be somebody's wife, a man she didn't even know, was completely and utterly insane. She wondered how she'd talked herself into it because now, in the cold light of day, the whole idea seemed ludicrous.

"Think of it like this," said Jason as he sat down next to her on the sofa with his breakfast. "It'll be like an extended holiday. Charlie is loaded so you can live in luxury for a while, spend all of his money and get a suntan. At the end of the day what have you got to lose?"

After listening to Jason going on about what a great opportunity it would be and how mad she would be to pass it up, Kate finally dialled Charlie's number. Convinced that he would have changed his mind, she was surprised when he invited her out to lunch. She agreed to meet him at an Italian restaurant in town and spent the whole morning fretting about it. Not wanting to give him the wrong impression she absolutely refused to doll herself up. It was only a business arrangement after all and when she arrived just after noon and saw him sitting at a table in the corner, she was relieved to see that he too was looking casual in jeans and a shirt.

"What do you want to drink?" he asked as he beckoned the waiter over.

"Just water please." There was no way she could handle any form of alcohol, just the smell of it was making her feel queasy. Two paracetamols followed by an ibuprofen chaser hadn't shifted her headache and the candle flickering in the centre of the table was making her eyes hurt. She needed a moment to calm her nerves so she picked up the menu and pretended to study it. The man sitting opposite her might be as annoying as hell but unfortunately for her, he was also incredibly sexy. And she didn't want to be drawn in by those gorgeous brown eyes.

"I was surprised you called," he said, pushing the top of the menu down with his finger so that he could see her. "And trust me darlin', not a lot surprises me. You haven't changed your mind then?"

"Why, have you?"

"No. Although I am wondering what I've let myself in for."

"Me too," she sighed, questioning herself for the hundredth time. She made a mental note never to drink again or who knew what else she might drag herself into. "Why don't you tell me about this business deal?"

"I don't think we should discuss that now. We've

got more important things to worry about."

"Like what? Our cover story?"

"No, like what we're having to eat. I'm bloody starving."

Kate scoured the menu. There were so many options she didn't know what to choose. The waiter arrived at their table and panicking, she ordered the prawns then instantly regretted it. She'd probably drip garlic butter all down her top. But she didn't want to cause a fuss by changing her mind so she just handed the menu back to the waiter and mentally cursed herself when Charlie ordered the far simpler option of a pizza.

Damn it, why hadn't she thought of that?

The restaurant was quiet and there were only a dozen or so people inside. She liked it, it was cosy and welcoming. She just wished she felt more relaxed. Charlie unnerved her in a way she couldn't describe and every time he glanced at her across the table, she dropped her eyes and studied her fingernails. She knew he was checking her out, wondering if he'd made the right decision.

Well that made two of them, then.

"Oh, I almost forgot." He reached into his jacket pocket, pulled out a thick brown envelope and slid it across the table. "This is for you. There's ten grand here. That should just about cover it."

Kate stared at it, unable to believe that such a huge amount of money was within her grasp. He was either seriously loaded or up to something seriously illegal to get his hands on that amount of cash at such short notice. The former was her preferable option; she was in enough trouble as it was without getting involved in some dodgy criminal enterprise that could see her behind bars for the rest of her life.

"Go on, take it," he said sensing her apprehension. "And don't worry, you're going to earn every penny."

The waiter arrived with their food and Kate was glad of the distraction. Her plate was placed in front of her and she stared in horror at her prawns. She hadn't expected them to come with their shells on. That served her right for not reading the menu properly. Charlie's pizza was served on a rectangular wooden platter and he immediately tucked in, ripping apart the cheesy crust with gusto and devouring the first slice within seconds.

"What's up? You not hungry?" He was already on his second slice and spoke with a mouth full of chicken and chorizo.

She glanced down at her plate and shrugged. She was about to explain her predicament when he whipped the plate out from under her and proceeded to rip the head and tail off each prawn. Then he turned them upside down, peeled off the shell and removed the black thread that ran along the back of each one. He returned her plate, wiped his hands on a serviette then tucked back into his pizza.

"Thanks," she mumbled awkwardly, feeling like an idiot.

The prawns were incredible, a good choice after all and so far not a drop of garlic butter had been spilt.

They ate in silence and when they were finished Charlie poured himself another glass of wine and topped up her water.

"So I've been thinking about what we should tell everyone. The easiest thing to do is stick as close to the truth as possible so we should say we met through Jason, went out for dinner and things developed from there. Spin some bollocks about a whirlwind romance, people really love all that, don't they? I don't want to make it too complicated as I'll only fuck it up. What do you think?"

Kate shrugged. "Whatever. Are you a love at first sight kind of guy then?"

"Fuck no, I don't believe in any of that bollocks."

Kate tried not to laugh; she didn't want him to think he was funny. "What are your friends going to say when I suddenly turn up? Won't they think it's a bit odd, this guy who doesn't believe in love at first sight coming home from England with a wife in tow?"

Charlie raised his eyebrows suggestively. "We'll just have to do a good job of convincing them, won't we?"

"I'm not having sex with you if that's what you mean. I might be doing this for money but I'm not a whore."

"I'm only messing around. Jesus, lighten up a bit will you? Are you always this uptight?"

"Only when I get mistaken for a prostitute."

"I think we're gonna have a great time, darlin'. You never know, you might even enjoy yourself."

"I doubt it," she muttered just loud enough for him to hear. He grinned but never said anything.

"How soon do you want me to fly out? The sooner the better, I suppose?" She knew that if she didn't leave soon, there was a huge chance she'd change her mind.

"I think that'll be best. I'll book you a flight as soon as I can arrange it. If you're sure?"

"I am sure," she said, eyeing the envelope on the table. It was an obscene amount of money and was more than enough to put down as a deposit on a flat the moment this farce was over.

"Right then, shall we make a toast?" he said raising his glass.

"What are we drinking to?"

He grinned. "Let's drink to marital bliss."

They chinked their glasses together and Kate couldn't help but smile. She had no idea what the next few weeks were going to entail but one thing she knew for sure, she certainly wasn't going to be bored.

CHAPTER FOUR

I t was ten to six on Friday morning. Kate's flight to Malaga was due to leave at eleven thirty and Clare and Jason were driving her to the airport. She had woken with a banging headache and a mixture of excitement and dread. She had agreed to be the wife of a man she didn't know, move to a different country and play a part in a game she didn't know the rules to. She really must have lost her mind.

"It'll be fine," said Jason as if sensing her mood. "Charlie is a great guy and a good friend. If you could just get your mind off Mark for a while you might even enjoy yourself."

He carried her suitcase to the car and rammed it into the boot with the rest of her luggage. Clare was already waiting in the passenger seat of his Audi A4 so Kate climbed into the back and stared out of the window. The sky was grey and overcast and a faint drizzle was in the air. It felt good to be escaping the unpredictable English weather and she was actually looking forward to waking up each morning with the rays of the hot Spanish sun shining down on her. It was one of the pros that weighed off against a huge list of cons she'd drawn up in the last twenty-four hours. At the top of the pros list was the ten thousand pounds she was being paid. She had to keep that uppermost in her mind or else she knew she'd call the whole thing off.

Gatwick was busy. It was mid-July and holiday season was reaching its peak. At check-in Jason heaved the luggage onto the conveyor belt and made a discreet exit so the girls could say their goodbyes.

"Well, this is it," said Clare, hugging her sister tightly. "It's not too late to change your mind."

"Actually, it is. I really need the money."

"I love you," said Clare as they parted. "Text me every day."

"I will," promised Kate. "I love you too."

"And don't fall in love with him…" she shouted out as Kate headed off towards passport control.

Huh, thought Kate with a grunt.

As if I could fall in love with that arrogant pig.

Charlie had booked her on a scheduled British Airways flight in Club Class and she had to admit, it was a fantastic way to travel. Sitting in luxury, her legs were stretched out in front of her and shortly after take-off the pretty blonde cabin crew member had magically appeared and offered her anything her heart desired. She was now looking out of the window at the fluffy white clouds below sipping champagne like a movie star.

It had been a week since she had met Charlie for lunch and she had spent most of that time fretting about him. Feelings of apprehension had been masked by a massive spending spree and by the time she'd settled her overdraft and her credit card bill, she'd spent in excess of two thousand pounds. Charlie had instructed her to buy a wedding ring so she'd visited a jeweller and bought an expensive gold band, refusing to buy a cheap one knowing that he could afford it and that she could sell it afterwards.

When the plane touched down her stomach lurched and she felt its entire contents gurgle. She knew instinctively it wasn't the three glasses of Moët & Chandon she'd just consumed; it was purely nerves at the prospect of seeing Charlie again. But it was too late for regrets. He was meeting her at the airport and, for better or for worse, she was going to become his wife.

It took twenty minutes to pass through security. The bored customs officer barely glanced at her passport and waved her on with a dull expression on his face. Welcome to Spain, she thought with a grin. Several other flights had landed within a few minutes of each other and hordes of holidaymakers were making their way to baggage reclaim, all competing for space at the carousels to collect their luggage. After battling her way through and retrieving her cases, she followed the throng of people ahead of her and the moment she cleared the barrier she saw him.

It was hard to believe that the temperature outside was soaring into the nineties as he looked so cool and relaxed. Wearing a loose-fit white shirt, denim shorts and a pair of flip flops, he was standing in the overcrowded arrivals hall with a pair of sunglasses perched on top of his head and a huge bunch of red roses in his hand. And he was just as gorgeous as she remembered.

He waved as she approached and though she tried not to be taken in by those sexy brown eyes, it was impossible. They had a force of their own and the smug look on his face told her he knew it. He glided towards her and in one smooth motion, pulled her into his arms. Without any warning whatsoever he crushed his lips down onto hers.

It was so unexpected that for the briefest moment she was caught completely unawares. His lips were soft and warm and the exotic scent of his after-shave infiltrated her senses. When he tried to slip his tongue into her mouth however, she abruptly pushed him away. The show of affection was un-called for and instantly she felt the colour rise to her cheeks. Her face was hot despite the air conditioning and her heart was beating ten to the dozen.

"What the hell are you doing?"

Charlie smirked and thrust the roses into her arms. "You are supposed to be my wife, remember?"

"Like I can forget." She peeled the fallen petals from her blouse. "Please don't ever do that again."

The way he grinned told her in no uncertain terms that he absolutely would but there wasn't anything she could do about that now.

"Come on," he said jangling his keys in her face. "The car's this way,"

Kate had two suitcases and a holdall, plus the handbag she wore diagonally across her shoulders. Charlie scratched his chin and stared at it all.

"Jesus, how long are you staying for? I don't think I'm gonna fit all this in the car."

There was no way she was going anywhere without her stuff but just as she opened her mouth to say so Charlie promptly held up a hand.

"Don't, I've got a hangover and I don't need it."

He took hold of the trolley and wheeled it towards the exit. The doors whooshed open and as they stepped into the mid-afternoon Spanish sunshine, the icy coolness of the air conditioning gave way to a burst of blistering heat. Kate sucked her breath in. She was completely unprepared and she didn't just mean for the surge in temperature.

Outside the terminal it was bedlam. There were people everywhere. Holiday company representatives were checking names on clipboards, directing tired but excited families to tour buses and repeatedly calling out instructions. Coaches crammed full of holidaymakers were manoeuvring out of parking spaces and taxis were being hailed by tourists holding maps that were flapping about in the hot breeze.

Charlie led her towards a sleek silver convertible BMW that was parked in a bay marked 'Coaches Only' and brought the luggage trolley to a halt beside it. As he loaded her cases into the boot he ignored the furious ramblings of the Spanish coach drivers as they honked their horns and raised their hands in anger at him. He slammed the boot shut and jumped behind the wheel. Kate slid unobtrusively into the cream leather seat beside him and with a loud roar and a screech of tyres, he reversed out of the parking bay and sped towards the exit.

It was a forty-minute drive to Marbella. Once they'd dropped off the toll road they joined the picturesque coast road and Kate allowed herself to be less irritated by Charlie overtly ogling her legs and relax enough to take in the breath-taking views of the Mediterranean Sea which stretched out in all its blue shimmering glory before them. The scenery was spectacular and as the wind whipped through her hair she stared into the distance and tried to force the stresses from her mind, a task that was particularly challenging seeing as Charlie was continually speeding up then jamming on the brakes to avoid hitting the cars in front of them.

"You're quiet," he said as he overtook a Lycra-clad cyclist with barely an inch to spare. Kate sucked her breath in and grabbed the door handle with white knuckles. He was a reckless driver and she was sure he was doing it on purpose.

"I'm just hoping I make it out of this car alive. Sorry," she said, realising how rude that sounded. "I'm just nervous, that's all."

"Nervous? You? I don't believe it."

He eased the car to a stop at a set of traffic lights and turned to face her. "Listen darlin', everything's gonna be fine." He removed his hand from the steering wheel and gave her knee a gentle squeeze. She flinched at the gesture, much to Charlie's amusement. "This isn't going to work if you freak out every time I touch you."

"I know, I'm sorry," she mumbled apologetically. But she hadn't been prepared for the physical contact or for the jolt of lightning that accompanied it.

"That's the second sorry in two minutes. Do me a favour will you, stop apologising and for fuck's sake relax?"

Although he was right, it was far easier said than done. The next few weeks she realised, were going to be so much harder than she'd ever imagined.

Kate had done her research on the area. She knew that Marbella was a glitzy and glamorous resort and their arrival into the town was heralded by an enormous stone arch which stretched high across the road, the word 'Marbella' expertly crafted on it. The traffic dwindled as Charlie took a right-hand turn and they continued along a block paved residential street lined with luscious palm trees and bushes bursting with colour. Another turning led them up a narrow lane on a slight incline, at the top of which was a gigantic set of wrought iron gates. Kate couldn't see anything on either side as the high stone whitewashed wall concealed whatever lay behind it. Charlie punched in a number on the gate entry keypad and slowly the gates slid open. They continued down a long block paved driveway, tall Cypress trees flanking either side of them and leading them to the place that Kate would call home for the next few weeks.

Set against the backdrop of the La Concha mountain, the three storey, contemporary white villa was simply incredible. Pulling off her sunglasses, she just stared at it, certain in the knowledge that her jaw had dropped. Charlie saw the surprised look on her face and grinned.

"What do you reckon? Think you'll be able to slum it for a few weeks?"

She couldn't answer him, she was too stunned to speak. She wasn't sure what she'd been expecting but it certainly wasn't this.

"Come on," said Charlie enjoying her reaction. "Let me show you around."

He unlocked the front door and she followed him inside. Large open planned spaces shaped the ground floor which gave the space a welcoming light and airy feel. The shiny grey kitchen was fully equipped with high-end stainless-steel appliances and expensive chrome fittings and led into a dining area with a highly polished glass table that seated eight. The lounge area featured a white corner sofa and subtle flashes of colour from sumptuous green scatter cushions. A modern fireplace housed a freestanding log effect fire and attached to the wall above it was the biggest flat screen television Kate had ever seen.

Bi-fold glass doors stretched from floor to ceiling and showcased the landscaped tropical garden and the large curved swimming pool which appeared to stretch all the way to the base of the La Concha mountain. Charlie folded the doors back against the wall, allowing them to step into the shade of a large seating area which ran along the entire breadth of the villa. It also doubled as an outdoor bar and BBQ area and deluxe rattan furniture and Cycas trees in terracotta pots furnished it.

"This is amazing," Kate said and it really was.

"I'm glad you approve. A friend helped me design it and trust me, it's taken a lot of time and money to get it looking like this. Come on, I'll show you upstairs."

He led her up a polished tiled staircase to the second floor. There were four heavy white doors; one led to a bathroom, two led to guest rooms and the fourth door led to the room that was to be hers. No expense had been spared in the decoration. High quality dark wooden furniture and crisp white Egyptian cotton sheets gave the room a chic hotel feel. In keeping with downstairs, floor to ceiling glass doors folded back to give access to a balcony which commanded breath-taking panoramic views all around her.

"Your bathroom is through there," Charlie informed her, pointing to a doorway. "My room's upstairs and don't worry, there's a lock on your door so you'll be quite safe."

She ignored his comment and they made their way

back downstairs. As she wondered into the kitchen Charlie disappeared outside to collect her luggage from the car.

"Get me a beer, would you?" he shouted over his shoulder.

"I thought you had a hangover," she mumbled as she opened one of the two tall chrome fridges. Expecting to see an array of lavish food and mouth-watering culinary temptations she was disappointed to discover that the contents consisted entirely of San Miguel bottles and pots of green and black pitted olives. There was also a piece of cheese on a plate which judging by its furry edges, had seen better days.

"I take it we'll be eating out tonight," she said as he came up behind her.

"Feel free to go shopping if you want," he said and took the bottle of beer out of her hand. Kate took a bottle for herself and popped off the top. "Why don't you go and unpack. Holler if you need anything."

Kate spent ages emptying her cases and arranging all of her belongings. She could've done it in half the time but was in no hurry to get back downstairs to Charlie. By seven o'clock she knew she couldn't put it off any longer. She had showered and changed into a clean pair of shorts and a vest top, just one of the many new outfits she'd purchased for the trip and went downstairs to find him. He was stretched out on a sun lounger engrossed in the sports page of The Sun. Thanks to the air conditioning inside she felt pleasantly cool but one glance at his half naked body and her temperature soared again. His tanned, muscular chest showcased a magnificent set of toned abs that could only mean he spent a lot of time working out. She tried not to stare but it was near on impossible.

"You took your time," he commented, his eyes peering out at her from over the top of the newspaper.

"I had a lot to do." She diverted her attention from his body and stared out at the beautiful garden. The sparkling blue water was beckoning her to jump into the pool but she'd just washed her hair and didn't want to get it wet again. Instead she sat down on the rattan lounger next to Charlie and let her body sink into the deep red cushion.

"Now that you're here we should go over the ground rules," he said as he folded his paper. "I don't cook and I definitely don't clean, I pay somebody to do that for me. And I don't want your shit all over my house."

"Don't worry, you won't even know I'm here."

"Good. And just so you know, we won't be going to the bar tonight. I thought we'd have a quiet evening in and get to know each other a bit."

"Whatever you want," she shrugged. "You're the boss."

He grinned as though the thought had never occurred to him before. "Yeah, I guess I am." He pulled his phone out of the pocket of his shorts. "First things first. I'm bloody starving. Do you fancy a pizza?"

Not having eaten since lunchtime on the plane, Kate was surprised by how ravenous she was. They sat outside beneath the covered area, the naya Charlie called it, and by the time they'd finished eating she had consumed a bottle of wine. She knew it wasn't a good idea, especially on top of all the champagne she'd drunk on the plane, but her nerves were all over the place and she needed it to calm her down. Charlie went off to fetch another bottle so she curled her legs beneath her and rested her head on the back of the chair. The sun had gone down, its golden rays replaced by brilliant orange streaks that stretched across the horizon. The beauty of it blew her away; she had never seen anything like it. Charlie didn't pay it any attention. She supposed he'd seen it a million times before and the effect had become lost on him.

"So how have your friends taken the news that you've suddenly got married?" she asked when he returned with the wine.

"Fucking shocked doesn't even come close to it. I think it's gonna take some time for them to get used to the idea." He looked her in the eye and grinned. "We'll just have to do a good job of convincing them, won't we?"

"You needn't worry," said Kate tartly. "I'll make sure you get your money's worth."

"I'm counting on it, darlin'."

She ignored his comment and let him refill her

glass. "I have to ask Charlie, is there a girlfriend tucked away somewhere that I should know about?" The question had entered her head on more than one occasion and she was curious. She also didn't fancy having her hair pulled out by a jealous lover. But Charlie shook his head.

"There's no-one."

"Surely there must be someone?" She was surprised. Despite the fact that his haughty arrogance was both irritating and annoying, he had the two other qualities that most women, although definitely not her, usually went for in a man; dangerous good looks and lots of money.

Charlie threw his arms wide open. "I'm free and easy and that's how I like it. Do you have a problem with that?"

"No, I just want to know what I'm up against, that's all."

"You can relax, it's just me and you, darlin'. And while we're on the subject, you can tell me what happened with you and your tosser boyfriend."

She threw him a death glare. Part of the reason she'd come to Spain in the first place was so that she didn't have to talk or even think about Mark. And the last thing she wanted to do was discuss him with Charlie.

"I'm interested, that's all. And seeing as we're gonna be stuck here together for a while you might as well give me the lowdown."

She sighed reluctantly; she supposed he was right. "I caught him in bed with his ex. We'd been together for almost eighteen months."

"Were you in love with him?"

"What do you think? We'd just bought a house together."

"Doesn't mean you were in love with him."

"I don't go around buying houses with men just for the fun of it, you know."

"So you're a serious one then?"

"If you mean that I don't flash my knickers at every Tom, Dick or Harry then yes, I suppose you could say that."

"Good to know," he said crossing his legs. "Because as my wife, I'll be expecting you to behave yourself."

"Don't worry, I'm all yours."

Immediately realising what she'd said, Kate felt the flames of embarrassment burn her cheeks. It was the bloody wine talking again; she knew she shouldn't have had that last glass. "What I mean is, for the purpose of this arrangement I'll give you a good performance." Realising that that didn't sound any better, she opened her mouth to continue but Charlie held up his hand.

"I'd stop there if I were you. You're digging yourself deeper into a hole."

"Oh, fuck off, you know what I'm trying to say."

He laughed. "Are you always this neurotic?"

"No, you just bring out the worst in me."

"I'll try not to but I can't make you a promise I probably won't be able to keep. So going back to your boyfriend," he said changing the subject. "I know someone who could sort him out for you, it wouldn't even cost you a penny."

Kate laughed nervously, unsure if he was winding her up. "I'll bear that in mind. Do that a lot do you? Sort people out?"

"Not me, that's more Mickey's thing. He's away on business at the moment but he'll be back in a few days." He narrowed his eyes, his expression unexpectedly serious. "Do yourself a favour and stay out of his way, yeah? If he gives you any trouble make sure you come and tell me."

She wondered what kind of trouble Charlie was referring to but he didn't elaborate and swiftly moved on.

"We'll go the bar tomorrow night and I'll introduce you to everyone. Don't worry you'll be fine, just don't go into too much detail, we don't want to end up telling conflicting stories."

Kate nodded; it was his show after all.

"Listen darlin', are you sure you want to go through with this because once we get started there's no backing out?"

Kate thought about it for two milli-seconds. What else was there to do, anyway? Wallow in self-pity thinking about her two-timing ex-boyfriend? "I'm sure. Look, I've even got the ring to prove it." She held out her left hand to show him the wedding ring she'd slid on her finger a couple of hours ago. It felt alien but she was sure she'd get used to it. Charlie took her hand in his and gently ran his thumb across the shining gold band. Her cheeks flushed at such an intimate gesture and she pulled away abruptly.

"You're gonna have to work on that," he said with a frown. "A wife who flinches every time I touch her will hardly be convincing, will it? You're acting like a born-again virgin."

"I'm sorry."

"Look," he said leaning towards her. "Why don't we make this really easy for the both of us? Let's go to bed, have a good fuck and in the morning we can get down to business."

"You're not serious?"

"Very."

"Is that your answer for everything,? Sex?"

"What's wrong with that?"

"Have you considered the fact that I might not even fancy you?"

"To be honest darlin', no."

"Well I don't. So stop trying to get into my knickers, it's not going to happen."

"If you say so."

She stood up carefully, not wanting to accidently brush against any part of him and give him the wrong impression. "I'm going to bed. Alone," she added just so that she was clear.

"You know where I am if you change your mind."

Like that's gonna happen, she mumbled to herself as she stepped inside the villa.

She took a quick shower to cool off. There was something about that man that got her all hot and bothered. He didn't have an insecure bone in his body and naturally assumed he could have anything or anyone he wanted. Well he was in for a shock, because she wasn't up for the taking. Changing into a pair of pyjama shorts and a camisole top she strolled out onto the balcony to take in the stunning night-time view one more time. The stars were twinkling above her head and there was a cool breeze blowing in from the sea. She could hear the sound of water but knew the villa was too far inland for it to be the soothing waves of the Mediterranean. She walked to the edge of the balcony and peered over the railing to investigate.

And that's when she saw him.

Swimming in the pool below, naked and illuminated in all his physical glory by the subtle underwater lighting, was Charlie. She watched, mesmerized by the sight of him. She knew she should look away but she just couldn't make herself do it. The muscular contours of his body glowed in the light as he glided effortlessly through the water. She had no idea how long she stood there or how many lengths of the pool he swam because she had lost the ability to think straight. After what she thought was just a few minutes but in reality was nearer fifteen, he emerged from the water. Picking up a towel from the sun lounger he wiped his face and then, as if in slow motion, he ran it over his washboard stomach and further down to his cock.

She gasped, then slapped her hand quickly over her mouth.

She would never hear the end of it if he knew she was watching him. But then she realised that maybe he was doing it on purpose, that he was showing her exactly what she was missing. Her heart hammered in her chest as she hurried back inside and collapsed onto the bed. He was playing games with her, that much was obvious.

The question she didn't dare ask herself was whether she wanted to play too; she wasn't entirely sure she could trust herself to answer.

CHAPTER FIVE

K ate didn't sleep well at all. Her dreams were haunted by wet and naked visions of Charlie and she was annoyed by the realisation that she fancied him so much. A full twenty minutes in the shower didn't help cleanse her mind of the images she feared would plague her from now until eternity and she cursed him under her breath repeatedly for his egotistical display of nudity. The man had no shame and certainly didn't deserve to look that good without any clothes on.

She eventually ventured downstairs and came face to face with him in the kitchen. He was wearing a pair of tight blue swimming shorts and her eyes automatically dropped to his body, absorbing the toned abdomen and rippling muscles. Angry for being so easily distracted she side stepped him and poured herself a coffee from the jug on the percolator and splashed some milk into it.

"I took your advice and whilst you were snoring I went shopping," he announced cheerily. "Did you sleep okay?"

"Yes, thank you."

She was hardly going to admit that she'd had erotic visions of him all night, was she? Feeling the need to put some distance between them she went outside and settled into a red cushioned wicker chair beneath the umbrella. It was only early but the sun was already hot and its rays were dazzling. She wished she'd put her sunglasses on as she was now having to squint in the bright light. She took a sip of her coffee. It was strong and she was grateful, she definitely needed a caffeine injection after her night of troubled sleep. Charlie sat down beside her, his mug of coffee in one hand and a slice of burnt toast in the other.

"What do you think of the view from your balcony, then?"

Kate baulked. The bastard knew she'd been watching him in the pool. She panicked, unsure of what to say. "What do you mean?"

"The mountain. What do you think I mean?" He was grinning; he knew exactly what he meant and they both knew it.

"I don't like heights," she lied quickly. "So I haven't been out there."

He smirked and took a bite of his toast. He knew she was lying but she decided to cut him off before he could wind her up even more. "What's the plan for today then?"

"I thought we'd do a bit of sight-seeing if you're up for it. I can't promise the view will be as great as the one from your balcony but it's still worth a look."

She grimaced; it was going to be a long day.

Charlie, true to his word, didn't cook so after Kate whipped up a breakfast omelette with bacon and mushrooms from the newly acquired groceries, she changed into a pair of shorts and another new top and they began a slow walk into town. Marbella was, without a doubt, one of the most beautiful places she had ever seen. It was a picturesque blend of modern luxury and old-world charm and its streets were lined with luscious green palm trees and white washed luxury villas that were set back from the road. The imposing La Concha mountain dominated the background, encompassing all it surrounded and rose to a magnificent peak under the skyline.

They negotiated the maze of winding cobbled streets of the Old Town and Kate was enthralled by the Spanish architecture and the centre, Orange Square, with its array of boutique shops and cafés and dozens of Seville orange trees. She stopped to take photos of The Old Governor's House, a sixteen-century mansion and visited the Church of Our Lady of the Incarnation, a baroque building which dated back to 1618. Charlie barely glanced at any of the scenery and spent most of the time firing off one text message after another on his phone.

They took a stroll along the seafront promenade and as it was almost two thirty, Charlie decided they should stop for lunch. Sitting on an outside deck area with views across to Gibraltar, Kate wasn't sure if it was the grilled sea bass or the deep blue Mediterranean Sea stretching out to the horizon that excited her more. Whatever it was, she was finally relaxing in Charlie's company. He was her personal tour guide and surprisingly knew a lot about the area. He regaled her with stories about the rich and famous inhabitants and every now and then he'd point out a man or a woman who had been embroiled in some scandal or another. To Kate it was simply a luxury holiday destination but to Charlie it was his home and he clearly felt it was his business to know everything that was going on in it.

It was late afternoon when they finally arrived back at the villa. Charlie promptly changed into his swimming trunks, grabbed a beer and headed outside. Kate took a quick shower, donned one of her new bikinis and was about to go and sunbathe when she spied a little old lady struggling down the marble staircase with a basket full of clothes balanced precariously on her hip.

Isaura Ruiz Sanchez had been employed by Charlie for two years. Paid a generous wage to clean and do his laundry, they were both happy with the arrangement. The news that Charlie had taken a wife whilst on holiday back in England had come as a complete surprise to Isaura, mainly because picking up the various skimpy items of lingerie from his bedroom floor and the frequency that she washed his sheets, hadn't made her think he was the marrying kind.

Isaura liked Charlie; he was fair and generous and had always been good to her and her family so when he had explained that his wife would be sleeping in a separate bedroom and gave her five thousand euros to ensure her discretion, Isaura accepted the money gratefully and asked no questions.

After all, what he got up to in the privacy of his own home was none of her business.

"Hola, hola, you must be Missus Charlie si?" Isaura reached the bottom step, short of breath and held onto the chrome railing to support herself.

Charlie had mentioned that he employed a cleaner but Kate had never imagined her being so old. In her mind, she had pictured a pretty young Spanish girl but this poor woman looked as if she was at least seventy. Despite the air conditioning that circulated through the villa the old lady was sweating profusely and her cheeks were rosy red. Kate leapt forward to relieve her of the basket but Isaura hastily pulled it away.

"No, no I take it 'ome," she insisted, refusing to hand it over. "Please tell Senor Charlie I 'ave it done tomorrow." She waddled out of the front door and headed down the long driveway towards the metal gates that enclosed the villa from the road.

Kate watched her go, livid. There was a fully equipped utility room in the villa so she couldn't understand why Charlie was making a little old lady do his washing when he was perfectly capable of doing it himself. Her anger rising, she marched off to find him.

Dozing on a sun lounger in the sweltering afternoon

sun, Charlie stifled another yawn. Being a complete philistine he'd been bored out of his head by Kate's enthusiasm over an old church and a crumbling, derelict building. He'd visited the Old Town when he'd first arrived in Marbella two years ago and had never seen much point in returning. But he'd made the effort anyway, figuring it was expected of him.

He rolled over onto his back and reflected on his present situation. Having a woman living in his house didn't bother him, it was the fact that they weren't sleeping together that he couldn't get his head around. It was a totally new experience for him; he was used to sharing his home but wasn't accustomed to not sharing his bed. And he was surprised by how much it bothered him. He liked sex and the one question that was burning at the back of his mind was how the hell was he going to cope for weeks on end without getting any?

He thought back to his naked swim last night and was jeered up by the knowledge that Kate had been watching him. Of course he knew he should've worn some trunks but it had been worth it just to wind her up. This morning she'd acted as though he was going to bite her and he'd had to stop himself from laughing. No wonder her boyfriend shagged someone else. She couldn't be much fun to live with but, he realised with a sigh, he'd soon find that out for himself. He was giving up an awful lot of his freedom to make this deal with Declan work. He just bloody well hoped it was going to be worth it.

All he wanted to do right now however, was drink

his beer and top up his tan; two weeks of the shitty English weather was enough to fade anything. He lathered some sun cream into his chest and settled onto the lounger thinking he'd take a quick nap but just as he was drifting off the sun suddenly lost its heat. Expecting to see a white billowing cloud floating overhead, instead what he saw was Kate and she was standing over him with her hands on her hips and a face like thunder.

"Do you mind?" he said shooing her away with his hand. "You're blocking the sun."

"Are you completely incapable of looking after yourself?"

He ignored her, he didn't have a clue what she was talking about anyway and was too busy checking out how good she looked in her skimpy blue polka dot bikini.

"Haven't you ever heard of a washing machine? Making an old lady do your laundry is immoral."

And then the penny dropped. "Ahh, you've met Isaura I take it?"

"It's disgusting, she's old enough to be your grandmother."

"I do pay her you know, not that it's any business of yours. Now if you don't mind, I'm trying to sleep." Actually, he was trying not to stare at her tits but thought it best not to mention it.

"It's five o'clock in the afternoon," she snapped angrily.

"That may be darlin' but tonight we're going to the bar and won't be home until the wee hours of the morning. So take my advice and get some rest, you'll be needing it." And he promptly rolled over. The sight of her in that bikini was giving him a hard-on.

Saturday night was the bar's busiest night of the week and they were already late. Kate had been in her room for hours trying to decide what to wear and Charlie, growing more impatient by the second, kept yelling up the stairs for her to 'get a bloody move on.'

She had tried on three different outfits before finally settling on a short green leopard print dress that matched the colour of her eyes. It was satin with blouson sleeves and a wrap over front. The belt was tied loosely around her waist and once she'd slipped on a pair of strappy silver sandals and grabbed her new clutch bag she decided she was ready. She paused for one final look in the mirror. Did she look good enough to be Charlie's wife? She would soon find out. She held onto the shiny chrome banister and carefully negotiated the steps down. One wrong move in these heels and it would all end in disaster. She reached the last step and was just about to congratulate herself on not breaking her neck when she saw the expressionless look on Charlie's face and froze in her tracks.

Shit.

She knew she should've worn the black dress.

This was a nightmare; he was going to call the whole thing off. Whilst she was under no illusion that he could've bagged himself a much prettier looking wife, she didn't think she looked *that* bad. Besides he'd already paid her the money, he couldn't back out of their deal now. She tucked a loose strand of hair behind her ear with shaking fingers, the ten grand and all her hopes of buying somewhere to live going up in smoke.

"Is it too late to change our arrangement?"

"What do you mean?" she stuttered, trying to hide her disappointment. She was damned if she was going to make it easy for him.

"I was thinking that we should skip going out and spend the evening fucking instead."

"You bloody idiot," she tutted dramatically. "You really had me going there."

"I hope so darlin' coz you've definitely got me going."

She rolled her eyes in exasperation. "Why is it always about sex with you? I already told you, I'm not interested."

"If you say so darlin'."

She stamped her foot like a child. "Stop it Charlie, it's really annoying. Now are we going out or not because I need a bloody drink?"

Chivalrously he held out his hand and gestured for her to lead the way. "Very well Mrs Mortimer, your wish is my command."

Unlike the super clubs of Puerto Banus, Bar Paraiso was a beach front music bar that attracted a cultured clientele. It was a chic venue where subtle tunes were played early evening and developed into a more sophisticated party atmosphere later in the night. Younger party-goers flocked to start the evening there before heading twenty minutes along the coast to enjoy the all-night club scene where they could boogie until seven am.

It was a twenty-minute stroll from the villa to the bar and when they arrived the outside terrace was packed. For Charlie, knowing that people wanted to spend their time and money at his bar was a buzz he would never tire of. Despite the vast amount of cash he had ploughed into buying the place and having it redecorated to his very high standards, it had taken a lot of hard work to make it a success. Although networking came pretty easy to him (he was a natural when it came to conversation), developing his reputation in the local community as a legitimate businessman had taken a lot more effort. But he'd achieved it and was now a world away from the delinquent he'd been in his youth. Those days were long behind him now and if everything went as well as he hoped it would, one last job with Declan would see his future finally secure. But right now, there was a more pressing issue on his mind. He took hold of Kate's hand and gave it a squeeze. He could feel her trembling and knew how nervous she was.

"You ok?"

"I don't think I can do it."

"Course you can, just relax, you're gonna be fine."

He wrapped his arm around her waist. She felt good next to him and looked as sexy as fuck in that green dress. He was desperate to kiss her and despite knowing he shouldn't, he decided that he bloody well would. He only intended to give her a quick peck but temptation got the better of him and he pulled her close, pressing his lips firmly against hers. Her mouth tasted fresh like minty toothpaste and her hair smelt of strawberries and cream. His head reeled and his groin stirred and he was just about to slip his tongue between her lips when she pulled away from him.

"What are you doing?"

"If we're going to do this darlin', we might as well do it properly. Come on, let's go."

Two hulking security guys dressed entirely in black were chatting with a group of girls who were sipping cocktails from glasses the size of fish bowls. When they saw Charlie approach they quickly shifted their attention back to the job they were being paid to do.

"Evening lads," said Charlie, pausing in front of them. "How's it going?"

"Yeah sound," replied one in a Scouse accent. He was tall and lean and tanned within an inch of his life. He adjusted his earpiece and gave Kate a discreet once over. Not so discreet however that Charlie didn't notice.

"Eyes on me, mate," he said, annoyed. He decided he didn't like the way his doorman was ogling his 'wife'.

"What? Sorry boss." The man looked sheepishly at Charlie and nodded.

"Any trouble?"

"No, it's been quiet so far, boss."

"Good, let's keep it that way, shall we?"

Charlie ushered Kate through the doors. This was it; this was the moment of truth, or in his case, the moment of deceit. He wasn't happy lying to his friends but an obscene amount of money was riding on the deal with Declan, enough for him to take care of Mickey and get out of the game for good. So not only did he hope that Kate could put on the perform- ance of a lifetime, he only hoped and prayed that he could do the same.

The bar décor was modern; it was all glass and mir- rors, lush foliage and contemporary lighting. There was a small raised dance floor where a DJ was housed, playing summer tunes that were neither overbearing in beat nor deafening in volume. Tables and chairs were occupied by what Kate could only describe as 'beautiful people'. Expensive handbags, designer shoes, false nails and fake breasts; it was like an episode of a reality tv show. She thanked God she had taken so much time with her appearance, especially as she acknowledged that every woman in the room had probably slept with her 'husband'.

Charlie gave Kate's hand an encouraging squeeze. "It might help if you smile darlin'. You are supposed to be in love with me remember?"

It took a while for them to make their way across the room. Charlie knew everybody and they all wanted to stop and chat. A legion of pretty waitresses wearing black walked the room, weaving in and out of the crowds balancing stacked trays of exotic cocktails, dispensing drinks and taking orders with the precision of Olympic athletes. It was serious stuff and business was booming.

Kate's eyes were drawn to a woman who was watching Charlie like a hawk about to swoop down on its prey. Her orange tanned skin glowed beneath the spot lights and the faux leather playsuit she was wearing was so tight it looked as if it had been sprayed on. There was something familiar about her but Kate couldn't put her finger on exactly what. And then it dawned on her. She tugged Charlie's arm and with a nod of her head she indicated in the girl's direction. "Isn't that Genevieve from that dating show on Sky?"

"Oh shit, yeah. Quick, let's move." Charlie made a sudden beeline for the bar, dragging her along with him.

"A friend of yours?" she asked as he whisked her along.

"Let's just say we know each other intimately and leave it there. She's a crazy bitch, had a thing for sucking feet."

Kate couldn't help but giggle; he was incorrigible. Suddenly a woman with bleach-blonde hair and foot long fake eyelashes blocked their path to the bar. Kate cringed as the woman wrapped her arms around Charlie's neck and kissed him hard on the lips.

"Oh my Gawd Charlie, I 'fort you was only going away for an holiday, I can't believe you've gone and got married."

"Easy, Tanya," said Charlie, pulling her off.

Kate was shocked at what passed as her outfit; a skin tight bodycon dress, its elasticity stretched to the limit across her fake breasts. It fell just below the cheeks of her arse and at the end of her long thin legs was a pair of three-inch snakeskin heels. She was, as was everyone else in the vicinity, an orange shade of brown and combined with the heavy make-up she wore, Kate assumed she must be another reality tv star.

"How did you do it, love?" she asked, turning her attention to Kate. "You've bagged the most eligible bachelor this side of the rock and I ain't gonna lie, I'm well jel." They were joined by a stocky built man with a piercing in his nose and a row of tattoos along both arms. He was carrying a pint of lager and a pink gin in a bubble glass.

"Ahh thanks, love, I'm fuckin' gasping. This is me hubby, Ray. You wanna watch it," she added to Kate, "the women round 'ere are lining up to claw your eyes out."

"Leave it out Tan," said Ray, taking a pull on his pint.

"Yeah leave it out," agreed Charlie and putting a hand in the small of Kate's back, guided her towards the bar. "Come on, let's get a drink."

Kate couldn't help but make a comment. "She seems like a nice girl."

"Yeah, a real diamond is Tanya."

"Shagged her as well, have you?"

Charlie grinned. "Not since Ray put a tracker in her knickers."

The bar was crowded. Although table service was generally the most accepted way to order, people still wanted to linger and chat at the bar. A tall, thin, athletic man with spiky blond hair and a goatee was shouting orders to a waitress behind the black marble counter. Due to the background music and the loud chatter Kate couldn't hear what he was saying but as soon as he noticed her standing there his face broke out into a huge grin.

"So, you *are* real then?" he said, dismissing the waitress who was now mouthing at him furiously. He reached over the bar and kissed Kate enthusiastically on both cheeks. "I thought Charlie was having me on. I can't believe you've actually married this tosser."

"Oi watch it," laughed Charlie.

"It's really great to meet you at last. I'm Phil."

Kate had already been given the low-down on Phil; close friend of Charlie and manager of his bar. Phil beckoned one of the waitresses over.

"Get us a couple of bottles of Bolly would you love? Tonight we're celebrating."

A red roped barrier separated the VIP section from the rest of the bar and access was supervised by a tall burly black man in a suit. He was wearing an earpiece which connected him to the club's security team and as he saw the three of them approach he immediately nodded at Charlie and unfastened the rope to allow them entry.

The area was occupied by a nefarious group, the club's high rollers was how Charlie described them to Kate. They were however, a mixture of local heavies, drug dealers and money launderers with a few Premier League footballers interspersed between them. Charlie didn't have a problem with any of them, just as long as they spent exuberant amounts of money and didn't push drugs in his bar he was happy.

Two waitresses arrived with a tray of glasses and half a dozen bottles of champagne in silver ice buckets. A loud chorus of cheers went up; Charlie knew it was going to be a heavy night. Whilst his friends were initially pissed off that he'd secretly gotten married, they'd soon got over it and were all keen to meet the woman who had finally forced him into submission. Whisked from one group to another Kate was an instant success. He couldn't deny she had class which was more than could be said for most of his friends for not only did she look the part but she was playing her role to perfection. He'd had his doubts that she'd be able to pull it off but she was creating a sensation and he couldn't have asked for more.

"Well you've certainly got me fooled," he whispered discreetly in her ear as she finished off her third glass of champagne.

"Didn't think I could do it, did you?"

"Course I did, I had every faith in you. But I reckon it's time to up the game."

She frowned at him. "What do you mean?"

"We need to seal the deal in front of everybody."

As she registered his meaning he saw the panic in her eyes but leaving her with no option and no chance of escape, he wrapped his arms around her waist.

"Don't you dare kiss me Charlie."

They both knew he was going to and he couldn't help the grin that formed on his face. He'd wanted to kiss her all night and was bloody well going to make the most of it. He moved slowly at first, barely brushing her lips with his own but as her body stiffened in his arms he increased the pressure tenfold. He could feel her resistance so in a gesture of pure possession he tightened his grip on the back of her neck and slipped his tongue into her mouth.

"Oi, Oi," came jeers from all around. "For fuck's sake you two, leave it out. Save it 'til later."

Everybody laughed as they parted. He knew that Kate was grateful for the interruption, he however, was not. He had a raging hard on and it wasn't going to go away by itself. He whispered into her ear, "Let's go home and fuck."

If she could've thumped him he was sure she would have. Instead she responded with a roll of her eyes, retrieved her handbag from the table and stormed off without even looking back.

Kate's head was spinning. She was dangerously close to being plastered. She needed a pint of water and a moment to calm down. Locking herself inside a toilet cubicle, she sat on the closed lid and rested her head against the wall.

What the hell was she doing?

It had only been a matter of time before Charlie wanted to get physical; his reputation definitely proceeded him on that score. But despite how attractive she found him there was no way she would allow herself to be intimate with him. She could barely handle him as it was.

She contemplated her choices. One, admit this whole thing was a big mistake and book a seat on the next flight home or two, put her game face on and get on with the job Charlie was paying her to do. Unwilling to face the repercussions of either option she decided to postpone the decision until she could think straight. She'd gotten through the hardest part of the night and had met all of his friends. All she had to do now was make it until bedtime. Not such an easy task when he kept touching and kissing her all the time.

The only thing she could possibly do she realised, was to have another drink. She slid back the bolt on the door and was just about to leave the safety of the cubicle when a female voice caught her attention.

"Did you hear about Charlie?"

Kate stood absolutely still, not even daring to breathe.

"I know, I can't believe it," said another voice, this one louder and with a strong Essex accent. "It all happened really quickly from what I hear, some kind of whirlwind romance. Funny, I never thought he was the marrying kind."

"Me neither. I reckon she's pregnant, that's the only way she'd catch him. Have you even seen her? She's nothing special and not exactly his type either. I thought he only went for blondes, that's why I dyed my hair anyway."

There was hysterical laughter and Kate shook her head as she continued to listen.

"It's all a bit funny if you ask me though, Mand. I mean think about it, when we were together we couldn't keep our hands off each other. We even used to sneak into his office and have sex on the desk but I've been watching the pair of them all night and they've barely laid a finger on each other."

"What are you getting at?"

"I'm just saying it's weird that's all."

"You're just pissed off because he broke up with you. Sounds to me like you're jealous."

So much for convincing people that she and Charlie were madly in love, thought Kate madly. As far as she was concerned the decision had now been taken out of her hands. She needed to stop any further rumours spreading or risk ruining the deal they'd made. There was ten grand riding on it after all.

"Excuse me ladies," she said, pushing past the two women and peering into the mirror. There was a gasp of shocked recognition when they realised who Kate was and that she'd been listening the whole time. She opened her bag and took out her lipstick, reapplied and pouted her lips then turned to both of them with a smile on her face. "Just so you know, I'm not pregnant and just because Charlie and I aren't all over each other it doesn't mean that we haven't been fucking each other's brains out all day. And maybe it's not the colour of your hair he got bored with love," she said addressing the one staring at her with her mouth open like a goldfish. "Maybe it's your irritating accent or your incessant need to fucking gossip all the time. Well I must dash, I've got to go and screw my husband. See you later girls."

She marched out of the ladies with her head held high. The rules of the game had changed and she wanted to win. And if that meant being the wife that Charlie wanted, then she was going to make damn sure that's exactly what he got.

The Johnson sisters descended on Charlie the moment Kate left his side. Blonde and beautiful, he'd fucked them both. Gemma, the taller of the two, pouted her botoxed lips at him like a schoolgirl. Ordinarily he would have ordered some drinks and enjoyed the attention, smug in the knowledge that those lips would be wrapped around his cock before the sun came up. But right now he couldn't have been less interested.

He was pushing his luck with Kate and he knew it but all he could think about was shagging her and the more she resisted, the more persistent it made him. He was also well aware that she'd just split up with her boyfriend and whilst *he* was convinced that the best way for her to get over her ex was to jump into bed with someone else, *she* clearly hadn't got the memo.

"Well you've certainly done it this time mate," said Phil arriving at his side with yet another bottle of champagne. The Johnson girls, realising they weren't getting any of Charlie's attention, stalked off with the hump. Phil topped up his glass and they chinked.

"She's way too good for you, you do know that right?"

"You're not wrong," Charlie laughed.

"I never thought I'd see the day. You, married? I'm sorry mate, I just can't get over it."

"Me neither," agreed Charlie, feeling the massive pang of guilt that was associated with lying to one of his best friends. He wished he could confide in Phil but he knew that his friend wouldn't only disapprove, he'd go fucking ballistic. Phil had watched Charlie's back for years and they'd been through a lot together. Charlie instinctively knew that Phil would be less than impressed by such an audacious plan and he also knew without the shadow of a doubt that he wouldn't want him to touch Declan Connors with a bargepole.

But it would all be worth it in the end, Charlie reasoned. A huge share in a multi-million-pound pay-off that would see him living in luxury for the rest of his life.

Surely, a few little lies were worth *that*?

Kate's eyes adjusted to the subdued lighting. The DJ had cranked up the volume and a group of girls had taken to the dance floor. Drunk on too many cocktails they were dancing and moving completely out of time to the music. When one of the girls lost her footing and fell to the floor loud jeers ensued. Kate felt sorry for her but had her own problems to deal with. Drama had never been one of her fortes but if she couldn't act like she was in love with Charlie then there had to be something seriously wrong with her. He was by far the most gorgeous man she had ever laid eyes on, he was sexy and although it pained her to admit it, he was very funny too. It couldn't be *that* hard surely?

Her pulse was racing and her heart was hammering with apprehension over what she was about to do. Charlie was deep in conversation with Phil when she approached, probably talking business she guessed.

"Here she is," said Phil with a smile. He passed her a glass of champagne and turned to get everybody's attention. "Right you lot, let's make a toast," he shouted at the top of his voice. He raised his glass into the air. "To the bride and groom."

There was a rowdy chorus of congratulations and Kate prayed nobody would notice her hands shaking. All eyes were fixed on her now and she knew that if ever there was a time to make her move, it was now. Pushing away the last traces of doubt she reached up onto her tip-toes, weaved her arm around Charlie's neck and kissed him. His eyes registered surprise but he responded willingly, snaking his arm around her waist and pulling her closer.

As kisses went, it was an incredibly good one. There was a round of loud clapping and banging hands on tables and when they finally broke free they both laughed at the commotion they were causing. Charlie's eyes silently questioned her so she leant into his ear. To anyone watching it looked as though they were making promises for later but in reality it was the complete opposite.

"Don't get too excited," she whispered. "I'm just keeping up appearances."

"Appearances my arse. Why won't you just admit that you want to shag me, darlin'?"

In as sarcastic a tone as she could muster she replied, "You're not paying me nearly enough to do *that*."

Negotiating the steps out of the bar had been easy enough but by the time Kate reached the pavement the night air hit her and her head began to spin. It was dark and although the promenade was illuminated she was struggling to see. She was also struggling to walk and could barely place one foot in front of the other. Kicking off her heels she held them tightly in her hand and swaggered from side to side.

"You're well pissed," said Charlie as he steadied her. "How much did you have to drink?"

Kate had no way of knowing. What she did know was that it had been a lot.

"You're not going to be sick, are you?"

"Are you kidding? I'm never sick."

Well that was a complete lie, thought Charlie to himself less than half an hour later. He was kneeling on the floor of the downstairs bathroom holding back Kate's hair as she vomited her guts up into the toilet.

"I'm so sorry," she said for the hundredth time as she retched then threw up again.

"Don't worry about it." He gave her an encouraging pat on the back and tried really hard not to be annoyed. He'd been in some crazy situations in his life but this was a first and it certainly wasn't the way he'd imagined the night ending at all. His grand plan of seducing her had gone up in smoke and disappointed didn't come close to describing how he felt right now.

Kate finally pulled her head out of the toilet and he dutifully wiped her mouth with a wet flannel. She'd been going for fifteen minutes and he was certain there couldn't be anything left in her stomach.

"Are you done?"

She nodded her head sluggishly.

"Good. Come on then, let's get you to bed."

He'd practically carried her all the way back from the bar and knew that she'd never be able to negotiate the stairs so he scooped her up into his arms. He took it slowly, mindful that any motion he made would probably result in her heaving down his four-hundred-pound shirt. She mumbled incoherently all the way, rambling and mumbling words that he didn't understand. In fact he had absolutely no idea what she was saying. The one thing he did know however was that this was all his fault. He'd been refilling her glass with champagne all night, the idea that she couldn't handle it never once occurring to him. They reached her bedroom and he kicked the door open with his foot. Two seconds after depositing her on the bed she was asleep. Undressing her came as naturally to him as breathing but he stopped himself, realising that he'd never hear the end of it tomorrow. Instead, he swept aside the hair from her eyes and kissed her lightly on the forehead.

"Night darlin'," he whispered softly and after giving her a final once over, he walked away before he did anything he knew she'd make him regret in the morning.

CHAPTER SIX

Somebody was operating a pneumatic drill, at least that's what it sounded like, but as Kate opened her eyes she realised that the noise was coming from inside her head. She ran her tongue over her teeth; her mouth was fuzzy and her throat was dry. And her head was banging relentlessly.

Her nerves had gotten the better of her. She'd consumed copious amounts of alcohol to get through the night and now, judging by the throbbing pain in her temple, she was going to pay the price. Uneasily she swung her feet to the floor. Her head spun and she thought she was going to throw up. She steadied herself and took a deep breath. She could smell sick. She looked down and whilst initially she was pleased to see that she was fully clothed, relief gave way to mortification when she saw that her dress was splattered in a trail of sticky, smelly vomit.

She crawled into the shower and stood beneath the rainfall showerhead. She could barely keep her eyes open as the water cascaded down her body and washed away the tiny chunks of food that once they'd sprayed out of her mouth, had become attached to her skin. She couldn't remember being sick, couldn't even remember coming home from the bar. She was grateful that Charlie hadn't left her in a gutter somewhere to rot but was annoyed that she'd allowed herself to get into such a state. It was the ultimate embarrassment and she knew he was never going to let her live it down.

A blisteringly hot day, there wasn't a cloud in the sky. The heat engulfed her as she stepped into the garden. Charlie was in the pool, trunks on she noted with relief. She adjusted her sunglasses over her reddened eyes and prepared herself for the almighty apology she needed to give him. But as she approached the poolside she took one look at his fit body and the words died on her lips. Instead she managed a very distracted and embarrassed "good morning."

"Try good afternoon," replied Charlie without so much as looking at her. "It's almost one o'clock."

"Is it? God, I didn't realise how tired I was."

"Or how drunk," he added in an undertone.

She couldn't argue with that. She'd let herself down badly and though she couldn't be certain, she'd probably let him down too. She sat on the edge of the pool and dangled her feet into the water, the coolness a welcome relief from the hot sun that was beating down on her. But it wasn't the heat from the sun that had her all hot and bothered. It was the mixture of mortification and shame over her actions and she knew the sooner she got this apology over and done with the better.

"I carried you home from the bar in case you were wondering," said Charlie before she had the chance to utter one single word. "And put you to bed after you chucked up in my toilet."

She put her head in her hands in disgrace. "I'm so sorry."

"So you said last night, about a thousand times in fact."

"I don't know what happened." Her mind was a giant void; she couldn't remember a thing.

"I'll tell you what happened, darlin'," said Charlie with a smirk on his face. "Too much bloody champagne. Maybe you should've told me you can't handle your drink."

"I can," she insisted. "I was just really nervous that everyone would see right through me. And then you went and kissed me and I just fell to pieces."

"When you kissed *me* you mean," he corrected.

Funny that the rest of the night was a blur but the memory of her kissing him was so real she could practically still taste him on her tongue. "I've got a perfectly good explanation for that," she said lowering her eyes to stare absentmindedly at her feet.

"Well let's hear it then." He flipped onto his back; he was enjoying this.

"I wanted to prove a point that's all."

"And that point was?"

She was going to kill him in a minute. She was embarrassed enough without him trying to wind her up. "I overheard two women talking about us and I didn't like it."

"You should know better than to listen to idle gossip. That's all the women do around here, that and try to shag anything with an American Express Gold Card." He was smiling and she couldn't help but smile too.

"I'm really sorry Charlie."

He tutted loudly. "What have I told you about apologising?"

She was about to say sorry again but stopped herself. There was one question however that she needed an answer to, even if it caused her untold grief and humiliation. She took a deep breath and said the words.

"Nothing happened did it…between us I mean? We didn't….you know….did we?"

"Now *that* I'm surprised you don't remember."

She felt the colour drain from her face. "*We didn't?*"

"Nah, course we didn't. You were practically unconscious darlin', it would've been a waste."

"You dick!" She splashed him and he swam over, pulled himself up and sat on the edge of the pool beside her. "Thank you for looking after me. I'm sorry I ruined the night."

"You didn't and you're welcome. But next time try to throw up *in* the toilet and not all over the floor. Isaura had her work cut out for her this morning."

Kate rolled her eyes; she was never drinking again. Ever.

Walking into the bar the second time wasn't as daunting for Kate. At just after nine o'clock it was still relatively early for the serious all-night party goers and as a result it wasn't as busy as it had been the previous night. She'd opted for a more casual look and was wearing a short khaki skirt with a cream wrap blouse and whilst she looked pretty cool on the outside, inside she was red hot and bubbling. Literally. She'd spent the afternoon sunbathing but had been so tired she'd dozed off to the sound of Taylor Swift singing her heart out on her AirPods. The result was obvious; without applying any sun cream to her back she had a serious case of sunburn.

Charlie was oblivious to her discomfort and looked as stylish as ever in a pair of Levi's and a white Ralph Lauren shirt. He was the kind of man that looked good in anything and not only did she know it, every other woman in the place knew it too. She wondered if she'd ever get used to the looks of adoring attention he constantly drew from the opposite sex.

Charlie retrieved a bottle of red wine and two glasses from behind the bar and led them to the VIP section. Jamal, whose sole responsibility it was to oversee the more important guests and the big spenders, released the barrier and with a nod of his head at his boss, waved them through. Charlie stopped for a quick chat then went on to greet a group of guests, half a dozen or so middle-aged English men who were having champagne poured for them by a pretty blonde waitress. She was being incredibly magnanimous considering they were whooping and jeering at her but Jamal had his eye on them, ready to step in if they got out of hand. After ordering them a round of shots on the house, Charlie ushered Kate to a quiet table at the rear of the section. But as he put his hand on her back to guide her through the effect of his touch on her extremely burnt skin caused her to jump three feet into the air.

"I thought we were past this." The irritation in Charlie's voice was clear and he sat down on the plush velvet sofa next to her tutting loudly. He was angry and had every right to be; she wasn't holding up her end of their deal.

"It's not that," she admitted reluctantly. "I've caught the sun on my back, that's all. I'm really sore."

"Why didn't you say?"

"And have you take the piss out of me? No thanks." Sun cream was Rule 101 and she didn't need him to remind her how stupid she'd been not to apply any.

He poured the wine and handed her a glass, not that she was going to drink it. The smell alone was making her wretch.

"You've got a really low opinion of me, haven't you?" He took a very large swig of Rioja and put his half empty glass back onto the table with a flourish. "Right, let's go then darlin'."

"Go?" she asked as he got to his feet. "Go where?"

"Home. I've got some fantastic stuff that'll sort you out."

"But we can't leave, we've only just got here."

"It's my bar, we can do whatever we want."

He shouted over to Phil who was collecting glasses from a nearby table and told him he would call him later. Kate remained in her seat, unsure whether he was serious.

"Well come on then, unless you want to sit here all night in agony?"

"I'm really sorry," she said as she got to her feet.

He rolled his eyes and cursed under his breath. "I swear to God if you say sorry one more time I'm going to bloody lose it."

They arrived back at the villa and Charlie retrieved a plastic tub from the bathroom. "What is it?" asked Kate, taking it out of his hand to examine it. It had no label and for all she knew it could be a voodoo potion from a witch doctor.

"Never you mind," he said seizing it back.

"It's not some sort of date rape drug is it? It's not going to render me useless so you can do all sorts of unimaginable things to me that I won't remember in the morning?"

"Trust me, darlin', anything I'd do to you you'd remember. Now take off your blouse."

"Excuse me?"

"Take off your blouse," he repeated. "There's no need to be shy, I've seen more of you in your bikini."

Although technically that was true, she still felt awkward unbuttoning her blouse in front of him. She could feel his eyes on her and as she slid it off her shoulders she realised how Little Red Riding Hood must've felt just before being gobbled up by the big bad wolf.

"You need to lie down."

She didn't move an inch, she was already standing there half naked and felt self-conscious enough without lying down in front of him.

"It's your choice," he said matter of factly. "We can either do it here or in the bedroom but either way the cream needs to stay on for a while so it can be absorbed into your skin. So unless you want to stand here all night?"

Kate quickly came to the conclusion that there was no getting out of this. Reluctantly she kicked off her heels and feeling more than a little embarrassed, she laid down on the sofa. It was soft and sumptuous and she sank down into it. She plumped a cushion and placed it beneath her head so she could rest on it. Charlie knelt down on the floor beside her and unscrewed the lid of the tub. Then he reached over and with extremely steady fingers, unfastened her bra strap.

"What the hell are you doing?"

"You want the pain to stop, don't you?"

She resigned herself to the fact that she had no choice but turned to face the back of the sofa so she didn't have to see the narcissistic grin on his face. He dolloped a huge blob of cream between her shoulder blades; it was so cold that it sent an unexpected chill down her spine.

"You did that on purpose," she said through clenched teeth.

"Shut up and stop being such a baby."

He placed both hands on her back and began massaging the cream into her skin. Her whole body was tense and she fought her awkwardness. Within a few minutes however, she knew she was going to have to tell him to stop. It wasn't that she felt uneasy anymore, it was the fact that she was enjoying it way more than she should be. And it was too intimate a gesture; she was half naked and his expert hands were roaming all over her. She felt him sweep her hair to one side and he moved his fingers to her shoulders, his thumbs moving in slow circular motions over her taut muscles.

"How does that feel?" he asked.

"Fine," she replied, her voice barely a whisper.

It felt more than fine; it felt bloody incredible. Slowly, and despite her best intentions, she started to relax. He applied another blob and distributed it lower down her back. It was quiet, the only noise being the sound of her erratic breathing and she knew instinctively it wasn't the relief of the sunburn that felt so good. It was the erotic way his hands were manipulating her skin. He had a really light touch and his fingers danced over her in a rhythm that had her hypnotised. And now they were venturing even lower to her hips and before she knew it had happened, a gasp of pleasure escaped from her mouth. Totally embarrassed by her reaction she panicked.

"Are you finished?"

"No."

"Well can you hurry up?"

"Why, is there somewhere you need to be?"

They both knew there wasn't. His fingers kept on moving, stroking and caressing her, keeping her locked in a trance. But when they tugged the waistband of her skirt she finally forced the fog from her brain and came to her senses. She sat up and clutched her blouse tightly to her chest with the full intention of walking away. But Charlie was kneeling in front of her, those sexy brown eyes working their magic.

"Come to bed with me."

He was serious and she knew that if she didn't look away right now she'd follow him blindly up the stairs. She faltered, afraid to open her mouth in case the word 'yes' fell out of it.

"You do realise it's the best way to get over your ex?" said Charlie, sensing her hesitation.

"And that's your opinion as a relationship expert is it?"

"It always works for me," he grinned.

"I appreciate the offer but I don't think it's that simple."

"It could be."

"I've just split up with my boyfriend. Jumping into bed with you is the last thing I need right now. Besides you're technically my boss and I know from personal experience that shagging the boss never gets me anywhere. I think it will be far easier if we keep this platonic."

"You and I have very different definitions of the word platonic."

"You're paying me to do a job Charlie and you need to let me do it." She wanted to look away but couldn't, he had her completely spellbound. "You're making this really hard for me."

"Me too darlin'," he said with a suggestive rise of his eyebrows but when she ignored his innuendo he relented. "Okay darlin' let's keep it platonic, although I think you're only kidding yourself. I'll back off if that's what you want. I won't even kiss you again unless you ask me to."

Kate felt confident in the knowledge that he'd be waiting a long time for *that* to happen. She stood up, desperately hugging her blouse to her chest. She needed to walk away whilst she still could. Another moment with him and she knew she was going to change her mind.

CHAPTER SEVEN

By morning the pain from her sunburn had completely dissipated. Looking in the mirror she saw that the redness had been replaced by skin that glowed a beautiful golden colour. Whatever had been in that miracle tub of Charlie's, it had certainly worked. After a quick shower she pulled on a short cotton dress and flip flops but as she headed for the kitchen to make a coffee she was distracted by voices drifting in from outside. Curious, she wondered out to the naya to investigate.

Sitting next to Charlie in a wicker armchair was a man. Certain that she hadn't met him at the bar, Kate assumed he must be Mickey. First impressions were somewhat disheartening; his legs were stretched out on the table in front of him, his trainers were on the ground in a heap and as he was wearing no socks, she was rewarded by the sight of his two, thin hairy feet. It wasn't an attractive look, made even less so by the un-ironed, baggy tee shirt he was wearing. He had beady little eyes and beneath a baseball cap which he wore backwards, his dark hair was greasy and unkempt. But what Kate found most unappealing was the loud wolf whistle he let out as she approached.

"Fucking hell Charlie, you never told me your wife was such a stunner. Fantastic tits."

Kate, too shocked by his comment to react, was relieved when Charlie came to her defence. He slammed his beer down onto the table with a crash and glared at Mickey as though he wanted to kill him.

"Don't be a prick Mickey, have some fucking respect."

Mickey threw his hands up and grinned. "I was only saying."

"Yeah, well don't. You're taking fucking liberties."

Mickey looked at Kate and gave her an apologetic shrug but she could tell he wasn't sorry. "So sweetheart, where was my invite to the wedding of the year then?"

"I've told you ten times what happened with the wedding," snapped Charlie irritably. "You need to lay off the drugs, they're fucking with your head." He tapped his finger on his forehead as if to prove his point. "Now for fuck's sake leave it out and stop winding me up." Charlie got out of his chair and taking hold of Kate by the arm, guided her back inside the villa.

"Your friend seems nice," she said sarcastically as soon as they were out of earshot.

"Yeah I'm sorry about that." He retrieved his wallet from his pocket and pulled out a fistful of notes.

"Here, take this," he said, stuffing them into her hand. "Why don't you go shopping, get your nails done or whatever it is that you girls do. Take the car," he added, handing her the keys. "I've got some business to sort out. Give me a couple of hours, yeah?"

Kate looked at the money in her hand. "But there's hundreds of euros here..."

Charlie shrugged. "Think of it as a bonus."

Could she really take any more of his money? she asked herself. It didn't seem right. But the thought of staying at the villa with Mickey was hardly appealing. Oh well, she thought with a shrug of her shoulders, she could always give it back if she didn't spend it. At least she would be out of the way of Charlie's creepy friend. She grabbed her handbag and shot out of the door.

Puerto Banus was four miles along the coast. Kate parked the BMW in a twenty-four-hour underground car park and spent almost an hour wandering around the famous marina, staring in awe at the array of super yachts and luxury speed boats that were moored there. It was a millionaire's playground; the women were draped from head to foot in designer clothes and the men drove red Ferraris and sleek looking Lamborghinis. It was sobering to realise that the clothes these people wore probably cost more than she earnt in a year and their jewellery alone could end world hunger. But this area was renowned for the rich and famous and they came here to flaunt their wealth. And Kate was fascinated to see how the other half lived.

The Marina Banus shopping centre was full of everyday high street brands, dozens of shops that Kate wondered in and out of but it was the Muelle Ribera with its designer boutiques that really captured her attention. She strolled along the street, glancing into the windows of Gucci, Dolce & Gabbana and Michael Kors, well aware that they were out of her league but still fascinated by the beautiful clothes on display. There were a few smaller boutiques and seeing a beautiful silk scarf in the window of one, she decided to buy it for Clare and send it home as a present.

Feeling hunger pangs in her stomach she stopped at a nearby bistro and ordered a salad for lunch which she thoroughly enjoyed despite its ridiculous price tag. She was shielded from the hot midday sun by a huge canvas umbrella and as she slowly sipped her glass of water she people-watched and took in the sights of the area. After lunch she wandered aimlessly along, not really looking for anything in particular when a dress in the window of a boutique who's name she couldn't pronounce caught her eye.

Her feet seemed to develop a mind of their own and before she knew it she was walking through the door. It was only a small shop, all marble tiles and spot lighting. There were only two rails of clothing on either side of the shop and a row of black curtained changing rooms at the rear. Two sales assistants were dressing a mannequin in a short blue dress but it was the red dress in the window that had captured Kate's attention.

The younger of the two sales assistants immediately descended on her and whilst she insisted she was only looking, within minutes she had been persuaded to try the dress on and was standing in front of the mirror in the changing room admiring herself.

The dress was flame red and long, falling to her ankles with a split on the left leg that reached all the way up to the top of her thigh. It was a halter neck and the straps fastened into a knot at the nape of her neck. She turned to see the view from the rear and wondered if she actually had the nerve to wear it out in public; her back was totally bare and the material pulled tight over her buttocks. She mentally congratulated herself on the foresight of undoing her bikini strap whilst she had been sunbathing and marvelled at how brown her skin looked and the amazing shape the dress gave her. She had never worn anything like it; she'd always avoided tight clothing thinking that she didn't have the body for it but even she had to admit, she looked stunning.

The shop assistant was fussing around her and mumbling in very rapid Spanish. Kate had no idea what she was saying but the look on her face told her that she approved. A pair of strappy red heels completed the look and when Kate eventually left the shop she'd spent almost six hundred euros. She hoped it was worth it, she'd never spent that amount of money on a single dress in her life. Buzzing from head to toe, she couldn't wait to wear the dress to the bar that night and made her way back to the car with a spring in her step.

Arriving back at the villa Kate was disappointed to find Mickey's black Porsche still parked in the driveway. She wanted to relax in the pool but not liking the idea of wearing her bikini around Charlie's creepy friend she slipped silently upstairs, deciding to take a long soak in the bath instead. She turned on the taps of the corner bath. It was huge and had pillows for two and an array of fixtures and fittings to operate the six massage jets and the four jacuzzi jets. It even came with lighting that illuminated the water. She peeled off her clothes and climbed in, turning a dial to increase the power of the jets. She closed her eyes and immersed herself into a deep state of relaxation.

It was only when she heard loud banging on the door that she realised she'd dozed off. As she came to she felt confused and disorientated; she had no idea how long she'd been asleep. She switched off the jets and got to her feet when suddenly there was a deafening thud followed by the splintering of wood as the door flew off its hinges and crashed against the wall. Standing in the now open doorway staring at her wide eyed was Charlie.

"Are you insane? What the hell are you doing?" She grabbed a towel from the rail and frantically tried to cover herself.

"You didn't answer me, I thought something was wrong."

"Like what? That I'd drowned in the bath? I was tired, I fell asleep." She had no idea what was going through his mind but he must've realised that he'd made himself look like an idiot because his face became a picture of red-hot embarrassment.

"I'm sorry, I wasn't thinking straight." He faltered momentarily and ran a hand through his hair. After a shake of the head he quickly regained his composure. "Maybe next time you should try answering your fucking phone, I've been calling and calling you."

She fought the urge to snap back at him; she was too busy trying to keep the towel in position and not lose her footing at the same time. "Can you just get out please? And make sure you get this bloody door fixed."

The stunning view from the rooftop terrace was usually enough to lift Charlie out of whatever mood he was in but right now he wasn't looking at the scenery. Instead he was sitting naked in his hot tub marvelling at what an absolute dickhead he was. He hadn't given the day-to-day practicalities of being a married man a second thought. Sharing his home with a woman was one thing, he'd lost count of how many had come and gone over the years, but none of them had ever lasted more than a few weeks or rattled his cage as much as Kate did.

It was blindingly obvious what was going on here; he was sexually frustrated on an epic scale and it was making him crazy. It was a well-known fact that the average man thought about sex at least nineteen times a day, and Charlie was in no way average. And now he was kicking down doors for no other reason than Kate not answering her phone. If it wasn't so ridiculous it would actually be funny.

He rested his head on the back of the tub and put his hand on his cock. It was still hard from seeing Kate naked in the bath. Not that there was fuck all he could do about it. Apart from a hand job of course, but the idea of tossing himself off in the hot tub made him laugh out loud.

How the hell had his sex life come to this?

What he needed was a good fuck to relieve the tension. But seeing as his 'wife' was having none of it and he couldn't get it anywhere else without being branded an adulterer, he knew he was screwed. And not in a good way.

Oh well, he thought to himself with a defeated sigh.

A wank it is then.

Unable to face Charlie after the embarrassing scene in the bathroom Kate stayed in her room and spent almost an hour on the phone to Clare. At eight o'clock she was painting her toe nails a deep shade of red to match her new dress when her phone rang again. The caller ID flashed 'Mark' and for one awful moment she actually contemplated answering it. Panicking, she rejected the call and a few minutes later received a text informing her that he had left a voice message. Tentatively she pressed the buttons and put the phone on speaker.

"Kate, it's me. Please call me back, I really need to talk to you. I know what I've done is unforgiveable but you have to believe me when I say I'm sorry. I really miss you and I know we can still make this work. I've given you some space to calm down but enough is enough. I need you to come home now."

"Bastard," she yelled throwing the phone onto the bed in a rage.

She finished getting dressed and looked at her reflection in the mirror. She pirouetted, admiring her curves with a newfound confidence. If only Mark could see her now. She blew herself a kiss and smirked; it would serve him right if she indulged in a night of meaningless sex with Charlie.

After all, two could play that game.

Charlie was lounging on the sofa, his hands locked behind his head and his long legs stretched out onto the glass coffee table in front of him. Having gained no relief whatsoever from his hand job earlier he was still in a state of frustration. In fact he was so preoccupied thinking about sex that he wasn't even aware that Kate had come downstairs, let alone moved to stand in front of him.

"What do you think?" she asked excitedly, giving him the full benefit of her ensemble. Jolted out of his reverie, his eyes combed over every delicious inch of her, analysed every curve and scrutinised the long flash of tanned leg that was revealed by the dangerously high split in her dress. Then she pirouetted and he clocked the wide expanse of silky-smooth flesh exposed on her back and totally fucking lost it.

"You're not wearing *that*."

The smile on her face fell. He could see that she was crushed but it was just too bad. There was absolutely no way she was stepping foot outside the villa looking like that.

"What's wrong? I thought you'd like it."

"Well I don't. You might as well be wearing nothing at all. Do you want every man getting a hard-on over you darlin'? You're supposed to be my wife, not a fucking whore. Now do us both a favour and change into something a little less slutty."

"I've seen what the women around here wear Charlie and this is conservative in comparison."

"How is that conservative?" he snapped, pointing at her chest. "You're not even wearing a bra."

"I can't, it'll ruin the look."

He was rapidly losing his patience. He ran his hand through his damp hair in frustration. "For fuck's sake, I'm not having this conversation with you. Go and take it off."

He turned and walked away before he ripped the damn dress off her himself. Never mind the fact that if he didn't fuck her soon he was going to lose his mind, the thought of her actually walking into his bar to be drooled over by every man in there made him irrationally insane with jealously.

He needed to calm down. He headed outside to get some air but there was none. Even though it was nine o'clock in the evening it was muggy and there was no respite from the day's intense heat.

"Bollocks!" he shouted loudly and fought the urge to punch something. He knew he was being unreasonable but there was fuck all he could do about it. After all, how could he explain it to her when he didn't even understand it himself?

The click-click of her heels sounded on the paving as she came up behind him. Despite his feelings, he knew an apology was in order. He'd been way out of line. But just as he went to speak she stuck her palm in front of his face and cut him off.

"Listen to me, you dickhead. This dress has just cost you nearly six hundred euros so you can either like it or lump it. I don't know what your problem is but I'm not getting changed so I either go as I am, or I don't bloody well go at all."

For a moment he considered slapping her across the face but he'd never hit a woman and wasn't about to start now. Tempted to call her bluff he quickly realised he couldn't; arriving at the bar without her wasn't going to convince anyone that they were happily married. And if word got to Declan that things weren't all they seemed it could jeopardise their deal. Against all his better judgement Charlie nodded. He had no choice and he knew it.

"Fine," he said, conceding defeat. "But I'm not fucking happy about it. And don't say I didn't warn you."

They walked into the bar looking every bit the happy couple. Charlie had a dynamic presence; the way he looked made the men envious of him and the women want him. Pity they didn't realise what a dick he is, thought Kate as she walked dutifully by his side. She felt completely deflated and it hadn't helped by the fact that he hadn't uttered a single word to her the entire way there.

The bar was crowded and Charlie effortlessly mingled with his patrons. As his wife, Kate stood beside him but it didn't seem to deter the women from making eyes at him and she found it annoying that they were being so obvious. Charlie, however, didn't seem bothered in the slightest and it seemed to Kate that he was deliberately flirting with them. Chatting and laughing, he was being perfectly charming to everyone.

Everyone except her.

After ten minutes of being completely ignored she downed the remainder of her gin and tonic and signalled to Phil to bring her another one.

"You two had a row?" he asked, depositing a huge bubble glass filled with pink gin and strawberries in front of her.

"No. He's just being a knob."

Phil belly laughed. "Oh my God, you two are so perfect for each other."

"You wouldn't think so right now."

She spied Charlie out of the corner of her eye talking to a beautiful blonde. Her fingers toyed with the stem of her glass, imagining that it was his neck and that she was strangling it. "Is he always in such high demand?"

"'Fraid so, love, it comes with the territory. Try not

to get too jealous, it's just business."

Kate baulked. "I'm not jealous Phil, I'm just trying to understand, that's all."

"Well this might help." He took a bottle of Sambuca from the shelf and filled a shot glass. He also filled one for himself and raised it in a toast. "Cheers, love." They chinked and downed the contents, Kate pulling a face as the liquid burnt her throat.

"God that's disgusting," she said, holding her glass out for more.

"Disgusting but addictive," agreed Phil and poured them another one.

A beautiful Spanish woman with long dark hair placed a silver clutch bag down onto the bar and gave Kate a radiant smile.

"Looks like I'm missing the party," she said in near perfect English. "You must be Kate. I'm Maria, Phil's girlfriend."

"About time, love," said Phil with a smile. "I thought you weren't coming." They kissed and Kate felt immediately envious; they were clearly in love and couldn't keep their hands off each other.

"I've heard so much about you," Maria said as she sat down on a barstool. "I wish I could warn you about Charlie but I just love him. Now come on, you need to tell me everything, how you two met, how he proposed." Maria downed the shot that Phil handed her. "And where did you get that dress? It's stunning. I absolutely love it."

"Charlie didn't want me to wear it," confessed Kate, her tongue loose after the Sambuca. "He told me I looked like a whore."

"He didn't?" Maria seemed genuinely shocked. "Oh ignore him, you know he doesn't mean it. He's just jealous. He wants to keep you all to himself."

Kate knew that wasn't the case but played along anyway.

"Would you like to dance?"

She contemplated Maria's question for only a moment; Charlie was still in deep conversation and paying her no attention at all, so what else was there to do?

"Sure. Let's go." She followed Maria onto the dancefloor and they nestled amongst the crowd to dance to a Summer anthem she had never heard before. The Sambuca and gin were giving her a warm fuzzy feeling inside which was just what she needed. People were moving all around them, dancing and singing at the top of their voices. One song merged into another and loving that the music was whisking her off to a place where she could forget everything, she happily let herself go.

For the second time that evening Charlie was feeling like a total shit. He'd been completely out of order earlier and downing one glass of Jack Daniel's after the other wasn't going to change that. Deliberately ignoring Kate all night wasn't going to help the situation either but he was still too disturbed by the sight of her in that dress to think straight.

Out of the corner of his eye he watched as Kate made her way to the dancefloor. The looks of appreciation she acquired along the way riled him and he wasn't fucking happy. Javier, the local Don Juan, was running his greasy eyes all over her and he didn't like how that felt one little bit. Relocating to the VIP section meant that he could keep himself appraised of the situation without being overtly obvious. He leant against the chrome railing and watched, his attention fixed firmly on her. Rick tried to talk to him but he brushed him off; he was too het up to engage in any kind of conversation. A group of lads on a stag party were eying Kate and Maria as they danced and it took all of Charlie's willpower not to leap over the railings right there and then.

His temper was flaring; he'd fucking known this would happen. Why hadn't she just done as he'd asked and changed the bloody dress? Because now he knew he was going to punch someone and it was all her bloody fault.

After dancing to four songs back-to-back Kate realised she needed the loo and negotiated her way off the dancefloor. After taking care of business she re-applied her lipstick and readjusted her messy bun, pushing a few misplaced strands back from her face. Despite feeling relieved that she still looked reasonably good, she still pretty much felt like shit.

Charlie's reaction earlier had really upset her. She'd wanted to look good for him but she should've known she couldn't pull it off. She didn't fit into his world of beautiful women and designer bodies and she was a damn fool if she thought otherwise. Not wanting to have him ignore her for the rest of the night she came to the reluctant decision to go and find him, if anything just to clear the air between them. But as she came out of the Ladies she collided into a man who had been approaching from the opposite direction.

"Oh my God, I'm so sorry," she gasped as she thudded against his chest. "I didn't even see you."

"It was my pleasure," said the man with a smile. He spoke with a heavy Spanish accent and was strikingly gorgeous in the way that only Latino men can be.

"Are you ok?" he asked, his smile revealing a set of white teeth that instantly dazzled her.

"I'm fine, honestly," she laughed. "I'm really sorry."

"I haven't seen you in here before. I'm Javier."

"Kate," she offered politely.

"Let me buy you a drink." He went to link his arm through hers but Kate pulled back. As flattered as she was, there was no way she could accept his offer.

"Thanks but no thanks. I'm here with someone."

"Are you? That's funny because I didn't see you with anyone. And I've been watching you for a while."

There was a playful glint in his eyes and Kate let out a nervous laugh. Her stalker senses suddenly activated, she made to leave but he took hold of her arm.

"Are you sure there's nothing I can do to change your mind?"

Despite his audacity she didn't feel threatened, she

knew he was just trying it on. She'd been hit on plenty of times and felt confident that he'd get the message but before she could spell it out to him, she glanced over his shoulder and caught sight of Charlie marching straight towards them. Without any warning whatsoever he grabbed hold of Javier by the neck and wrenched him backwards, then he drew his fist and punched him straight in the face. Javier went down instantly, the crack of bone sounding like a twig being snapped as his nose broke. Javier clutched his face in agony, the blood seeping through his fingers and spurting down onto his shirt.

"What the fuck, Charlie. What the hell was that for?"

"Because you dumb cunt, that's my wife. And you've just put your greasy fucking hands all over her."

Charlie moved in for another punch but Javier scurried back as fast as his butt could shuffle him. Two men approached, looking as though they were about to intervene but one look at Charlie's face made them swiftly turn around and head in the opposite direction.

"I didn't realise she was married to you. Honestly, I had no idea. She looked like fair game to me." Javier realised he'd said the wrong thing when Charlie lunged at him again. He tried to move but wasn't fast enough and Charlie grabbed him by his shirt and lifted him from the ground. Two buttons flew into the air and there was a rip as the material tore apart.

"You wanna say that to me again, you greasy fucking dago?"

Javier knew he was in for a kicking and grimaced. He held his breath, waiting for it to come, but Charlie didn't hit him. Instead he gave him an almighty shove that sent him crashing back down to the floor.

"What the hell are you doing?" shouted Kate in disbelief, unable to comprehend what she was witnessing. "Leave him alone."

"You be quiet," he said pointing an accusing finger at her. "I'll handle this."

"*I* was handling it."

"Yeah, it really looked like it, darlin'."

Kate threw her hands into the air. "What's the matter Charlie? Are you afraid I was tempted?"

"None of this would've happened if you'd have just listened to me. I told you not to wear that fucking dress but you knew best didn't you? Well look where it's got you darlin'. I hope you're fucking happy."

"Unbelievable!" she screamed as she stormed off towards the exit.

"Where the fuck are you going?"

"Anywhere you're not."

"Get back here."

She ignored him. She had to get away from him and fast.

Charlie was pacing the floor of his office with a large Jack Daniels in his hand. He was fired up, his adrenaline was pumping and he wanted to kick the place down. His knuckles were red from the punch he had thrown and he knew that in a few hours' time they would be as sore as hell. But he wasn't sorry. Seeing Kate with Javier had infuriated the fuck out of him. The Spanish twat was lucky he hadn't broken both his legs.

Phil was leaning against the desk, doing his best to calm Charlie down. "It'll be fine. Surely she must know what you're like, she did marry you after all? Buy her some flowers, tell her you're sorry and it'll all be over by bed time."

Mickey, coked out of his eyeballs, was taking a different approach altogether. "Fuck her. Let's go to that strip club they've opened down the marina and get some pussy."

Phil turned to Mickey. "Are you a fucking idiot, or what? This is his wife we're talking about here. He needs to go find her and sort this out."

"Who fucking cares?" said Mickey. "She's a distraction. Two weeks back in England and he's like a love-sick puppy. It's fucking sickening."

"I am standing here, you know." Charlie gulped down the remainder of his drink and slammed the glass down on his desk. "But Phil's right," he said to Mickey. "You are a fucking idiot. I'm going to find her and I suggest you stay out of my way."

Kate sat down beneath a palm tree on the sand and stared out into the night. In the far distance she could see the illumination of passing boats and cargo ships and overhead, the sky was sprinkled with stars. She could hear music and laughter in the background and coupled with the sound of the waves lapping against the shore it felt really therapeutic. In fact she thought she might stay there all night.

The beach was practically deserted with the exception of a couple walking hand in hand whilst their dog, a blonde Labrador, was frolicking with a ball and splashing in and out of the water. She slipped off her shoes and let her feet sink into the sand. Although it was still warm, she suppressed a shiver. And she sensed Charlie's presence even before she heard him speak.

"I've been looking everywhere for you."

"Well it looks like you've found me," she said drily. "Have you come to apologise?"

"No. He deserved it."

"And I deserved it too, did I? Being ignored all night just because you didn't like my dress?" She stared up at him, eagerly awaiting his answer but he didn't respond. Instead he ran a hand over his chin. Admitting he was wrong clearly wasn't something that happened often. But that was too bad. She wanted an apology and wasn't moving until she got one. "I don't need you to come in all fists blazing just because someone actually bothered to take the time to talk to me, which incidentally, you failed to do all night. And there was no need to break his nose. What the hell were you thinking?"

"I wasn't thinking," he admitted with a shake of his head. "I just reacted."

"You were out of order."

"I know. I'm sorry."

She sighed at his pathetic attempt of an apology. "Oh, come on Charlie. Say it like you mean it."

"I'm sorry," he said again but this time with a bit more conviction. "There, are you happy now?"

Kate shrugged. She was far from happy but it was a start.

"But I did tell you not to wear that dress. It was pretty fucking obvious what was going to happen when you turned up looking like that."

"Looking like what? A whore?"

He at least had the grace to look away. "I didn't mean that, I don't know why I said it."

"I honestly don't know what your problem is. It's just a bit of leg, Charlie."

"It's not just a bit of leg though is it? Half of your body's on show."

"Careful," she warned. "You're starting to sound like a jealous husband."

"Of course I'm bloody jealous. You've turned me into a fucking crazy person."

"I'm guessing you don't get turned down very often."

"No actually I don't."

"Well you're just gonna have to learn to live with the disappointment. You might jump into bed with everyone you meet but I don't." She snatched her shoes from the sand, stood up and began walking. After taking a dozen steps she turned to him. "Well are you coming or not? Unless you expect me to walk home by myself?"

He jogged up alongside her and linked his arm through hers. "I really am sorry. I'll make it up to you, I promise."

"Yes you will Charlie," she agreed. "And you can start by not being such a dickhead."

CHAPTER EIGHT

C harlie spent the following day trying to make things up to her. Albeit, she knew he was only trying to protect his investment but even so, he was caring and attentive and nothing seemed to be too much trouble for him. He made lunch and cleared away the dishes afterwards, he even loaded the dishwasher and figured out how to turn it on. Kate was impressed but the real test came when she refused point blank to accompany him to the bar that night.

"I just can't face it," she admitted but amazingly he seemed content to leave her at home. Secretly she knew he was relieved to be spending a night away from her. He left the villa just before ten o'clock and didn't return until six the next morning. She heard him creeping past her bedroom door and assumed that he'd spent the night screwing some blonde. Turning over, she buried her face in her pillow but somehow never quite managed to get back to sleep.

The food that Charlie had purchased when she had

arrived was all but depleted so whilst he was still sleeping she pinched the keys to his car and drove to the local supermarket to stock up with fresh fruit and vegetables, bottled water and other essentials. Surprisingly the shelves were littered with English branded food so she filled the trolley and loaded it all into the car. She spent the rest of the morning busying herself with chores. She had no intention of letting Isaura do her laundry so she washed her dirty clothes and finding an old piece of rope in the pool room, she fixed a line between two palm trees in the garden and hung it all out to dry. Then she changed out of her shorts, donned another new bikini and settled by the pool with her book.

Charlie finally came downstairs mid-afternoon looking tired and bleary eyed. He was just stifling a yawn when he caught sight of the row of lacy underwear on full display in the garden.

"Jesus, it looks like a brothel."

"Well you'd know," said Kate icily, barely glancing up from her book.

He ignored her jibe and slumped down on a sun lounger. "God, I feel like shit."

"That's what you get for staying out all night. What you need is a nice greasy fried egg sandwich." She grinned as he pulled a face. "I'll tell you what, seeing as you're suffering I'll make you some lunch."

Fifteen minutes later they tucked into a delicious chicken and bacon salad that Kate put together from the fresh ingredients she had bought that morning. They ate in companionable silence and when they finished Charlie promptly fell asleep in his chair.

The dress that Kate chose to wear to the bar that night was a far cry from the one that had gotten her into so much trouble two nights previously. In a beautiful coral colour, it was a knee length fit and flare, showing hardly any cleavage whatsoever and was something she was sure even her mother would approve of.

She sat chatting to Maria whilst Charlie worked the bar and for the first time, she acknowledged the un-remitting demands on his time. Despite having Phil as his manager and a string of staff, he still ensured that his guests were catered for and that everything was running as it should be. He was constantly aware of everything going on around him and at one point she saw him leap between two men who were having a heated disagreement and physically drag one of them outside by the throat.

Mickey was also working and although she couldn't be certain, she'd felt his eyes on her several times. Charlie seemed indifferent towards him and she noticed that he didn't laugh and joke with him as he did with everyone else. There was definitely something off about their relationship but she just couldn't put her finger on exactly what.

It was just after eleven when Charlie finally grabbed a minute and came and sat down. Phil was also on a break and the four of them enjoyed a bottle of wine together. Phil and Maria were all over each other, kissing and cuddling like a couple of love-sick teenagers, making Kate feel more than a little awkward. She was aware that as newly-weds, she and Charlie should be displaying the same kind of affections. Charlie must've felt it too because after fifteen minutes of watching the two of them slobbering all over each other, he grabbed Kate's hand and pulled her up.

"Come on," he said with a sigh. "Let's get the fuck out of here."

The promenade at night was spectacular. Bustling with people, it had a vibrant and busy atmosphere. Street entertainers were playing music and tourists were sitting lazily outside bars and restaurants, sipping drinks and soaking up the ambiance. Charlie ordered two kebabs from a small counter that was sandwiched between an Italian restaurant and a souvenir shop and set a path towards the beach. It was completely deserted so they kicked off their shoes and walked through the sand, coming to rest under the gently swaying branches of a palm tree.

As they ate their food Charlie's phone rang twice. The first time it was Phil angling for some help back at the bar and the second time, Kate swore she heard the shrill voice of a woman shouting down the phone at him. But Charlie just calmly pressed the end call button and slipped the phone back into his pocket.

"Who was that?" asked Kate as she popped a piece of grilled chicken into her mouth. "One of your many girlfriends?"

"What's it to you?"

"Nothing. I'm just curious, that's all."

"Could've fooled me. Jealous are you?"

"Oh don't make me laugh."

"So you don't care who I fuck as long as it's not you." He ripped a piece of pitta bread apart with his teeth. "Why is that?"

"Because," she said as she licked the mayonnaise off her fingers. "I've just got rid of one cheating bastard, do you really think I want to get involved with another one?"

"Just so we're clear, I don't cheat. I've never been unfaithful to anyone in my life. I just lose interest so I move on."

Maybe that's what Mark had done, thought Kate suddenly. The idea had never occurred to her before but perhaps that's what had happened. Her mind was suddenly awash with the possibility that she was to blame for their breakup. So she didn't want to make love three times a week anymore but that was because she was tired after being at work all day. And when she came home there was the cooking and the cleaning and all the other mundane jobs that came with being an adult. But that was real life, wasn't it?

Not according to Charlie.

Her phone beeped indicating that she'd received a text message. Grateful for the distraction she fished it out of her bag, checked the name on the caller ID and let out a disappointed sigh. She was about to put the phone away but Charlie snatched it out of her hand.

"Speak of the devil," he said seeing Mark's name on the screen. She tried to grab the phone back but his arms were too long and he held it way out of her reach. "Let's see what the tosser has to say for himself."

He put on a voice and started to read. *"I'm truly sorry for all the pain I've caused you. You are the best thing that has ever happened to me. I love you and I'm begging for your forgiveness."*

"Ugh," he said tossing the phone onto the sand. "I've just thrown up in my mouth. Trust me darlin', you've had a lucky escape."

"It is romantic though," she mused out loud.

"Romantic? Come off it. He wouldn't know romantic if it jumped up and bit him."

"And you would?"

"Darlin', I am the definition of romance. I can make you feel as though you're the only woman in the world."

"Until you get bored and move on," she reminded him. "You are a Casanova and I quote, 'a smooth-talking charmer who has mastered the art of attracting and seducing beautiful women into the bedroom.'"

Charlie burst out laughing. "Is that what I am? And there I was thinking I was just irresistible." His laugh was deep and infectious, much like his personality. He was so bad on so many levels and she found herself laughing too.

"Can I ask you something?"

"If you must."

"Have you ever been in love?"

He shook his head.

"What, never?"

"No."

"That's really sad."

"Not for me darlin'. It's easier that way."

"Easier for who?"

He raised his eyebrows. "What is this? Twenty questions?"

"I told you, I'm curious. I'm just trying to figure out what makes you tick."

"Yeah, well you know what curiosity did."

He stood and began unbuttoning his shirt. It was a muggy night but was it really necessary for him to take off his clothes? The one thing she didn't need right now was a close up of his torso.

"What are you doing?"

"Going for a swim. Coming?"

She thought he was joking until he unfastened his jeans. He slid them down his legs and when they bunched at his ankles he pulled them off with one hand.

"You're not serious?"

"Don't tell me you've never been skinny dipping? Honestly you don't know what you're missing." And in one swoop he pulled off his boxers.

She threw her hands up over her eyes and screamed. "Put your pants back on you idiot." But instead he threw them at her. They landed in her lap and as he ran to the water's edge she flung them after him. But she too was distracted by his silhouette as it basked in the moonlight to protest further and she couldn't take her eyes off him as he waded into the water. He dived into a gentle wave and yelled at her to join him.

"Fat chance," she mumbled under her breath. After repeatedly telling him she wasn't interested, what would it look like if she stripped off all her clothes and went running into the sea with him? No, she wasn't going to do it. No way. She trusted herself even less than she trusted him, and that was saying something.

He finished his swim and sauntered back up the beach towards her. Honestly, the man had no shame. She didn't know where to put her eyes so she concentrated on a very interesting grain of sand in her lap, keeping her head down and refusing to look up until he was dressed. He didn't make any attempt to grab his clothes however. Instead, in one rapid motion, he swooped one arm under her legs and snaked the other around her back and lifted her from the ground. She screamed in protest as he carried her to the water's edge. He stepped into the sea with her thrashing around like a mad woman in his arms.

"Don't you dare drop me, Charlie," she screamed, but it was too late. He let go and she went down with an almighty splash. Her head went under the water and she emerged seconds later, her hair dripping and her coral dress clinging ridiculously to her body.

"What?" he asked innocently when she glared at him. "You needed cooling off."

"Did I? Well let's see how you like it."

She whooshed her hands through the sea and showered him with a giant wave of water. He didn't move and the splash caught him full frontal. He laughed so she lunged at him, but he was way too fast for her. He stepped to the left and kicked her leg out from beneath her. She went under the water again but when she resurfaced this time she swam away so he couldn't catch her. Not stopping until there was at least a two-metre gap between them, she flipped over onto her back and grinned at him in triumph.

"Not so quick that time, were you?"

He dived below the water and came up beneath her, grabbed hold of her around the waist and launched her into the air. She came crashing down with her mouth open and as she went under she swallowed at least half a pint of sea water. Coughing and spluttering she broke the surface and tried to catch her breath but he was on her again. She managed to dodge him but lost her footing on the sea bed and slipped. She kept her head up this time but he'd snuck up on her. He laughed as he tried to push her down but she refused to go down without him.

There was a scramble of arms and legs but they clung to each other, neither of them wanting to be the first to let go and admit defeat. After a minute of thrashing together beneath the surface, they both came up gasping for air. They'd drifted to shallower waters and Charlie's lower body was barely immersed in the water. He was way too close for comfort and even in the moonlight, she could see his cock rising just beneath the surface. She swung round in embarrassment and glanced up at the night sky. It was a mistake and too late she heard the rippling of water as he moved in behind her. He brushed her hair to one side and let his fingers trail across her shoulder. He pressed up against her, his breath hot on her skin as he whispered into her ear.

"I said I wouldn't kiss you again unless you asked me to."

His lips nuzzled her neck and she shivered, not from the cold but from the illicit desire he was invoking in her. Goosebumps formed on her skin, her physical reaction to his touch and she gasped, a throaty sound that came from deep within. Her breath turned into vapour as it hit the night air and swirled like mist around them. She couldn't speak, couldn't even make her lips move. There were a thousand reasons why she should tell him to stop but at this moment she couldn't think of a single one. She closed her eyes and leant her head back against him, overwhelmed by how incredible her body felt at his touch. His hand snaked around her waist and crept slowly upwards to her breasts.

"You're driving me crazy," he murmured into her ear as he gently squeezed her nipple between his fingertips. She gasped, a combination of passion and the crashing thump of a reality check; what the hell was happening? She needed to get control before it was too late.

"Stop...," she breathed quickly. "Please Charlie,

stop."

He twisted her around, so fast her head spun. "Are you fucking kidding me?"

"I can't do this," she said, putting her hands against his chest to prevent him from coming any closer.

"Yes you can. We're both adults, it's simple."

"For you it may be simple but I've just split up with my boyfriend."

"What's that got to do with anything? It's just sex darlin', just easy, no strings attached, uncomplicated sex. Besides, revenge sex is the best sex and I guarantee that by morning, you'll have forgotten all about him."

She didn't doubt that for a moment but that was beside the point. "It wouldn't be right Charlie."

"Jesus, what do you want from me?"

"Nothing. I just don't want the added complication."

"Do you want me to make you fall in love with me? Is that it?"

She shrunk away from him, horrified by the thought. "That's not even funny."

"Alright darlin', whatever you want." He threw his hands up in defeat. "I'm not going to beg. It's your loss."

He turned and walked away, making for the shoreline and although her heart knew she'd made the right decision, her head was declaring its utter disbelief. What woman in her right mind would turn down an opportunity to have sex with a man like Charlie?

One thing she knew for certain, he was spot-on. It was definitely her loss.

CHAPTER NINE

They were due to visit Declan at his villa in Seville at the weekend but after last night's debacle at the beach the relationship between them had turned distinctly frosty. Charlie knew it would take Declan less than five minutes to see past their rouse if Kate continued to be angry with him so keen to smooth things over and get their relationship back on an even track, he decided to throw a small party at the villa.

He spent the whole day offloading crates of beer from the car and organising food, refusing all of her offers to help and insisting that she relax by the pool and work on her tan. He invited a dozen or so of his closest friends and by eight o'clock that evening he was sitting at his outdoor bar with a large Jack Daniels in his hand waiting for the first of his guests to arrive.

As he listened to the soft soulful music that drifted through the wireless speaker he sipped his drink and wondered whether Kate was actually going to be joining him or not. She'd been in her room for hours, trying to avoid him no doubt. They both knew they had to put on a show for everyone tonight and he wasn't sure how that was going to play out. He was also praying that she wasn't going to wear some racy little number that would set his pulse racing again. His life would be far simpler if he just accepted that she was never going to have sex with him but her continued rebukes had the opposite effect on him; part of him enjoyed winding her up but the other part was desperate to get into her knickers. And it wasn't in his nature to give up so easily.

"Sorry," said Kate apologetically as she came breezing outside in a cloud of Chanel No 5. "I was on the phone."

His eyes roamed over her. Her hair was piled up on the top of her head in that messy bun thing she did and she had a light dusting of make up on her face, not too much, just a shimmer of pink lip gloss and a touch of blusher. He felt his groin stir; it turned out she didn't need to be wearing a racy number at all because just one look at her in that short pale green dress was enough to get him going. He opened his mouth to say as much but thought better of it. Best leave off with the comments or she might disappear again and the evening would be over before it had even begun.

Fillet steaks and lobster were being served by a local catering company hired especially for the evening and the Bollinger was flowing by the bucket load. There were about twenty guests in all and most of them Kate was already familiar with. There were the odd few that she didn't recognise but Charlie played the gallant host and introduced her to each of them. As his wife she was the subject of a lot of attention but luckily her lack of acting skills didn't seem to be a problem as conversation flowed easily and she was soon chatting and laughing like she'd known them all forever.

Mickey was the last of the guests to arrive and made a grand entrance with a young girl clinging onto his arm. Wearing a leopard print mini skirt and a see-through black mesh blouse with a lacy bra beneath it, Kate thought she looked like a hooker. Mickey made a bee-line for the bar and began knocking back champagne, following each glass with a brandy chaser. Kate caught the look of disapproval on Charlie's face and wondered again what their story was. She didn't have time to ponder it however, as dancing commenced and everyone looked as though they were having a great time. Especially Charlie, she noticed, who was observing Mickey's hooker out of the corner of his eye. She was standing by herself at the poolside, swaying her hips to the music and jiggling her boobs like a pro. Mickey wasn't paying her any attention, he was too busy getting smashed at the bar, so she was putting on a performance for everybody else instead.

"I think she's a prostitute," Kate whispered into Charlie's ear as she crept up behind him.

"I think you're right. Come on, let's dance." But Kate baulked as he pulled her close to him. "Relax, I'm not gonna try anything. We just need to do our thing, that's all."

She knew he was right but being in such close proximity wasn't going to help her body overcome it's ridiculous attraction to him. She also knew that she had no choice. A ten-foot barrier between them wasn't going to cut it tonight, especially in front of so many of his friends.

The moment he slipped his arms around her waist however, she knew she was in trouble. Her hands travelled over his hulking biceps and slid around his shoulders; was it really necessary for his tee shirt to be so tight? She tried to keep eye contact to a minimum by concentrating on what was happening around her. Phil and Maria were smooching, surprise surprise, Rick was talking to another man whose name she couldn't remember and Mickey's prostitute was grinding on down to Drake who was singing about hot love and emotion.

But those brown eyes and the intoxicating smell of Charlie's aftershave soon put her into a trance. Her nipples were rigid and she wondered if he could feel them poking into his chest. She wished he didn't have such an effect on her but there was nothing she could do. But just as she caught her fingers unconsciously caressing his neck there was an almighty shriek from the pool. Mickey had either jumped in or been pushed and was trying to pull his hooker girlfriend in with him. There was a splash as she hit the water and jeers erupted all around them.

Charlie immediately broke his hold and stood glaring at them. "For fuck's sake, why is he always such a prick?"

Rick, passing on his way to the bar, shrugged. "Fucking prick," he agreed. "I've a good mind to tie a concrete block to his feet and push him back under, the dickhead. I'm just getting a refill mate, do you want one?"

"Yeah and make it a large one, I fucking need it."

It was almost midnight and the party had really got going. Phil was making cocktails and offering them to anyone who was brave enough to drink them. After knocking back a Pina Colada, which she thought should be renamed Rum Colada seeing as that was obviously the only thing in it, Kate was feeling light headed and was dancing on the grass with Maria and Rick's wife, Sharon.

"You should go steady on that," said Charlie, looking at her empty glass with a frown. "We both know what happens when you drink too much."

"Leave her alone, Charlie," admonished Maria. "She's enjoying herself."

"Yeah, leave me alone," agreed Kate.

"Fuck me, is there an echo or what? I'm only saying girls." He threw his hands up in the air and walked away, chuckling to himself. "Kate knows what I'm talking about, don't you darlin'?"

"I know I shouldn't say this seeing as you two have just tied the knot," said Sharon as she watched him walk away with a wistful expression on her face. "But I just fucking love him. What I really want to know though love, is what he's like in the sack?"

Kate smirked because unbeknown to Sharon, she was wondering the exact same thing.

The music became louder as the drinking got heavier. Kate spotted Charlie on the patio, dancing in the arms of a young girl. A waitress from his bar, she was sure her name was Precious or Paris or something. She was wearing a tight black dress and had the most amazing pair of legs Kate had ever seen. Charlie was whispering something into her ear and when she threw her head back and laughed, Kate felt green-eyed with jealously. It was ridiculous; it wasn't as if they were really married for heaven's sake, he could do what he liked. She drained her glass with the intention of getting another and drinking her way to oblivion when she saw Mickey purposefully striding towards her. She moved to try and dodge him but it was too late.

"I think we got off on the wrong foot."

His voice was slurred. Not surprisingly he was really drunk and if she wasn't mistaken, he was on more than just alcohol. His eyes were dilated and heavily bloodshot and they roamed over her like a racing horse owner inspecting his thoroughbred. He looked painfully thin and she wondered if he was ill; his Lacoste polo shirt was at least three sizes too big and was tucked into frayed jeans that were being held up by a tattered brown leather belt. Kate took a step backwards. Mickey had no concept of personal space and his breath stank. She was tempted to waft her hand under her nose but didn't want to appear rude. He was Charlie's friend after all.

"Here," he said and thrusted his glass towards her so that she could take a sip. "Let's have a drink and get to know each other better."

There was no way she was putting her lips on his glass; she had no idea where his mouth had been. And she certainly didn't want to get to know him any better. She'd already seen enough to know that they were never going to be holding hands and singing Cum Bi Ya together.

"I was just going to the bar," she said and seeing a chance to escape went to walk away. Unfortunately he put his hand on her arm and stopped her.

"There's something you need to understand, sweetheart. Charlie and I have a very complicated relationship and I don't want anything getting in the way of that."

"By anything I take it you mean me?" said Kate not liking where this conversation was heading.

Mickey gave her a wide grin. "You got it, sweetheart."

The grip he had on her arm was a little too firm to be friendly and the look in his eye made her feel uncomfortable. She just wanted him to leave.

"I don't know what it is you're trying to say Mickey but I can promise you I won't be getting in anyone's way, especially yours. I've no intention of stopping Charlie doing anything he wants to do."

"Good. Because we have history together and you coming along makes me uneasy. It was all very sudden wasn't it, you and him?"

"Yes, I suppose it was."

"I'm not gonna lie to you sweetheart, I'm finding it all a bit hard to swallow. You see Charlie was never the settling down kind and now all of a sudden you're here and I'm wondering what's going on."

"Nothing's going on. We love each other." She tried to sound as believable as she could but after three Pina Coladas she wasn't sure how convincing she was. "Look Mickey, I know it all happened very quickly and you just want what's best for him but so do I. I love him and he loves me."

"You're not his type though, are you? But lucky for you," he said leaning in closer. "You're definitely mine. So why don't we slip off somewhere a bit quieter and really get to know each other?" He trailed his finger down her arm until it settled at her wrist then drew small circles with his fingertips.

She flinched; he was coming onto her, only an idiot would think otherwise. Alarm bells rang in her head. She needed to extricate herself from this situation and quickly. She didn't want anyone to see them and think she was a willing participant. Her eyes darted over to Charlie but he was engrossed with the waitress from the bar and wasn't paying them any attention. Phil and Maria were nowhere to be seen but thankfully she managed to catch the eye of Rick who whether he realised what was going on or not, seemed to be heading straight for them.

"There you are," he said taking hold of Kate's arm firmly. He turned to Mickey and in a not so friendly tone, said, "go and sort your girlfriend out Mickey, she's pissing in the bougainvillea."

There was no mistaking the heated look on Rick's face and for the briefest of moments she thought there was going to be trouble between them. Thankfully Mickey lowered his eyes and walked away, leaving Kate staring after him in a state of relief.

"Oh God, thank you," she blurted as soon as Mickey was out of earshot.

Rick furrowed his brows and gave her a hard stare. "Are you okay?"

"No I'm not." She wasn't sure how much to tell Rick so she just rolled her eyes. "Is it me or is he just fucking weird?"

"Nah, it's not you love. The lift don't reach the top floor, know what I mean?" She did know what he meant and Rick's description summed up Mickey perfectly. "Come on, let's get you a drink, you look as if you need one."

The bar was only small and Rick went behind it to pour her a shot of Tequila. As soon as he handed it to her she downed it in one and indicated for him to pour again. She didn't care whether the night ended with her head down the toilet, all she wanted to do was to forget that the last ten minutes had ever happened.

"Was he hassling you?" asked Rick studiously.

She decided it best not to elaborate, not wanting to be the cause of any trouble. So she shook her head.

"What is it with him and Charlie? I don't understand their relationship at all."

"I think that's best coming from him, love. Listen, a word of advice. Steer well clear of Mickey, he's a bit of a loose cannon. He can't help it, it's just the way he is."

Thankfully Kate didn't see Mickey again. He left shortly after Rick dispatched him to go and deal with his girlfriend and never returned. She was relieved. Without Mickey around she could get back into the party spirit. She was quite drunk now, not totally wasted but sozzled enough to be dancing to a Steps song with Maria. Charlie was talking to yet another young girl; this one was blonde with red lips that were so full, it looked as if they'd been stung by a bee. He caught her watching him and smiled but determined not to let him see how bothered she was, she stropped off to the bar.

"What's the matter darlin'?" asked Charlie following her. "Am I neglecting you?" He went to put his arm around her shoulders but she threw him such a filthy look he didn't bother. "Come on, don't be like that, what with us being newlyweds and all."

"Why don't you run back to your little friend?" Kate nodded in the direction of the girl. "It looks like she's missing you."

"Now, now, don't be a bitch," he tut-tutted. "Her name's Zoe and she's Phil's sister. And there's nothing going on between us. Just so you know, I'm not into little girls."

"What are you into then?" Kate could've kicked herself the moment she asked the question but it was too late to take it back now.

"Funny you should mention that. You see there's this sexy brunette, about so high." He indicated an area somewhere between his chest and his chin. "She's wearing a green dress and has her hair up which incidentally, I find really fucking hot. The thing is she's got a really shitty attitude and refuses to admit she's into me."

"What makes you think she's into you?"

"Because darlin', when I touch her I feel her tremble and that tells me everything I need to know." He traced his thumb across her lips and sure enough, she quivered.

"So what are you going to do about it?" she asked, her voice barely a whisper. She couldn't move if she wanted to, she was totally rooted to the spot.

"I'm gonna flirt with every woman here and make her insanely fucking jealous."

"Good plan," she agreed. "But will it work?"

He kissed her softly on the cheek. "I don't know. We'll just have to wait and see, won't we?" He walked away, throwing her a wink over his shoulder.

Kate let out a breath. He was incorrigible and he knew it.

The bastard.

Music was still filtering through the speakers but the volume was low. It was four o'clock in the morning and only a handful of people remained, most of them sprawled out on the rattan furniture in a drunken stupor. Charlie felt good. After their performance tonight, nobody would ever suspect that he and Kate were anything but a happily married couple. In fact, with the lack of action in the bedroom department, he was starting to think that they actually were. That's why he needed to screw her and fast, if only to relieve some of the tension he was feeling.

He'd been watching her for the last fifteen minutes trying to decide when to make his move. She was pleasantly drunk, not to the point where she didn't know what she was doing but pretty plastered nonetheless. He felt no shame in hitting on her whilst she was intoxicated, some of the best sex he'd ever had was with drunken women. Alcohol was definitely the best way to lubricate a woman's knickers. Get them tipsy and then lay back and enjoy the ride.

"What are you smiling at?" Kate sashayed over to him, dancing to a Camila Cabello track that was playing softly in the background.

"I was just wondering when to get the bucket ready."

"Just because I was sick that one time doesn't mean it's going to happen again."

"Are you sure about that?"

"Yes, I'm sure."

"Good, because I can think of better ways to end the night than holding your head down the toilet."

She eyed him coyly. "I've had a really great time tonight, thank you."

The praise was unexpected and he smiled. "It was my pleasure, darlin'."

"I want to go for a swim," she said, surprising him again.

"Do you now?" he frowned. "In the state you're in, you'll probably drown."

"Then you'll just have to save me, won't you?"

She strolled to the edge of the pool and peered down into the water. Then slowly she pulled up her dress. For one excited moment he thought she was going to take the whole thing off but she stopped at her knees. She threw him a suggestive smile; she knew exactly what she was doing, the little bitch. He couldn't take his eyes off her as she stretched her foot out and began to dangle it into the water. But just as she leant forward she began to wobble and appeared to lose her balance. He shot towards her to save her from falling in but she let out an excited laugh and jumped to the side.

"Umm...someone's playing games," he said, impressed and annoyed at the same time.

"Maybe," she grinned. "Or maybe your plan has worked and I'm insanely jealous."

"Well make up your mind darlin', because you're fucking killing me here."

"Dance with me."

He didn't need to be asked twice so he pulled her into his arms. She looked up at him expectantly, a hot and heavy glimpse full of passion and promise. A flirtatious move if ever he'd seen one. If she was eye-fucking him then surely that had to be a good sign?

Somewhere in the recess of his mind he heard someone calling his name but didn't dare answer for fear of ruining the moment. He'd waited a long time for her and wasn't about to let the opportunity slip through his fingers.

"Let's go to bed," he whispered into her ear.

She didn't answer but she didn't pull away either. She was battling with her conscience; another good sign. He could see she was contemplating his offer and was on the verge of accepting when she suddenly lowered her eyes.

"I've never been into casual sex."

He wasn't surprised; that was obviously why she was so uptight.

"What if you break my heart?"

"Darlin'," he said with a sigh. "It's already broken."

She looked up at him with those smouldering eyes and at that moment he just snapped. That was it, he'd had enough. No more fucking about. He grabbed hold of her and threw her over his shoulder in a fireman's lift.

"What are you doing?" she shrieked loudly.

"I'm taking my wife upstairs so I can fuck her. Is that alright with you?"

"But there's still people here...."

"So what? It's about time we consummated this marriage and we're gonna do it before you change your mind."

He slapped her on the arse and carried her shrieking into the house.

Throwing her down onto his bed he stripped off his clothes as fast as he could. He climbed on top of her and kissed her. She responded eagerly, her tongue teasing and probing and their kiss hot and breathless. He eased her dress up her thighs but taking things slowly wasn't going to cut it. It had to come off. He was desperate to get a look at her and as he glided the material up over her head he wasn't disappointed. She was wearing a lacy strapless bra and a matching pair of white knickers but they would have to go too. The bra was easy; he inched his arm behind her back and unfastened it single-handedly. Her breasts were smaller than he was used to but they were perfectly formed and he wasted no time sucking them into his mouth. She cried out as he snapped the elastic of her knickers, he hadn't meant to be so rough but if he didn't get inside her soon he was going to explode. Almost too late he remembered a condom and grabbing a packet from his bedside drawer he ripped it open with his teeth and rolled one on in double time. He had no patience for foreplay and got straight to it.

He thrust his cock inside her and they both groaned. As they gained momentum she let out a series of little cries that almost finished him. She was so wet and tight, he could barely control himself. He knew he should take his time, get to know her body and the things she liked but honestly, the way she was urging him on, it was as if she needed to come as fast as he did. She gripped his arse with one hand, the other was raking her nails across his back and her lips were on his. He kissed her hard, catching her moans in his mouth and he thrust harder and faster until at last, he felt her pussy contracting around his cock. Even in such a frenzied state, he cared enough to ensure she came first and as she gasped and writhed beneath him, he finally let himself go. It had been forever since he'd had a good fuck and his climax felt out of this world.

This was exactly what he needed.

It was the perfect way to end the night and was the ultimate achievement. He'd finally screwed her. It was going to put a smile on his face for the rest of the week.

CHAPTER TEN

I t took Kate two milliseconds to realise that she wasn't in her own bed. The sheets that caressed her skin were the crispest cotton and the scent that lingered in the air was masculine and strong. She propped her head up on her elbow and took a good look around. Charlie's bedroom was a lot less pretentious and a lot more unassuming than she'd imagined. She wasn't sure what she had expected but there was no sign of any notched bedposts, no handcuffs dangling from the headboard and no sex toys or gadgets strewn across the floor. Not exactly the shagging pad she had pictured in her head but instead a light, bright airy room with spectacular views across to the mountain. There was even a beautiful terrace with a scattering of exotic palms. The only thing missing she realised, was Charlie.

She rolled onto her back and stared up at the ceiling. Amazingly, after all the alcohol she had consumed last night she didn't have a hangover. Not even a huge blank void where her memory should be. Instead she felt warm and fuzzy and the incredible satisfaction of having had the most amazing orgasm of her life.

She held a hand to her forehead and recalled how she'd ended up in Charlie's bed. He'd literally driven her crazy with jealousy all night. His repeated come-ons and the knowledge that he wanted to have sex with her had finally made her throw caution to the wind and go for it. But along with the after-sex glow her body was basking in, was the realisation that she had done the one thing she'd promised herself she'd never do.

She'd had a one-night stand.

She grinned; why on earth had she never had one before?

She felt fantastic, at least her body did. Her head was still trying to catch up with the fact that it was a one-off and definitely wasn't going to happen again; Charlie had made his feelings perfectly clear on that score. He hadn't hung around for a repeat performance either which was fine by her. It wasn't as if she hadn't known he only wanted to get into her knickers. He was a bloke after all.

But now that he had, she hoped that things would finally calm down between them and that he'd finally allow her to get on with the job in hand.

Yeah, she thought to herself. Like anything was ever *that* easy.

It was almost eleven o'clock by the time Kate showered and strolled downstairs. The villa had been thoroughly cleaned and there was no evidence that the party last night had ever taken place. Isaura was loading the last of the glasses into the dishwasher when Kate entered the kitchen.

"Buenos días Missus Charlie, you have a good time at the party, no?"

Kate recalled the orgasm Charlie had given her and nodded. She'd definitely had a good time at the party.

"Mister Charlie, he outside," said Isaura pointing to the garden. "Let me get you some coffee."

Kate felt anxious about seeing Charlie again. What if the sex hadn't been as amazing for him as it had been for her? What if he'd found her dull and boring and that was the reason he'd left before she'd woken up? There were so many questions going through her head but deep down, she wasn't sure she wanted the answers.

They might make her feel even worse.

Charlie was sitting in the shade when she stepped outside. If things were going to be weird between them then now was the time.

"Morning," he said flashing her a wide grin. "You snore."

Instantly she felt herself blushing. "I do not!"

"Trust me darlin', you do. Sit down, I've made you some breakfast."

"Thank you," she muttered awkwardly. She saw the croissant and glass of orange juice on the table and pulled out a chair.

She'd never been in this situation before. What

was one supposed to say the morning after the night before? And did he really have to stare at her like that? She sat down and took a nibble out of the croissant but cursed as the pastry crumbled down her chin. She brushed the crumbs away and took a sip of orange juice. The ice cube clanged against her teeth and she slurped, making an awful noise that turned her cheeks even redder.

Charlie propped his arm up onto the table and cupped his chin in his hand. He was enjoying her discomfort and could see how embarrassed she was. He was about to say something when his phone vibrated on the table. He picked it up and frowned.

"I don't mean to shag and run darlin' but I've got to go to work. There's some stuff I need to take care of at the bar. Have a swim or read a book or something, I won't be long."

She stopped chewing, trying to think of a suitable response but she couldn't think of anything to say. Charlie got to his feet and as he walked past her he swooped down and kissed her on the head.

"And just so you know," he said with a wink. "You come like a goddess."

Charlie switched on the air conditioning in his office. Well he called it an office, it was more like a stock room really. There were crates of alcohol stacked three or four deep, sanitation supplies that wouldn't fit in the cleaning cupboard and boxes of champagne and beer glasses to replenish the never-ending round of breakages.

He pulled out the swing chair and sat at his desk. After his two-week sabbatical in England his paperwork was behind and he had a stack of bills to pay. Phil was an excellent bar manager but paying the suppliers was Charlie's responsibility and he knew he'd let it slide. He sorted through the mess on his desk, piling invoices on one side and receipts on the other and made a couple of phone calls to get some urgently needed stock delivered. This part of the job he found a ball ache; he'd much rather be on the other side of the bar, knocking back drinks and chatting with the customers.

His phone rang. He saw that it was Mickey but couldn't be arsed to answer it. He let the call ring out knowing that Mickey would leave a voicemail which he wouldn't bother listening to either. Nothing he had to say interested him. He'd turned up at his house last night off his head on drugs and had made a complete spectacle of himself. The only reason he hadn't laid one on him was because he hadn't wanted to lose his rag in front of Kate. He shook his head; Mickey had always been a fucking liability.

He picked up an invoice but couldn't make head nor tail of it. His mind had wondered off and he was picturing Kate lying beneath him, groaning like a wild animal as he fucked her. He was a selfish prick and he knew it and once he'd gotten into her knickers he'd been so sure that it would be mission accomplished. Now however, as he thought about her naked body and their hard fucking, he realised it might take one more shag to get her out of his system. He felt his cock stir and he grinned.

"What are you so happy about?"

Phil's voice came out of nowhere and disturbed Charlie's erotic daydream, putting paid to his impending hard-on. He strolled into the office with a stack of receipts in his hand and added them to the pile already on the desk.

"I'm no expert at mind reading but I'm guessing it's that wife of yours?"

Not for the first time, Charlie felt the heavy pang associated with lying to his friend. He wasn't proud of what he was doing and he certainly didn't want to hear the reproach in Phil's voice when he discovered he was making deals with a lowlife like Declan Connors.

"What are you doing here?" asked Charlie changing the subject. "Why aren't you at home sleeping off your hangover?"

Phil made a face. "Maria's mother's visiting."

Charlie knew only too well how Phil felt about the delightful Senora Alonso Ramos. Disappointed by her youngest daughter's choice in boyfriend, the old bag never missed an opportunity to slag Phil off and tell Maria how she could do so much better than an Englishman. Phil perched on a crate of champagne positioned in the centre of the room. There were few people that Charlie trusted and he could count them on one hand. Jason was one but he was five thousand miles away and yes he could pick up the phone for a chat, but it wasn't the same. Phil was another and the way his friend was staring at him it was almost as if he knew that something was going on. Charlie squirmed in his chair. He was going to tell him; if he didn't tell someone soon his head was going to explode.

"What would you say if I told you that Kate and I weren't really married?"

"What do you mean you're not married?" asked Phil blankly. "Wasn't it a legal ceremony?"

"No, there was no fucking ceremony. That's what I mean, we're not married."

"Then why are you saying that you are? Sorry mate I don't get it."

"Kate isn't my wife Phil, it's a con. She's only pretending to be my wife so that I can pull a job with Declan Connors."

"Declan Connors?" Phil's eyes widened in surprise. "What the fuck do you want to get hooked up with him for?"

"It's complicated."

Phil threw his arms wide open. "I've got all day mate."

Charlie ran a hand through his hair. They'd certainly pulled some shit together over the years but this was a first. "Declan's branching out. He's putting a team together to raid a security depot in Brighton and he wants me in on it."

"I thought your days of running around with a shotgun were long gone, unless I'm mistaken?"

"I won't be there for that, he needs Jack and knows he can't have him without me."

Jack Mortimer was an expert hacker, a computer

geek who at the young age of twenty-four could slice through firewalls like a knife through butter. With Jack inside the system, the security protocols would be disabled enabling them to walk into the facility, lift the cash and walk straight back out again. Jack also happened to be Charlie's nephew and wouldn't work with anybody else.

"Okay I get that he's bringing you in to get to Jack but why do you need a wife?"

"That's where it gets interesting. Have a guess who Declan's married to now?"

Phil shrugged his shoulders in a 'fuck knows' gesture.

Charlie said the word, "Francesca," and could barely believe it himself.

Phil did a double take. "As in your ex-wife Francesca?"

"The one and only."

"Fuck me, she gets about. No offence mate."

Charlie grinned. "None taken, it's not like we were love's young dream, was it?" Charlie shook his head to rid himself of the memory. "Declan's a jealous fucker and can't stand the fact that we have history together but he needs me. He ain't fucking happy about it and because I don't want him putting a bullet in my head I'm gonna put on a show, convince him I'm not interested in Francesca, which by the way I'm not, and give us both one less thing to worry about."

"So, let me get this straight. You're pretending to be married to Kate in order to convince Declan Connors that you haven't got the hots for his wife who coincidently you were married to more than ten years ago. And all to make him feel better and spare his feelings. He's a career fucking criminal Charlie and the only reason he ain't banged up is because his brief's as bent as a nine-bob note. Have you lost your fucking mind?"

"It's a lot of money Phil."

"I should fucking hope so. What does Mickey say about it?"

"Well that's just it," said Charlie reluctantly. "Mickey's not involved, you've seen what he's like lately. He glassed that waiter the other week just because he spilt a drink on him and now he's smuggling drugs for the Albanians. Mad fuckers they are, they're the slit your throat now, ask questions later type. That's why I need to do this job, Phil. I can pay Mickey off and retire for good. It's been five years since Jamie died and I think I've paid my dues, don't you?"

Phil contemplated everything Charlie had told him. "I get it, I really do but don't you think you've gone to extremes this time mate?"

"For that kind of money there's not a lot I wouldn't do."

"I just hope Mickey doesn't find out what you're up to."

"I can handle Mickey."

"And what about Kate? Can you handle her?"

"Don't worry," said Charlie with a grin on his face. "I've got her exactly where I want her."

Charlie finished his paperwork and poured himself a large brandy. After his conversation with Phil, he couldn't get Jamie out of his head. The memories came flooding back and he could still remember the events as if it had been yesterday. What had started as a bar fight had turned deadly and it had all been his fault.

The images engulfed him and although he willed himself not to be, he was back at the bar in his local pub enjoying a quiet drink with some friends. But in Southwark where he grew up that was unheard of. A rowdy crowd had breezed through the door just before the barmaid called last orders and were making a nuisance of themselves, yelling and jeering until Charlie decided that he'd had enough. His temper flared and against Jamie's pleas to leave well alone, he punched one of them in the face, followed in quick succession by a chair over the head and a snooker cue in the stomach. All hell had broken loose and Jamie had unwittingly got involved, as did Phil and Jason but after just a few minutes of violent fighting the opposing gang ran out of the door.

In all the confusion nobody noticed that Jamie was lying on the floor with a ten-inch blade sticking out of his stomach. By the time Charlie saw it, it was too late to do anything, the knife had pierced Jamie's liver and he was already bleeding out. Charlie cradled his friend's head in his hands as in between spitting mouthfuls of blood, Jamie had made him promise to watch out for his younger brother,

Mickey. Charlie had sworn he would; crazy with grief, he would've agreed to anything.

He spent the next week on a drunken rampage. The police hadn't managed to locate the man who had stabbed Jamie but Charlie did. And when Jason finally pulled him off, the man was already unconscious with a fractured skull, two broken legs and a ruptured spleen. They left him in an alleyway behind a public car park to rot.

Charlie had long ago accepted the blame for Jamie's death. The guilt he carried would never leave him. And no matter what messes Mickey found himself in, Charlie knew that he would always bail him out.

But now the situation was getting serious and Mickey's involvement with the Albanians changed everything. It was only a matter of time before the shit really hit the fan.

CHAPTER ELEVEN

Set in the Sierra Morena mountain range, twenty-five minutes from Seville stood the impressive home of Declan Connors. In a typical Spanish design, the single storey farmhouse-style villa had white stucco clad walls and terracotta roof tiles which gave it a typical Andalusian feel. Tall, tower like chimneys adorned both ends of the property and ornate ironwork graced the windows. A wide, elegant archway led to the imposing wooden front door.

Charlie switched off the car engine and sensing Kate's apprehension, put a reassuring hand on her knee.

"Don't worry, darlin', it's going to be fine."

"That's easy for you to say," she replied as her stomach churned. "What if I make a mistake and he realises we're faking it?"

"He won't. Just remember everything I told you and try to act naturally."

Kate rolled her eyes. She hadn't been able to act naturally since crawling out of Charlie's bed. Everything was riding on her ability to convince Declan that she and Charlie were in love but how was she meant to do that when she couldn't even look him in the eye and flinched hopelessly every time he touched her?

"Okay, I've got this," she said steeling herself and blowing out a breath. "Shall we set a code word or something, just in case I need rescuing?"

"Darlin', this aint a James Bond movie. Come on, let's go."

Francesca Connors was the most beautiful woman Kate had ever seen. She glided out of the front door with the grace and self-assurance of a catwalk model and floated towards them in a pair of denim hot pants and a flamingo pink bikini bra. Her slender body and long legs were a perfect shade of brown and her long blonde hair glowed like a halo on top of her head.

"Charlie! It's so good to see you."

She tossed back her hair theatrically and threw her arms around him.

"Hello Francesca. You look great, darlin'."

Francesca gave him the dazzling benefit of her perfect white smile. "It's been too long."

"Yeah? Well let's not get carried away, ey?" He removed her hands from his neck and wrapped an arm around Kate's shoulder, pulling her towards him. "This is my wife, Kate."

Francesca gave Kate a smile that didn't quite reach her eyes, it just fizzled out somewhere between her botoxed lips and her surgically enhanced cheek-bones.

"Where's the old man?" asked Charlie, checking out the silver Aston Martin parked in the shaded car port.

"He's out the back waiting for you."

"Is he still pissed at me?"

Francesca threw her head back, swished her long hair and laughed. "You know what he's like. He can hold a grudge forever but it won't stand in his way of making money. Come on, follow me."

With a combination of stone and white painted walls, the house was just as impressive on the inside as it was on the outside. Wooden beams ran along a high-ceilinged entrance hall and led to an open planned living area which was stylishly decorated in various shades of cream and beige. The furniture was solid oak and on one side of the room a baroque fireplace stretched from floor to ceiling. A corridor paved with patterned terracotta tiles led to an indoor covered bar area which opened out directly onto a picturesque courtyard with potted palms and sumptuous wicker furniture. Sitting at the table was a man. He was older than Kate expected and from the deep-set wrinkles around his eyes she guessed he was somewhere in his late fifties. He had narrow oval shaped eyes and thick bushy eyebrows that were in need of a good manscape. The inch-long jagged scar which ran along his left cheek ruined any hope of him being handsome and left him looking stark and dangerous instead.

"Charlie," he said in a heavy Irish brogue. "How ya doing?"

Both men shook hands gingerly. "It's good to see you again, mate." Charlie made introductions and as Declan gave Kate the once-over she felt the intense scrutiny in his eyes.

"Now if you don't mind, Francesca's gonna give you a tour of the house while me and this fecker here talk business. Give us a little while, yeah? We've things to discuss."

Whereas the exterior of the house was entirely traditional, the interior was the exact opposite. As Francesca showed off room after room of expensive artworks and lavish decorations, Kate couldn't shake the feeling that Francesca would be more comfortable showcasing herself rather than her beautiful home. She was definitely the kind of woman who demanded attention and having been dismissed by her husband to give her the grand tour, Kate got the impression that she wasn't entirely thrilled about it.

It was only when they arrived at the end of a galleried corridor and stood in the doorway of yet another extravagant room that Francesca seemed genuinely happy.

"This is my daughter's bedroom," she said as they stepped inside.

The room was decorated in pale pastel colours and resembled a page from a story book. An exquisite mural of a castle was painted on one wall, with its high turrets reaching to the ceiling. A four-poster bed took centre stage in the room, sitting in the middle of which was a little girl. She was the image of her mother; blue eyes with smooth skin and luscious blonde hair that fell in locks to her waist.

"Mummy!" she cried excitedly. "Have you come to play with me?"

"No sweetheart, I've brought someone to meet you. This is Kate, say hello. Kate, this is my daughter, Maya."

"Hello Maya, it's lovely to meet you. I love your room."

Maya gave Kate a shy smile.

"Maya has just turned four," said Francesca.

"And for my birthday daddy brought me a horse!" said Maya excitedly.

Kate was impressed. When she was four, she'd been presented with a gift-wrapped toy from a McDonalds Happy Meal. Money clearly wasn't an issue for the Connors family.

The grounds were equally as imposing. There were multiple seating areas around the villa and accessed on a lower level via a stone staircase was the lagoon style swimming pool. It's freeform shape and gentle curves wound its way through the perfectly manicured lawn and culminated in a waterfall with a tanning ledge where two wooden sun loungers were positioned.

It was unbearably hot and as they made their way back to the villa Kate was perspiring in the heat. The July sun had reached its peak and even though it was now almost six o'clock in the evening, she could still feel its intense heat burning down on her shoulders.

When they reached the inner courtyard Declan and Charlie were drinking whiskey and chatting easily which Kate took as a good sign. She didn't know much about their relationship as Charlie had been sketchy on the details. What she did know however, was that Declan was possessively jealous when it came to his wife. She could definitely understand why; with Charlie's movie star looks and devilish charm, what man wouldn't feel threatened when he was around?

Francesca headed to the kitchen so Kate pulled out a chair next to Charlie. As soon as she sat down he placed his hand on her thigh, conjuring up images that had no business being in her head right now. Charlie threw her a cheeky grin; she was sure he was thinking the exact same thing.

Declan poured her a glass of Sangria from a jug overflowing with exotic fruit. "So tell me then Kate, how did the two of yers meet?"

She took a long sip, using the time to mentally prepare herself. She was off balance, and not just because Declan was waiting for an answer. Charlie's fingers were stroking her skin and the little circles he was drawing with his index finger were making her quiver. Didn't he realise he was making her hotter than the Spanish sun? She put her hand on top of his, applying just enough pressure to warn him to quit with the fondling. Then she gazed lovingly into his eyes and batted her eyelashes at him like a good wife.

"It was a whirlwind romance," she told Declan with a dreamy smile. "He completely swept me off my feet."

"Aye, he does that, doesn't he?"

Kate couldn't tell if Declan was being sarcastic. He had a hard stony face and wasn't giving anything away so she just smiled and continued with the story that she and Charlie had rehearsed; they'd met via a mutual friend, went out to dinner, feelings developed between them, it was love at first sight etcetera, etcetera. When she reached the end Charlie leant in and kissed her, not a quick peck on the cheek but a slow, lingering kiss on the lips that made the hairs on the back of her neck stand up. She blushed; to an observer it looked as though the kiss was the promise of more to come. To Kate it was her internal warning system telling him to back the fuck off.

"That's grand," said Declan raising his glass. "Let's have a toast to the two of yers." They held up their glasses and chinked. "So how do you like my home?"

"It's beautiful," admitted Kate truthfully. "And I've met your daughter."

"Ah, my little angel. You truly don't know what love is until yer have a child, to be sure. Yer planning on starting a family?"

"You must be joking!" Immediately realising her slip up, Kate laughed. "I mean not yet. Soon though, hopefully."

Declan laughed too; a haughty Irish laugh that came from deep within his belly.

She didn't even dare turn to look at Charlie.

Francesca arrived with dinner. A selection of Tapas dishes, there was a gorgeous lamb casserole like nothing Kate had ever tasted, beef meatballs in a tomato sauce, mushroom croquettes and chilli prawns. They ate hungrily and easy conversation flowed throughout the meal. Charlie had a natural ability to hold people's attention and Kate had to admit, it was one of his most attractive qualities. Along with those sexy brown eyes and that incredible body of course.

Francesca must have thought so too because twice Kate caught her staring wistfully at Charlie when her husband wasn't looking. Pity she didn't do it when Kate wasn't looking because whilst she knew she had no right to be, she couldn't help but feel annoyed. For all intents and purposes Charlie was *her* husband so when he popped a prawn into her mouth and proceeded to kiss off the chilli sauce that dripped from her lips, Kate was only too happy to oblige. It was an intimate gesture that felt shockingly good. But when he went on to squeeze her leg beneath the table and idly ran his fingers under her dress, she thought that maybe they were both taking their performance a little bit too far.

By nine thirty the sky had turned black. Ornate iron lanterns lit the courtyard and Citronella candles burnt on the table, casting flickering shadows and dispersing a sweet lemony scent into the air around them. Declan and Francesca disappeared to put their daughter to bed leaving Kate and Charlie alone beneath the full moon and an array of twinkling stars.

"You've been amazing tonight," said Charlie in a hushed whisper.

"Stop it," said Kate slapping him playfully on the arm. "You're embarrassing me."

Charlie put his finger under her chin and turned her face to his. "You've even convinced me you're in love with me."

"I'm just doing my job. You know, the one you've paid me ten thousand pounds to do?"

"And you've earnt every penny, darlin'. In fact, I think you deserve a bonus, don't you?"

She knew he was going to kiss her and didn't tell him not to. Their lips met and their tongues entwined, the heat from their mouths emulating the heat that was already pulsating between her legs. Her body was on fire, especially when he ran his hand along her thigh.

"When we get home I'm going to do things to you that are gonna blow your mind."

She gasped, a release of shock and excitement. She went to protest but he held a finger to her lips.

"Don't bother talking yourself out of it, we both know it's going to happen."

"I thought we were going to keep this professional?"

"Oh I'll be professional, trust me. I'm very good at what I do."

"You're leading me astray Charlie."

He kissed her again and the worst part of all was

that she knew she was bloody well going to let him.

They said their goodbyes at midnight. With the roof up and Charlie's foot pressed firmly on the accelerator they began to eat up the two hundred or so kilometres back to Marbella. The air in the car was charged with sexual tension. Every time Charlie changed gear he 'accidently' brushed his hand against her leg and the one time she reached for the air conditioning button he reached for it too, causing their fingers to collide and linger together for a few moments.

The kissing started the minute he pulled the car into the driveway. They went inside but didn't make it past the kitchen. Hoisting her up onto the granite worktop he tore her knickers down and buried his head between her legs before she could protest. As his tongue danced over her clitoris she cried out, writhing against him as he licked and sucked. With one hand on his head and the other gripping the worktop she grinded herself into him, urging him on. Something was digging into her bum but she didn't care and as she threw her head back she felt the thud as it connected with the wall. But all she could think about was Charlie's tongue as it slipped inside her and the orgasm that was threatening to engulf her. When she came she cried out, gripping his hair with her fingers and gasping loudly as the wave washed over her.

"You taste amazing," he breathed against her thigh as he nipped at her skin with his teeth.

She couldn't talk, her head was tilted back and her eyes were closed, revelling in the ebbs of her climax. He pulled her against him and she wrapped her legs around his back and her arms around his neck.

"Time to give you that bonus now," he said as he carried her towards the stairs.

She buried her head against his chest and smiled. "Oh really? I thought you just did."

CHAPTER TWELVE

They were due to return to Seville on Saturday and this time they had planned to spend the weekend there. Kate was feeling apprehensive. Having sex with Charlie was one thing, keeping up the façade twenty-four seven was something else entirely; one little slip and she could ruin everything. By Saturday morning she was feeling sick. Literally. It had been years since she'd had a migraine, but the symptoms were all there; the pounding headache, the nausea, the sensitivity to light. Charlie wanted to call Declan and cancel but knowing how important it was to him, she wouldn't hear of it.

"Don't worry," she said as he loaded their overnight bags into the car. "I've taken some pills, it'll wear off."

It didn't. And by the time they reached Seville, she felt awful. Her vision had blurred and she couldn't focus properly. The minute she stepped from the car the dizziness kicked in and she had to grab hold of the car door to steady herself. Ignoring her protests,

Charlie whisked her straight off to the guest bedroom.

"I'm so sorry," she mumbled as she climbed onto the bed.

"Stop apologising for fuck's sake. It's my fault, I should've called the whole thing off."

"I'll be fine, I just need to sleep."

He pressed the button on a control panel on the wall and the shutters came down, blocking out the sunshine and instantly darkening the room. "I don't want you to move. If you need anything send me a text. Here's some water," he said, placing a bottle on the white bedside table. "I'll check in on you later."

Francesca was lounging by the pool in a provocative red bikini and Charlie being Charlie, he gave her a thorough visual inspection. The tiny triangles of material barely covered her silicone enhanced double-d breasts and automatically drew his eye to her ample cleavage. The high leg bikini bottoms also left little to the imagination. She was a good-looking woman, there was no denying it, but surprisingly, he wasn't struck by a lightning bolt of lust in his loins; the sexual desire he'd once felt for her had dissolved as quickly as their marriage had.

He dived into the pool and swam a dozen lengths. He desperately needed to cool off. The drive from Marbella had been a pain in the arse; stuck behind one tractor after another on the winding rural roads, he'd lost his patience and almost driven head on into a lorry in his haste to overtake.

"Where's Declan?" he asked as he pulled himself up onto the side of the pool. Desperate to avoid antagonising him, the last thing he wanted to do was spend time alone with his wife whilst she was wearing her showpiece of a bikini. Declan's paranoia went beyond the realms of normal, a result of Charlie being married to her all those years ago no doubt.

"He's on his way back from the stables with Maya. How's your wife?"

He detected a trace of jealousy in her voice but chose to ignore it. He wasn't in the mood for her bitching; he'd had enough of that when they were married. "She's sleeping, she's got a fuck of a migraine."

"Are you sure it's a migraine? She looked tired to me. You forget how well I know you Charlie. I still remember your tendency to keep me up all night." She fluttered her eyes and tossed back her long hair, letting it fall seductively over her shoulders. "Tell me again, why didn't it work between us?"

"Come off it, Fran, it was a long time ago. What are you bringing it up now for?"

"We were good together."

"Don't make me laugh. It was a train wreck and you know it. Getting hitched on the back of a three-day bender wasn't the greatest idea I ever had."

Francesca shrugged her shoulders. "It was okay for a while."

"Six months in an alcoholic stupor was hardly the prelude for a long and successful marriage, was it? Don't make it out to be something it wasn't, darlin'.

It would never have worked anyway, we were too young and too bloody stupid."

"The sex was good."

"I don't remember much about that," said Charlie, peering down into the water.

"I'd be happy to jog your memory if you like. For old time's sake."

Charlie couldn't believe his ears. "Are you fucking crazy? Aside from the fact that I'm not bloody interested, Declan will cut off my balls and ram them down my throat. Please Francesca, for both our sakes, keep your bloody knickers on."

"Well you can't blame a girl for trying," she huffed and jumped into the water.

Charlie let out a breath. If Declan knew what his wife was thinking there'd be fucking murders. He'd been so preoccupied in faking his relationship with Kate that he'd forgotten what a nightmare Francesca could be. And now she was bringing up their history together, a part of his life he wanted to forget.

Why couldn't she just leave it in the fucking past where it belonged?

Declan returned from the stables with Maya and whilst Francesca put her down for a nap, Charlie followed him into his study. Dark wood panelling and high bookcases made the room dark and masculine and hanging on the wall as a centre piece above a wooden console table was a painting by Salvador Dali, The Great Masturbator. Interesting choice thought Charlie to himself as he looked at it.

He didn't see the appeal, but then again he wasn't a collector of fine art. He was also trying to figure out whether it was the genuine article or a very convincing fake. Either way, he didn't like it so what difference did it make?

In front of the heavy wooden desk were two faded brown armchairs and under his feet, a thick brown shagpile rug. It was the kind of room more suited to old men smoking cigars in their slippers. In contrast to the rest of the villa, it was really old fashioned. Declan gestured for Charlie to take a seat and as he did so, Declan pulled the stopper out of a crystal decanter. On a silver tray were two crystal glasses and Declan poured two fingers of whiskey into each of them.

"Let's get down to it," he said as he handed Charlie a glass. "Is Jack on board?"

"He is," confirmed Charlie.

"And he knows what I want?"

"The alarms to be disabled, the security protocols to be overwritten and access to the vault."

"Aye. You make it sound like a piece of piss."

"For Jack it is. Not for me, I don't have a fucking clue."

"Which is why I need you on the backup team. You're going to hold the family of the Security Manager so if it all goes tits up, we can use him to get into the vault."

Charlie frowned; this was news to him. He'd once made a name for himself banging heads for a living and metering out a particular type of punishment using whatever weapon was available to him at the time. Now however, fifteen years on, he wasn't sure he had it in him anymore.

"Surely you didn't think it was just an introduction I was after? Besides I need someone who can pull the trigger and you have a certain reputation, or at least you used to have. Unless you've gone soft?"

Charlie hadn't gone soft but that didn't mean he wanted to kidnap an innocent family and terrorise them. "I've been out of the game a long time Declan."

"Do yer think I'm an idjit? It's in yer blood, same as it's in mine. Besides, it's not gonna come to that. All you need to do is keep that boy of yours on a tight lead and nobody will get hurt."

Charlie gulped down the rest of his whiskey. If this was what it was going to take for a share in the forty-million-pound prize, then he would do it.

But it didn't mean he was happy about it.

Kate eyes focussed on the red neon numbers of the clock on the bedside table. She didn't know if she was more surprised that she'd slept twenty hours straight or by the fact that Charlie was in the bed next to her, spooning her with one arm stretched high over the pillow and the other draped loosely across her body. She didn't want to wake him but the moment she stirred he tightened his grip and pressed himself hard up against her.

"Morning darlin'. Feeling better?" He yawned and nuzzled his lips into her neck.

"Charlie, what are you doing?"

"Saying good morning. What are *you* doing?"

"Wondering why you're lying naked next to me."

"I'd have thought that was obvious."

She didn't know why she was so surprised. "We're not really married, you know."

"Course we're not, I probably wouldn't want to fuck you if we were. Has your headache gone?"

"Yes."

"So you're feeling better then?"

"Yes."

"Good. So can we please fuck?"

He was unbelievable. And he was turning her into a raging nympho.

After breakfast, Charlie and Declan had more business to discuss so they went into the study and closed the door behind them. As Kate swam in the pool with Maya, she tried to put Charlie's 'business' out of her mind. She was beginning to feel uneasy; every time she tried to talk to him about it he shrugged her off and changed the subject which only drew her to the conclusion that it had to be something illegal. Exactly how illegal she didn't know and deep down she wasn't sure she wanted to find out.

As much as she hated to admit it, she liked Charlie. She hadn't meant to but he was so good looking and had such a wicked sense of humour that she was drawn to him on a whole other level. And then of course there was the sex. There wasn't a word in the dictionary even close to describing how good it was.

Convinced that a man like him would put his own needs above all others, she couldn't have been more wrong. This morning he hadn't even allowed her to touch him until he'd given her two orgasms, one with his mouth the other with his fingers. Only then had he let her return the favour. She was rewarded with a third orgasm that nearly blew her head off.

A splash of water brought her back to the present and she realised she'd been daydreaming. She pushed away all thoughts of orgasms and filed her suspicions of Charlie's illegal enterprises to the back of her mind. She turned the key and locked them in tightly; she didn't want to think about them anymore. She didn't want to spoil the day.

Francesca joined her in the swimming pool wearing a white bikini which looked as if it had been selected from the 'slut shelf' at Ann Summers. Totally unsuitable for swimming, she must have only worn it to flaunt her perfect body and make Kate feel completely inadequate. It worked. In comparison, her yellow two piece from New Look looked like something her own mother would wear.

"So tell me about you and Charlie," said Francesca as she adjusted her Prada sunglasses and flipped onto her back. As she floated on the surface of the water, Kate noticed that even her feet were pedicured; ten highly polished toes sticking up into the air, looking pretty and glamorous. Kate doggy paddled her way to the edge of the pool and leant against the side wishing she'd put her glasses on; the sun was so bright and was shining straight into her eyes.

"Is it a torrid love affair or do you think you'll last the course? He's not really great on commitment you know."

"Are you speaking from experience?"

"I'm trying to give you the benefit of my wisdom."

"Well there's no need," said Kate with a tight smile. "Charlie and I are very happy."

"He gets bored easily, you know. He has the attention span of a fish when it comes to women."

"I'm aware of that."

Kate wished she'd shut the fuck up. She obviously didn't approve of her but that was too bad. "Look Francesca, I appreciate that you two were close once, but it was a long time ago." How long ago, she wasn't sure, because Charlie had been sketchy about the details. "Yes we married very quickly but we're in love."

"I was in love with him too. And we'd only been together for a month when he asked *me* to marry him."

Kate's knees almost gave way. Francesca and Charlie had been married? What the actual fuck?

She saw the smug expression on Francesca's face and suddenly it all made perfect sense. The warm embraces, the lingering looks she gave him, Francesca being so standoffish with her. She'd dismissed it thinking she was being silly but now it was glaringly obvious. Francesca was his jealous ex-wife.

"You did know we were married? Charlie wouldn't be keeping me a secret from you, would he?"

"Of course not," she lied. "We don't have any secrets."

"Are you sure? I bet I can tell you things about

Charlie that will make your hair curl."

Francesca was about to say something when Maya swam between them and demanded that Kate watch her dive off the edge of the pool. Kate was glad of the distraction. Francesca was proving to be the bitch from hell and she couldn't wait to get away from her.

Inside their en-suite bathroom Charlie was taking a shower. Kate could hear the water pounding against the glass door so she sat down on the bed to wait for him. Despite how angry she was, it was taking all of her willpower not to join him. She could barely imagine how incredible sex with him in the shower would be.

She stopped herself abruptly; who was she kidding? There was going to be no more sex. He had lied to her about Francesca and as a result, she'd had to endure Francesca's constant sexual remarks the entire afternoon.

Has he done *that* thing with his tongue yet?

Has he tied you up?

Have you had a threesome?

It had taken all of her self-control not to punch her in the face. If it had been Francesca's intention to wind her up, she'd done a bloody good job.

The shower stopped. Momentarily distracted by the image of Charlie running a towel over those chiselled abs, she quickly shook her head in despair. What the hell was the matter with her? She needed to stop thinking about sex and focus.

He emerged from the doorway, too busy tying his

towel around his waist to realise she was there. As soon as he saw her a smile crept over his face and he immediately let go of the towel. It fell to the floor in a heap. He made a move towards her but she leapt off the bed and marched to the other side of the room.

"For crying out loud Charlie, is that all you ever think about?"

He cocked his head to one side, looking genuinely bewildered. "What's up with you?"

"What's up with me?" she echoed incredulously. "Did being married to Francesca completely slip your mind or did you just not want to tell me?"

The guilty look that flashed across his face was unmissable. "Oh that."

"Yes that. And I've had to spend the entire day hearing about your torrid love affair and sexual escapades. How do you think it felt to listen to Francesca describe every perverted sex act you two performed together?"

"*You what*?"

"And that's not the half of it. It was the absolute highlight of my day to hear how you loved to fuck her up the arse."

Charlie threw his head back and laughed. "Well that's a load of bollocks. She's winding you up, darlin'."

"And the part about you two being married?"

"No," he admitted reluctantly. "That part's true."

She let out a long breath, unsure if she was disappointed or just plain jealous. "Why didn't you tell me? At least then I would've been prepared. She completely blindsided me Charlie and made me feel like an absolute idiot. I had to pretend that I knew all about the two of you and to be honest, I'm not sure my acting skills were that convincing."

Charlie retrieved the towel from the floor and wrapped it around his waist, correctly assuming that there'd be no sex for him tonight.

"I'm sorry, okay? Is that what you want to hear?"

"Well it would be a start."

"I just didn't want to pile any more pressure on you. I knew you were nervous and thought it would be easier if you didn't know the truth. I was wrong." He shook his head and sighed. "You shouldn't listen to a word she says, she's off her fucking nut. She even tried it on with me yesterday."

"I hope you told her to fuck off?"

"No, I fucked her up the arse. What do you think?"

"It's not funny, Charlie."

"I'm not laughing. In fact I'm seriously fucked off that she's telling you crap like that. Why d'you think our marriage lasted exactly five minutes?" He tapped his finger against the side of his head. "She's mental. A total fruit loop."

"You're not still in love with her then?"

"Which part of what I just said aren't you getting? She's a basket case. And Declan's welcome to her. Now stop being so jealous, it doesn't suit you."

Kate was about to argue that she wasn't jealous but what was the point? They both knew she'd be lying. But now she was wondering what else Charlie wasn't telling her. She was rapidly being pulled out of her depth here and needed to keep her head above the water for fear of drowning. "Is there anything else I should know?"

"If you're expecting me to confess all my sins darlin', we might be here a while."

"I was thinking more about the job with Declan."

"That," he said frankly, "is something I definitely don't want to talk to you about. And don't ask me to because you won't want to hear it. Trust me, you're better off not knowing."

"It's something illegal isn't it? Is it dangerous?"

"Darlin', I'm touched that you're concerned for my welfare but seriously, let it drop. Now get your arse in the shower, we're going to be late for dinner."

Feeling refreshed after a cool shower, Kate took a stroll out into the courtyard. She wasn't looking forward to spending another evening in the company of either Francesca or Declan. Charlie had promised they'd leave first thing in the morning and truth be told, she was glad. Declan seemed pleasant enough but Francesca was a right piece of work. Clearly still in love with Charlie, Kate knew she'd pounce on him the minute she turned her back.

The sky was beautiful; there was a warm orange glow encompassing the sun as it slowly made its descent. She stared up at it, enjoying the moment. The constant buzzing of the cicadas had finally ceased and the air was still and quiet. It was just at that moment that she heard raised voices coming from inside. Francesca's voice was high pitched and frantic. Kate listened, wondering whether Declan had finally discovered that his wife still had the hots for Charlie but the words she heard weren't of betrayal. They were of worry and fear.

"I've already checked and she's not there. If you weren't shut away in that bloody office of yours all day you might've seen her."

"Don't blame me. You have one fecking job to do and that is to take care of our daughter. Where the feck can she be? Look again, she's got to be hiding somewhere."

"She's not," shouted Francesca. "I've looked everywhere and I can't find her."

Kate's pulse raced; Maya was missing. Guessing that she had probably wondered off and was playing in the huge grounds surrounding the house, she ambled off and began exploring the garden to find her. She couldn't see Maya anywhere so she decided to widen her search. Descending the curved stone steps towards the pool area, something in the water suddenly caught her eye. Her entire stomach contents heaved as she realised it was Maya.

Shouting at the top of her lungs, Kate ran as fast as she could to the pool. Kicking off her flip flops she dived straight in, slicing through the water and plunging to the bottom of the pool. Reaching Maya, she scooped her into her arms then pushed up with her legs as hard as she could in order to propel them to the surface. She heaved Maya up onto the poolside and as she pulled herself out alongside her, she realised instantly that Maya wasn't breathing. Her lips had turned blue and her skin was grey. She checked for a pulse; there wasn't one.

Kate went into automatic pilot. Instinctively she tilted Maya's head back to free her airway and pinched her fingers over her nose. She sealed her mouth over hers and blew five rescue breaths into her. She checked to ensure her chest was inflating, then performed thirty chest compressions, counting aloud with each one.

Declan and Francesca fell to their knees beside her but Kate wouldn't allow their frantic screaming to distract her. After the chest compressions she repeated the rescue breaths, then repeated the chest compressions again. Time seemed to pass in slow motion; there was no movement from Maya and Kate was beginning to feel that she was too late, that the little girl was already gone. But suddenly Maya began to cough and a river of water gushed from her mouth. Kate flipped her onto her side and let her cough until the coughing turned to tears.

Kate sank down onto the poolside. There was nothing more for her to do. Francesca cradled her crying child in her arms as Kate watched, traumatised by what had happened. She hadn't thought about any of it, she'd just reacted. She hadn't even known whether she was performing CPR correctly. All she knew was that if she didn't do something Maya would die.

Charlie's arms wrapped around her and he held her tight. She was shaking uncontrollably and dripping water all over him but he didn't seem to care.

"I'm alright," she said as she collapsed against him. "I'm just glad I got to her in time." Her teeth were chattering and she felt an involuntary shiver run down her spine.

"You should take her to the hospital," she told Declan. "She needs to be checked over."

Declan didn't argue and lifted his daughter into his arms. He carried her towards the house, a fretting Francesca close on his heels. Kate waited until they were both out of sight before dropping her head onto Charlie's chest.

"That was pretty fucking amazing," he said as he kissed the top of her head. "Where the fuck did you learn to do that?"

"I saw it on the telly once. I didn't even know if I was doing it properly."

"The fact that she's alive says you were. Come on, let's get you inside, you're shaking like a leaf."

The cool air conditioning that circulated through the villa made her shiver even more. Charlie insisted on pouring her a brandy which she didn't want but she necked it anyway and felt the instant warmth flow through her body. Whilst she peeled out of her wet clothes Charlie went into the bathroom and switched the shower on. Exactly thirty seconds later he was standing in front of her, completely naked.

"Well you didn't actually think you were going in there by yourself, did you?"

CHAPTER THIRTEEN

The bungalow-style villa that Phil shared with Maria was a far cry from the pokey bed-sit Charlie had shared with him and Jason fifteen years earlier. Flanked by towering hedges, the villa was painted entirely in white and was bursting with colour from the dozens of flowers in fragrant bloom and the luscious green palms that were planted outside. Charlie parked the BMW and ascended the two stone steps to the porch and duck-ing out of the way of a hanging basket teeming with flame red geraniums, gave the door an almighty bang.

"To what do I owe this pleasure?" asked Phil, open-ing the door in his underpants. "You do realise I've only been in bed for a few hours mate." He yawned loudly, not bothering to cover his mouth. Charlie was rewarded with a bird's eye view of his tonsils and an unmistakeable waft of morning breath.

"I just fancied a chat. Stick the kettle on."

Charlie wandered on through to the lounge and slumped down on the sofa. He loved Phil's home;

whereas his own was modern and contemporary, the bungalow was typical old style with white-washed interior walls and rustic style furniture. It had a traditional and homely feel to it and it always made him feel relaxed. Which was just what he needed at the moment he figured, what with everything going on inside his head.

Phil returned with two steaming mugs of coffee. He handed one to Charlie and sat down in an old leather recliner which judging by its threadbare cushion and worn-out leather, was clearly used more for comfort than for style. He curled his long hairy legs beneath him and took a swig of coffee.

"How did it go at Declan's?"

"One fucking drama after another, but that's what you get when Francesca's around." Charlie took a sip of his coffee; it was creamy and full of sugar, just how he liked it. "She spent the whole time winding Kate up with bullshit sex stories from back in the day. Honestly mate, I swear to God I'll never understand what makes her tick. Then the fun really started when her daughter nearly drowned in the pool. Kate found her and performed CPR, fucking amazing it was."

"Jesus," said Phil, wide-eyed. "Sounds like a right nightmare. So how are things going with you and Kate? It's game on then is it, the two of you?"

Charlie furrowed his brows. "What d'you mean?"

"Don't look at me like that, it's obvious you're shagging her. I can read you like a book."

"Yeah, as usual my cock's run away with me. But

like I've said before, it's nothing I can't handle."

"Really?" said Phil unconvincingly. "Unless you're falling in love with her, of course."

The coffee went up Charlie's nose and shot out of his mouth, spraying the front of his shirt. He dabbed himself down with a dirty sock he found wedged in the side of the sofa then lunged it at Phil's head, hitting him squarely on the nose. "Don't be fucking stupid."

"I'm not being stupid. You just seem very happy, that's all I'm saying."

"What's not to be happy about? The deal's going according to plan, Declan's off my back about Francesca and I'm getting laid. It's a no fucking brainer mate." He kicked off his shoes, swung his legs up onto the table and clasped his hands behind his head.

"If you say so. But from where I'm sitting it looks like more than a game to me."

"It's a business arrangement Phil and besides, she's not even my type."

"Oh that's right, I forget how fussy you are."

Charlie huffed. He was getting the right hump now. He hadn't come here to get all touchy-feely with Phil about his relationship with Kate.

"It's just sex," he said flatly.

"You carry on telling yourself that if it makes you feel better. Look mate, you're welcome to stay as long as you like but I've been up all night working and I'm knackered. I'm going back to bed. Do me a favour, will you? Shut the door when you leave."

Charlie closed his eyes as Phil padded back to the bedroom. He was also knackered, but not because he'd been working. He had in fact spent all night screwing. The sex was pretty fucking fantastic, even if he did say so himself. And afterwards, instead of rolling over and falling asleep as he usually would, he'd laid there with Kate and they'd talked for hours. He'd told her things about himself he'd never revealed to anyone. Details about his violent father and the beatings he'd endured as a kid. He'd also told her about his time spent at a Young Offenders' Institution. Not being an over sharer, he hadn't been looking for pity or sympathy but her silent acceptance of his past was completely unexpected. If she'd been shocked or appalled, she certainly hadn't shown it. Which brought him back to the dilemma that was currently raging inside his head.

Was it just a game they were playing or worse, was he actually falling in love with her? He stifled a yawn and grinned.

Nah, course he wasn't, because that would just be fucking ridiculous.

Kate finished her lap of the pool and settled down on a lounger with her book. She'd started reading it when she'd first arrived at the villa over a week ago but was still on the first chapter. She attempted to lose herself in the intricate plot but after only a few minutes she put it down again. She couldn't concentrate, she had too much on her mind. Well only one thing really, she admitted to herself begrudgingly.

And that was Charlie.

After dropping her back at the villa this morning he'd disappeared and she hadn't seen him since which had given her some much-needed time to reflect on her present position.

She'd known he was a bit of a character; the revelation about his chequered past only confirmed it. What she was having trouble getting her head around was that she didn't care. And that worried her. A lot.

As much as she hated to admit it, she was seriously attracted to him. Yes, he had irritated the hell out of her when they had first met but she was now drawn to him in a way she would never have expected. His bluntness, once infuriating, she now found refreshing; he said what was on his mind and didn't care who he offended in the process. As a result, she knew exactly where she stood with him.

Deep down she couldn't shake the sense that she was falling in love with him. It could just be the intoxicating pull of lust, but all she knew was that when she was with him, he made her feel like she was the most desirable woman in the world. A skill that was already on his list of many qualities.

Her phone buzzed and she was pleased to see it was Clare calling. She filled her sister in on everything that had happened over the last few days, minus the part about having sex with Charlie (she didn't want to have to listen to her sister gloating about *that*), and they chatted for well over an hour. When the call ended her phone immediately rang again and assuming it was Clare calling her back she answered without checking the caller ID. Mark's cheating voice reverberated through her ear and she almost dropped the phone in surprise.

"Kate? Thank God I've finally caught you. Please don't hang up I need to talk to you."

She rolled her eyes in annoyance. Why hadn't she looked at the screen? Mark was the last person she wanted to speak to right now. She wasn't in the mood to listen to his regrets and excuses.

"Have you been getting my messages?"

"All three hundred of them."

"And what do you think?"

"About what?"

"About us starting over. I really want to put this behind us."

She sighed and ran a frustrated hand through her hair. "How many more times do I have to tell you Mark? It's over."

"Look, this would be much easier if I could just see you. Can I come round?"

"No."

"Why not?

"Because I'm in Spain."

"Spain?" He sounded confused. "What the hell are you doing in Spain?"

"What do you think I'm doing?" She hadn't meant to snap but he was getting on her nerves now. "Look Mark I'm really busy, I have to go."

"When are you flying back?" he asked quickly. "I can pick you up from the airport."

"I don't know when I'm coming back."

"How can you not know? Exactly what the fuck's going on Kate? You need to come home, you've got responsibilities here. We have a life together."

"After what you did we have nothing together."

There was silence on the line and she pictured him pacing up and down, getting more frustrated by the second. Mark loved to be in charge and she could only imagine how annoyed he was that the conversation wasn't going his way.

"Listen to me Kate. I'm not willing to give up on our entire relationship just because I had a moment of weakness."

"A moment of weakness? Is that how you're justifying it to yourself? We're done Mark."

"Come on, I know you don't mean that."

She stared at the phone in disbelief. What was it going to take to get through to him?

"I'm going to say this one last time and please, get it through your thick head. Even if you got down on your knees and begged me, I would never take you back. You've made a complete joke out of everything I thought we had. As far as I'm concerned you can crawl into a hole somewhere and die. And stop ringing me or I'll report you to the police for harassment."

She pressed the end call button and for one mad moment, considered lobbing the phone into the pool. She allowed herself a triumphant smile. If he didn't get the message after that, there was no hope for him.

"Wow! Remind me never to piss you off," came a deep drawl behind her. She swung round, surprised to see Charlie standing there. "I must say, my balls have just shrivelled up. The tosser from the office must be shitting himself. It's a pity it's not a crime to be a pathetic spineless bastard because the jury would throw the book at him."

Kate couldn't help but laugh. "Was that too much?"

"Fuck no, I'm proud of you darlin'. And I think you deserve a large glass of something expensive for wasting your time on that prat, don't you?" He brandished a bottle of champagne which he'd been concealing behind his back and poured them each a glass. "Let's finish the bottle and head to the bar. I feel an all-night sesh coming on."

The evening was in full swing when they arrived. It was one round of endless partying after another and Kate was losing track of time on a frightening scale. The champagne had already made her feel wobbly but at least it allowed her to put her conversation with Mark out of her head. She didn't want to waste any more time thinking about him.

Charlie was in a good mood. He was his usual charming self, laughing and joking with his customers and friends and she couldn't help but admire the way he effortlessly moved from group to group. He had a natural affinity with people and they flocked to be around him.

Unlike Mickey who was sitting alone at the bar, sipping beer from a bottle and staring moodily ahead into the distance. He didn't hold people's attention for long and they moved on quickly to get away from him. Kate could sympathise with them. After his audacious flirting with her at the party last week she'd be happy to never be alone with him again.

Sharon and Maria pulled her into their booth in the VIP section and they cracked open another bottle of champagne. Sharon regaled her with stories of some of the seedier patrons of the bar and Kate was shocked by how many infamous characters, adulterers and general bad boys there were amongst them. Throw in for good measure a sprinkling of television celebrities and it became a haven for the insalubrious and the unsavoury.

And the atmosphere was electric.

Kate threw all caution to the wind and swigged back one glass after another, not caring in the slightest that the night would probably end with her head down the toilet again.

Charlie extracted himself from a group of Premier League footballers who were celebrating their recent lifting of the championship title from a rival club. They were getting more riotous with every minute and had taken over half the bar with their troupe of wives, girlfriends and hangers on. He wasn't worried, he knew several of them anyway and although they were loud and boisterous, they were all behaving themselves. His phone started to vibrate in the pocket of his jeans and knowing he wouldn't be able to hear a damn thing with all the noise and the music playing, he set off for the privacy of his office.

As he opened the door however, he forgot all about his buzzing phone. Kneeling on the floor in the middle of the room was a man and standing over him, a gun in his hand, was Mickey. The man had taken several punches to the head. He had a bruised cheek and an open cut on his eyebrow was oozing blood down the side of his face. Charlie had never seen him before and had no idea who he was.

"What the fuck's going on?" This was the last thing he'd been expecting and his temper was frayed.

"This cunt owes me a grand," announced Mickey boldly.

Charlie took a closer look at Mickey and could see that his eyes were dilated. There was a white powder residue beneath his nostrils; he'd been on the cocaine again. He realised he needed to get hold of this situation quickly, before Mickey's drug induced state caused him to do something stupid. The last thing he needed was a shooting in his bar. A couple of cracked ribs and bruises he could explain, a bullet hole in the head was not as easy.

"Why don't you put the gun down Mickey and we can talk about this, yeah?"

"There's nothing to talk about. I did a job for him and I want my money."

"Job? What job?" Charlie didn't know anything about a job.

Mickey waved the gun erratically from left to right. He was completely bombed and the euphoria was rushing through his body, preventing him from thinking clearly. He hopped from one foot to the other like an excited child.

"His old woman was playing away and needed a slap. I obliged, for a fee of course but now he's refusing to pay me."

So Mickey had reached a new low and was knocking women around. Charlie shook his head in disbelief. These two idiots were as bad as each other. There was no justification for hitting a woman no matter the circumstances. Part of him wanted to walk away and let them kick the shit out of each other; this whole sorry mess had been brought on because the idiot on his knees wanted to teach his wife a lesson. Affair or not, he should simply have left her. But there was the small matter of the gun and in Mickey's hands never had a weapon been more deadly.

"Is this true?" Charlie asked the man on his knees.

The man nodded silently in confirmation.

"Then for fuck's sake just pay him the money."

"I'm not paying him a penny. He was only meant to knock her around a bit but he beat the shit out of her. She's got a tube stuffed down her throat and the doctors say she'll never walk again."

Charlie felt sick. Not only had Mickey beaten a woman, he'd sunk so low as to cripple her. He shook his head in utter despair. "For fuck's sake Mickey, what is wrong with you?"

"She wouldn't listen, the stupid bitch. What was I supposed to do? Anyway, enough of this bullshit." He pressed the barrel of the gun into the man's forehead, so hard that it caused an indentation on his skin. The man closed his eyes, muttering silently to himself. He looked absolutely terrified.

"Don't do anything stupid Mickey," urged Charlie. "Put the gun down and let's sort this out."

"There's nothing to fucking sort out." Mickey, losing patience, swung back his hand and smashed the stock of the gun into the side of the man's temple. The man slumped forward, howling in pain. It didn't knock him out which was surprising as it had been a hell of a blow, but it did create a huge gash in his eyebrow which instantly released a spurt of thick red blood. Mickey then hawked up in his throat and discharged a frothing mouthful of spit into the man's face.

The drugs had taken hold of Mickey. He was sweating heavily, huge droplets of water were dripping from his brow and had pooled on his upper lip. Charlie knew that any attempt to vilify Mickey could end up with the gun either being pointed at himself or being fired accidentally and he was keen to avoid both scenarios. He placed a steady hand on Mickey's shoulder and gave it a squeeze.

"Let me deal with this. I'll get you your money."

Mickey drummed his fingers against his forehead as he tried to come to a decision. Charlie realised that he wasn't capable of rational thinking and was about to give up all hope of getting through to him when Mickey finally relented and handed him the gun. Charlie pulled out the clip, cleared the bullet from the chamber and placed the gun and its components onto the desk. He let out an inward sigh of relief; that was the hardest part over. Now he needed to try and salvage this situation without anyone losing face, including Mickey who he was now considering shooting in the head himself.

"Who the fuck are you?" barked Charlie, looking at the man on the floor in disgust.

The man touched the cut on his face and stared at the red blood on his fingers. "John," came his barely audible reply.

Charlie lost his rag. "Speak up prick, I can't fucking hear you."

"John," the man repeated, louder this time and more confidently which must have taken some balls because his whole body was shaking. "My name's John."

"Well John, it looks to me like you've got yourself into a bit of a situation. Tell me, do you love your wife? Even though she's a fucking slapper who's been putting herself about?"

The man nodded, not daring to speak.

"That's what I thought. So because I'm a reasonable man and you've caught me on a good day, I'm going to make this easy for you. Either pay Mickey the money you owe him or I'll finish the job he started on your wife and trust me, you won't be burying her in an open casket when I'm finished with her. Do you understand what I'm saying?"

Charlie's calm but deadly tone rattled the man enough for him to nod his head.

"Good. Now give me your wallet. Give me your

wallet," Charlie repeated when the man didn't move. "Are you fucking deaf?"

John reached into his pocket, retrieved a black leather wallet and held it out. Charlie snatched it from his shaking fingers and delved inside. There was about five hundred euros in there. He took it, handed the cash to Mickey and tossed the empty wallet to the floor.

"This will do for now but I want the rest tomorrow. Come here to the bar and give it to me in person. And you wanna make sure you're here by midnight mate, because if I have to come looking for you it will put me in a really bad mood." Charlie crouched down beside him and said into his ear, "Now fuck off before I change my mind."

John rose unsteadily to his feet and clutching the side of his head he fled from the room. Charlie watched him go, a sick feeling in the pit of his stomach. He was back to extorting money through violence and intimidation and he hated it. It didn't matter that Charlie had no intention of going after the man's wife, the fact that he'd said it out loud made it real.

And he hated himself for it.

"Nice one, mate," said Mickey as soon as they were alone. He was busy counting the cash with sticky, eager fingers and as Charlie watched, his adrenaline started to pump. He needed to lash out and Mickey was going to earn himself a punch in the face for putting him in this position.

"Don't nice one me, Mickey. You put me in an impossible situation, what was I supposed to do?"

Mickey shrugged; he didn't give a shit. Charlie felt his temper spike. He fisted his hand and was about to take a step towards him when the office door swung open and Kate appeared in the doorway looking like an absolute vision in her short pink dress.

"I thought you'd be in here. Rick sent me to find you, says he needs to talk to you about something."

Charlie took a deep breath and counted to ten in his head. It was a calming technique he'd picked up over the years to help control his temper. Slowly, as if by magic, he felt his heart rate steady to a more normal pace.

"Are you okay?" she asked with a slight incline of her head.

No he wasn't fucking okay, but that wasn't her fault. And he was damned if he was going to take it out on her. Suddenly Mickey became the last thing on his mind. Because he could, he ran his eyes over her and took in her gorgeous tits and her long brown legs and realised that there were other things he'd much rather be doing.

Fuck it, he thought to himself. I'll deal with Mickey later.

Kate felt quite drunk. It was just after two in the morning and she was walking arm in arm with Charlie as they casually strolled home to the villa. She was holding her ridiculously high heeled shoes in her hand and was treading carefully along the pavement trying not to step on any foreign objects.

She was desperate for a wee. She should've gone before they left the bar but she couldn't be bothered, a decision she was now seriously regretting. They continued to walk at a steady pace, but due to Charlie's long legs, it was taking her two strides to keep up to his one.

"So what was that all about with Mickey then?"

Being his usual vague self when it came to details, Charlie shrugged. "Nothing for you to worry about."

"It didn't look like nothing."

"Like I said, it's nothing for you to worry about."

He clearly wasn't in the mood for talking but that was just tough because she was. After all, anything was better than thinking about her bulging bladder.

"Okay, so if you won't tell me about Mickey, how about telling me what Rick wanted?"

"It was just business."

"You're being vague."

"I'm not. I just don't want to discuss it with you. I am allowed to have some secrets you know. But I'll tell you what," he said, seeing the look of disappointment on her face. "Ask me a question about anything else and I'll answer it."

"No you won't."

"I will, I promise."

"Alright," she said, accepting the challenge. "Tell me about your deal with Declan."

He tut-tutted. "Seriously?"

"Okay, okay," she relented. It had been a long shot anyway. So she asked him the one other question that had been burning at the back of her mind. "Why me?"

"Huh?"

"Out of all the women throwing themselves at you, why did you pick me to be your wife?"

"Well that's easy," he said with a grin. "Jason told me what a pain in the arse you are and begged me to take you off his hands. What else could I do? At the end of the day he's one of my best mates and he's pulled my nuts out of the fire so many times that I figured I owed him one."

The fact that he was making jokes proved he didn't want to talk about that either. But at least it sounded better than admitting he'd been desperate. She punched him playfully on the arm.

"You're a dick."

"Why thank you."

They turned the corner into the next street and walked the rest of the way in silence. Charlie punched the code into the control panel mounted in the wall and the side gate automatically opened to allow them entry. He unlocked the front door and they both stepped inside, Charlie heading for the kitchen and Kate for the downstairs bathroom. She only just made it in time. She sat on the loo and put her head in her hands. She was tired and more than a little drunk. What she needed to do was go straight to sleep. Charlie however, had other ideas and pulled her into his arms the moment she stepped into the kitchen.

"Let's go to bed."

"I'm not sure I want to." Well she had to make him

pay for ignoring her questions somehow.

"You're not going to make me beg are you?"

"Maybe."

"You are wearing my ring on your finger, darlin'. Aren't wives supposed to do what their husbands tell them?"

"It's not 1950 anymore Charlie. Besides, I never said I'd love, honour and obey you, did I?"

He hoisted her up into his arms. "You didn't say you'd fuck me either and look where that got you."

She couldn't help but laugh. "True. But isn't a girl allowed to change her mind?"

"Only if it means I get what I want."

She met his lips in a long provocative kiss and as he carried her towards the stairs, she had no doubt in her mind that he was about to get exactly what he wanted.

But that suited her just fine.

Because it was exactly what she wanted too.

CHAPTER FOURTEEN

When Kate eventually made her way downstairs just before noon the next day, Charlie wasn't home. Isaura was already cleaning and after they shared a coffee together, Kate went for a swim whilst Isaura tried in vain to find some clothes to wash; an impossible task seeing as Kate had already done the laundry. She hadn't got her head around having a cleaner, it was an unadulterated indulgence that didn't sit well with her. Her parents had brought her up to be independent and responsible for her own needs. Relying on other people to do things for her was not a concept she was familiar with.

When Isaura left Kate made some lunch and chatted on the phone to Clare. She'd just loaded her plate into the dishwasher and was about to go for another swim when she heard the unmistakeable sound of a key turning in the door. She felt a flutter of excitement; it was ridiculous and she knew it. She heard footsteps but as she turned towards them, the smile died on her face. The man standing in front of her wasn't Charlie. It was Mickey and he was staring at her with a cocksure grin on his face.

"Hello sweetheart. The old man home?"

Kate was shocked. She wasn't aware that Mickey had his own key. The euphoria she'd been feeling gave way to bitter disappointment. "He's not here," she said before mentally kicking herself. What was the use in telling him that?

"Pity," he said without a trace of regret in his voice. "I need to see him about something."

Feeling more than a little awkward, Kate motioned towards the door for him to leave. "I'll let him know you called." But instead of heading to the door, Mickey sauntered off in the direction of the lounge. She went after him but he threw himself down on the sofa, kicked off his trainers and stretched his legs out onto the table in front of him.

"Get us a beer would you, love?"

Kate felt uneasy. She remembered Charlie's warning about him and realised in hindsight that she should have told him that he'd come onto her at the party. But it was a little late to think about that now. Standing there in just a bikini and a sarong she felt exposed and was aware that Mickey was openly gawping at her. She retreated to the kitchen on the pretext of getting him a beer but instead took her phone from her bag and scrolled through her contacts. She reached Charlie's number and pressed the screen to call him, mumbling under her breath for him to hurry up and answer. But the call rang out and when she dialled him a second time, he still didn't pick up.

"Who are you calling?"

The sound of Mickey's voice made her jump and she stuffed the phone back into her bag. "I've just spoken to Charlie. He said for you to go and that he'll catch up with you later."

"Did he now? I'll tell you what, why don't I hang around anyway? We can have a drink while we wait for him."

He opened the fridge and pulled out a bottle of prosecco. He popped the cork and retrieved two champagne flutes from the cupboard. Kate watched him pour and accepted the glass despite having no intention of drinking it.

"Cheers!" said Mickey and downed the entire contents in one. Then he retrieved her handbag from its position on the worktop and proceeded to delve inside.

"What the hell are you doing?" asked Kate, horrified. He was invading her personal space and she wasn't happy about it.

"You wouldn't be lying to me, would you?"

Mickey retrieved her phone and jabbed at it with his finger. Luckily he couldn't get past the fingerprint id. He tossed it aside, knowing it was useless to him.

"You do realise that he's probably cock deep in some blonde, right?"

"Okay Mickey, that's enough. I think you should leave."

Kate turned to head for the door but was caught by

surprise when Mickey suddenly lunged at her. The champagne glass slipped through her fingers to the floor, shattering on the marble tiles with a crash. She was spun around and slammed full pelt into the island. Grabbing a fistful of her hair, Mickey viciously pulled her head back then smashed it down against the hard granite surface. Pain shot through her cheek and she yelped in agony.

"What the fuck are you doing?" she shrieked. "Get off me!"

Mickey lowered his head until his lips were against her ear. "Charlie's had his fun," he hissed, so vehemently that she actually felt the spit showering her face. He ran his tongue along the side of her cheek, his saliva leaving a wet trail on her skin. "It's only fair that I have mine."

She struggled to break free but he slammed her head back down onto the worktop again. The pain ricocheted through her whole body this time and her head began to thump.

"I hope you like it rough, sweetheart," said Mickey as he clasped his hand around the back of her neck and pinned her down. She had a sudden vision of him raping her and as he forced her legs apart with his knees the thought became a reality. Thrashing out blindly with her arms, her hands frantically searched the surrounding area for something to grab. Her fingers made a connection, she had no idea with what but whatever it was, she was grateful. She gripped the object and swung it round. As it connected with the side of his head it gave him just enough pause to enable her to wriggle free. As he recoiled from the blow she made a frantic run for the door. Tiny pieces of glass imbedded themselves into her feet as she flew across the room but she couldn't think about that now. She had just one thing on her mind; she had to get out of the house.

She grasped the door handle with her fingertips but was yanked back and dragged across the kitchen floor by her hair. Her head was on fire and her feet couldn't get a grip, causing her to slide wildly across the tiles. She sank her fingernails into Mickey's flesh and dug her nails into his arms but it was no good. He was just too strong. When they made it to the lounge he hurled her down onto the sofa but she immediately jumped to her feet, seeing a chance to escape. A sharp slap across the face knocked her to the ground. Her head connected with the floor and though she fought against it, she started to lose focus and the room became dark.

"Don't you pass out on me, you bitch. I don't want to fuck a corpse."

Mickey's voice filtered into her consciousness and another slap brought her round but everything was still fuzzy and she had no co-ordination. She tried to move her legs but the signal from her brain wasn't reaching any other part of her body. She felt a vicious tug as her bikini top was pulled from her and rough squeezing as Mickey's hands clamped down on her breasts. She couldn't believe this was happening. Any moment now she was going to wake from this nightmare. But as she felt Mickey's hand slip between her legs she knew it was no dream. And her only chance of getting away was to fight.

But her head was so heavy and her legs felt like lead. She squeezed her eyes shut and prayed to God for the strength to move.

The strip club that had newly opened in Puerto Banus was heavy on opulence and glamour. Gilt framed prints adorned the walls and private booths were furnished with red velvet. Red lighting illuminated the exotic dancers who were either performing on the stage or strutting around serving drinks in three inch stilettoes and not a lot else.

The fact that it was only early afternoon hadn't discouraged any customers. Groups of men, either on stag dos or lad's holidays, were enjoying the delights that were on offer. And there were plenty.

Charlie was sitting between Phil and Rick in a booth and they were leering at a tall, model-thin redhead who was sliding up and down a chrome pole wearing nothing but a silver thong. Her tits, while overtly fake, were shimmering with oil and bouncing around joyously as she dry-humped the pole. Rick was practically drooling, much to the amusement of the others.

The music changed to a faster beat and another girl came out onto the stage. This one was Asian with shiny black hair in the shape of a bob. She was of slight build and stature but nobody was paying any attention to her height; they were too busy looking at her small but perfect round tits and her see-through lace panties as she performed the splits in front of them.

"Fuck me, I'd love to get a piece of that," said Rick almost spitting out his pint.

"In your dreams," laughed Phil, sipping his JD and coke.

Charlie wasn't sure what he was doing there really. So far he'd sat for two hours and although he'd felt the stirrings of a hard-on, (he'd have to be deaf, dumb and blind not to), he hadn't felt a single urge to screw anyone. Least of all the redhead on the pole who was seductively removing her panties now, much to the joy of the crowd. Whooping and jeering came from all directions as she parted her legs to reveal her pussy; clean shaven and sparkling with glitter.

"Ch-rist," said Phil excitedly. "That should come with a public health warning."

Out of nowhere an image popped into Charlie's head. Kate was dancing seductively in front of him, naked except for a pair of black hold up stockings and her high heels. Shit, he realised suddenly, he had an almighty erection. He needed to get a hold of himself. He called the waitress over and ordered another round of drinks. They arrived, courtesy of a topless blonde beauty, and Rick pulled out a roll of cash and started peeling off notes.

"How about a private dance ey, lads?" He waved his money at the waitress who smiled in agreement. She was extremely bendy and all three of them craned their necks to follow her from one flexible position to the next. She used the available space to her advantage and mounted the table, causing their drinks to spill everywhere. That was probably the idea realised Charlie, as this would encourage them to order another round and spend more of their money.

The waitress smiled at him; she was pretty, in a sluttish kind of way. Heavy made-up eyes and red pouting lips, just the kind of girl he'd usually go for. She thrust her tits at him and fondled them, cupping and squeezing them enthusiastically in her hands, then threw her head back and made soft mewing noises as her hands travelled towards her pussy.

Phil and Rick were enjoying the show and so was Charlie, but not as much as he imagined he would when he suggested they check the place out. The girl pushed back on her arms and thrust her hips forward, grinding and simulating sex with all the accompanying panting and writhing.

"I think I've just come in my pants," said Rick excitedly.

The girl began to wind it down and dismounted from the table in one fluid movement. She gave them a wink and held out her hand. Rick slapped the cash into it.

"Worth every penny love," he sighed dreamily.

She blew them a kiss and walked away, leaving them all grinning like a bunch of naughty schoolboys.

"I don't think I'd have the energy to keep up with her all night," said Phil as he took a pull on his pint.

Charlie laughed. "Me neither, mate. I wouldn't

mind giving it a try though."

"Thought you were a happily married man," said Phil with a sly wink. "It's strictly no access all areas now, don't forget."

Charlie hadn't forgotten. And the sooner this deal with Declan was over the better.

"Come on," said Rick. "Let's get out of here. I need to go home and bang the missus before I lose the urge."

They dropped Rick home first. He turned and gave them a thumbs up before he disappeared through his front door, grinning like a Cheshire cat. Charlie talked Phil into coming back to the villa for a drink; it was the only way to stop him ripping Kate's clothes off the moment he walked through the door. But when the taxi pulled up, Charlie was surprised to see Mickey's Porsche parked in the driveway.

"What the fuck's he doing here?"

He met Phil's eyes and they both shared the same uneasy feeling. Charlie leapt out of the cab leaving Phil to pay the fare. He unlocked the door but as soon as he pushed it open his sixth sense immediately alerted him that something was wrong. As he walked into the kitchen he saw broken glass and spilt champagne on the floor. And that's when a scream pierced the air. Racing into the lounge he came to a thunderous halt as his brain processed what was happening in front of him.

Lying on the floor, being held down by Mickey, was Kate. She was fighting like crazy as he pinned her to the ground with one hand and was frantically trying to pull his jeans down with the other. Charlie vaulted over the back of the sofa and lunged at him so hard that they both went hurtling across the room, smashing into a lamp table. The lamp crashed to the floor and shattered, sending ceramic splinters flying like a grenade that had just exploded. They grappled for a few minutes, both of them struggling to gain the upper hand but Charlie was by far the stronger and fuelled by rage and fury, he laid into Mickey with all of his might.

"You sick fuck," he bellowed as his knuckles cracked against the side of Mickey's head. The blow sent Mickey sideways but Charlie grabbed him by the hair and bounced his head up and down against the floor, really fucking hard. He pulled his arm back viciously, causing Mickey to yelp out in pain. He added a double jab to the kidneys and sank his knee into the small of Mickey's back, preventing him from moving. But somehow Mickey managed to free himself and attempted to crawl away on his knees. Charlie was on him again and with another punch to the face, he heard the unmistakeable crunch of bone as Mickey's nose split open. Blood erupted and sprayed onto his shirt, but Charlie took no notice. All he wanted to do was inflict as much pain as physically possible. He struck Mickey in the head again but as he pulled back his fist for another strike a hand grabbed hold of his arm, stopping him mid-air.

"Easy, mate," said Phil cautiously.

"Get the fuck off me Phil." Charlie shrugged himself free and with a right hook cracked the side of

Mickey's face. Mickey hit the floor with a thud.

"Come on mate, that's enough." Phil came up on Charlie from behind and seized both of his arms, wrenching him away before he could throw another punch. Charlie was like a man possessed, shouting and lashing out but Phil had a firm grip. "You're gonna end up killing him for fuck's sake. You don't want to do it mate, not here, not in front of her."

Phil's words penetrated his angry haze; his was the voice of reason that Charlie needed to pull himself out of his trance. He took several deep breaths, trying to dampen the rage that had taken over him. He counted to ten in his head, reaching nine before his breathing returned to anywhere near its normal state. He peered down at Mickey. He was cowering in the foetal position covered in blood and groaning in pain. It would have to be enough, for now at least. He made a silent promise to finish him off later, away from his house and away from Kate who was rocking in the corner of the room like a crazy woman.

"Get him the fuck out of here Phil. I don't care where you take him, just get him out of my sight."

Phil touched Charlie's shoulder reassuringly. "Leave him to me, you go and sort your wife out." Phil hauled Mickey to his feet and dragged him from the room.

Charlie's hands were shaking, his fists bloody and sore but right now that was the least of his worries. Kate was clutching her knees to her chest, trembling uncontrollably. Blood was oozing from a gash in her eyebrow and her right eye was swollen to twice its size; it had already turned a deep shade of purple. Her cheek was inflamed, she'd taken a blow to the head, maybe more than one he realised as he looked at the cut on her lip. He felt a burning rage in the pit of his stomach but it wasn't anger. It was guilt.

He'd been totally consumed by his deal with Declan, the only thing on his mind the money. He'd whisked Kate away from her home, dangled thousands of pounds in front of her eyes like a prized carrot and thrown her slap bang into Mickey's crosshairs.

It was his own damn greed that had caused this.

He dropped to his knees beside her and watched as a lone tear fell from her bloodied eye and rolled down her swollen cheek. She was a mess. Aside from her facial injuries her hair was sticking up in every direction and her arms were covered in scratches where she'd tried to fight Mickey off.

For the first time in his life he didn't know what to say. No words were going to make this right and he was an idiot if he thought he could smooth things over with a wink and a smile. He'd never been the soft and sensitive type but the moment her eyes met his, he knew he was finished.

"I'm so sorry Charlie," she said as she sank her face into his chest. Her skin was cold and she was shivering; he needed to warm her up and fast. He wrapped her in his arms and rubbed his hands over her back and arms, trying to get her circulation going.

"What the hell are you sorry for? This isn't your fault, darlin', it's mine." Unburdening his inner feelings wasn't going to do either of them any good right now, he knew what he'd done and he'd have to live with it, so instead of pouring his heart out to her, he helped her to her feet. "Come on, let's get you up." She was wobbling all over the place and fell unsteadily against him. "I've got you, darlin'," he said and lifted her into his arms. He needed to clean her up and the only place he could think of to do it was upstairs, away from the carnage that surrounded them.

Arriving at her bedroom he kicked the door open with his foot and set her down gently on the bed. She was trembling so he pulled the sheets around her, both for warmth and to protect her modesty; she'd just been through hell and he wanted her to know that she was safe with him.

"I'll be right back," he said and left the room in search of the things he needed.

Alone on her bed, Kate was determined to hold herself together. Although she couldn't stop her body from shaking she could definitely stop herself from having a mental breakdown. She was lucid enough to realise that if Charlie hadn't arrived home when he had, Mickey would have raped her and she'd be in a much worse position than she was in now. Despite the pain in her head and the cuts on her face she'd been lucky.

And she knew it.

Charlie came back holding a green first aid box. He opened the lid and tipped the entire contents onto the bed. "Right," he said as he went through it all. "What have we got here?" He tossed aside the crepe rolled bandages and various packets of different sized gauze and settled on a sachet of alcohol-free cleansing wipes. He ripped open the packet. "This is probably going to hurt."

She winced as he gently dabbed her eye; it was really sore and she was having trouble seeing out of it. Her eyelid felt heavy and she could feel the pressure building behind her eye socket. She had to congratulate Mickey on his fighting skills; he'd done a brilliant job.

"I think you should see a doctor. This is really nasty."

She winced again when he touched her cheek but sucked up the pain. She noticed that Charlie's knuckles were red and bleeding; he wasn't complaining so she wasn't going to either. She glanced down and saw the bright red blood smeared across the sheets and remembered the glass she'd dropped in the kitchen. She hoped Isaura had the Spanish version of Vanish as those stains were going to be a bastard to get out.

Charlie brandished the tweezers at her. They looked tiny in his massive hand. "I can't promise this won't hurt."

He extracted three pieces of glass from her feet. They were only miniscule shards but were razor-sharp. When he was content that all the pieces had been removed he disappeared downstairs and returned a few minutes later with a glass of brandy and two large oblong shaped white pills.

She looked at them dubiously.

"Do you trust me?"

She nodded. With her life.

"Good. They'll help you relax."

Without hesitation, she swallowed them down.

"You're going to fall asleep now," he said as he gently placed a kiss on her forehead. "But I'll be here when you wake up, okay?"

She let her head fall back onto the pillow and as Charlie covered her with a thin blanket she closed her eyes. Within minutes she fell into a deep, dark abyss and gravity pulled her under.

CHAPTER FIFTEEN

The Lady Catherine was a fifty-four-foot Predator Sunseeker motor yacht that was permanently moored in the luxury marina at Puerto Banus. Not the largest of the Predator range by far, it only boasted a single level living area and accommodation for up to six guests, but it still held its own amongst the million-dollar yachts and super cruisers that were berthed either side of it.

As Kate walked along the pontoon she pulled the brim of her hat down over her face and ensured that her dark glasses were in place. She might have looked like a celebrity trying to evade the paparazzi but inside she felt more like a domestic abuse victim. She didn't want anyone to see her, didn't want to have to explain the cuts and bruises on her face and especially didn't want anybody looking at Charlie with the presumption that he was the man who had put them there.

She followed Charlie onto the teak bathing platform and ascended the three shiny steps to the cockpit, an outside seating area with a teak table sitting between two light grey leather bench seats, one of which could be adapted to form a large sunbathing area. Charlie went inside so she proceeded into the saloon where there was another seating area and a sideboard that housed a wine cooler and doubled up as a wet bar. Charlie went to the helm station and began pressing buttons on a dashboard that to Kate, looked like something from the Starship Enterprise.

Having absolutely no nautical knowledge whatsoever Charlie explained to her that the front of the boat was called the bow and the rear was called the stern. It didn't make any difference to her; it wasn't like she was going to become the next Lord Nelson of the seas. She wasn't even sure she wanted to be here really. Not having set foot outside the villa in a whole week she had somehow let Charlie talk her into getting away for a few days but the reality was, she was still shaken by what had happened with Mickey. She was having constant flashbacks, repeatedly asking herself what she might have done to provoke him and if there was anything she could have done to prevent it. She'd had more than a few sleepless nights where she'd tossed and turned and woken up sweating and in a state of confusion.

Charlie had arranged for the locks to be changed and a state-of-the-art alarm system to be installed at the villa and although she had felt safe enough to be alone, Charlie hadn't allowed it. But instead of spending time with her he'd retreated into his office and spent hours on the phone, his conversations sometimes becoming so heated that she could hear him shouting through the walls. She had no idea what was going on because he hadn't confided in her so she just assumed that it was all to do with his business deal with Declan.

What she found hardest to cope with however weren't the days she spent alone by the poolside, but the invisible barrier Charlie had erected between them. Since the attack he hadn't once attempted to come near her, in fact the physical intimacy they'd previously shared was now non-existent. She didn't blame him. After all, why would he want her now that Mickey's disgusting hands had been all over her?

"Why don't you go and unpack," said Charlie, his voice interrupting her reverie and bringing her back to the present. "I'll get us moving."

Kate descended a narrow flight of shiny teak steps into the lower lounge. To the right there was a seating area with a table and opposite, on the left, a small galley which consisted of a sink, built in oven and two ring hob, a worktop area and various wooden cupboards including one that concealed a fridge. A small breakfast bar separated the galley from the lounge area. Straight ahead was the forward cabin, set in an inverted 'v' shape with two single beds and windows on both sides hidden behind unopened horizontal blinds. The walls were light grey and there was a flat screen television mounted between two doors, one which led to a tiny bathroom with a toilet, basin and shower and the other back to the lounge area. With a pang of disappointment she noticed Charlie's overnight bag at the foot of one of the beds. The invisible barrier between them was clearly still in effect.

She made her way along the tiny passageway and entered the master cabin. A huge double bed was in the centre covered by a satin quilted bedspread and matching pillows. Ochre coloured cushions gave it a splash of colour and complemented the teak furniture and teak wooden panelling on the walls. A doorway led to a bathroom, only slightly larger than the one in the forward cabin but again housed a toilet, basin and walk-in shower. She tossed her hat onto the bed and retrieved her bag from where Charlie had intentionally left it on the floor, leaving her under no illusion that the purpose of this trip wasn't to try to restore the physical gap between them, but to simply enjoy a change of scenery.

Feeling somewhat disheartened, she began pulling her clothes out of the bag when she felt the sudden murmur of the engines coming to life. She didn't want to miss anything so she left her clothes where they were, grabbed her hat and climbed the stairs back up to the main deck.

"What do you think?" asked Charlie as he manoeuvred them out of their berthing and negotiated the route to exit the marina. Kate stared at the other boats in fascination as they passed. The view was captivating. Tall sailing boats and super yachts with multiple decks, hot tubs and one even had its very own helicopter pad.

"It's incredible. And I can't believe you named your

boat after me."

"Huh?" He threw her a confused look and she laughed.

"My real name is Catherine. Well that's what's on my birth certificate anyway. Kate's just the name I use."

"Someone's been keeping secrets," he said with a grin.

"If it's good enough for the Duchess of Cambridge then it's good enough for me."

"So what do I call you?"

"You can call me milady."

He laughed. "There's a few things I'd like to call you but milady definitely isn't one of them. Do me a favour and grab me a beer?"

She opened a cupboard door to reveal a wine cooler stocked to the brim with bottles of white wine and Becks. She grabbed one, popped the top and handed it to him.

"I didn't have you down as a man of the sea."

"I'm not," he confessed. "I won her in a high stakes poker game."

"Lucky," said Kate with a low whistle.

"More like stupid. Pissed out of my head on whiskey it seemed like a good idea at the time." He smiled at the memory as he set them on route out of the marina. "I took a two-day crash course in motor cruising and the rest I picked up from the Frenchman who owned her. It was just as well my five cards were less shitty than his, I was so bombed I'd bet the bar. Christ knows how I would've explained that to

Phil."

Within minutes Kate completely got the whole sailing thing. The sun was in her eyes and the wind was on her face. She savoured the sensation, enjoying the cool breeze on her cheeks. She drifted off into her own little world and allowed herself to indulge in the fantasy that this was her life now, here in Spain, with Charlie. But of course it wasn't and reality hit her like a sobering slap around the face. Her illusion shattered, she opened her eyes just as Charlie took them on a series of high-speed manoeuvres that left her knuckles white and her heart racing in her chest.

"Stop showing off," she yelled, holding on to her sunhat to prevent the wind from taking it.

Charlie grinned; he obviously thought it was funny. He cut the speed and they cruised along the coastline. The landscape was incredible and Kate was mesmerised by the enormous jagged rocks that edged into the sea and the rugged mountains that erupted from the ground and reached high into the sky. They encountered endless small coves and Charlie dropped the anchor near a small deserted beach with a scattering of tall palm trees that resembled the backdrop of a Bounty advertisement; it literally *was* paradise.

He killed the engine then proceeded to peel off his tee-shirt and kick off his trainers and then he dived in spectacular fashion off the side of the boat. There was an almighty splash and Kate peered over the chrome railing to watch him glide gracefully beneath the water. Making a split-second decision she decided to join him; the water looked so inviting she couldn't resist. She hurried to her cabin and changed into a bikini but just as she was leaving she caught sight of her face in the mirror and came to an abrupt stop. She'd tried to avoid looking at herself for the past week but there was no mistaking the hideous mess that Mickey had left. Her right eye, although no longer swollen, was still red and sore. The inch-long cut on her eyebrow had crusted over but now looked angry and raw where she had picked at the scab. Her cheek was still a browny-yellow colour, thanks to Mickey cracking her head against the worktop; the doctor said she was lucky not to have broken her cheekbone. The cut on her lip had healed but it was no wonder Charlie didn't want to kiss her anymore. The Bride of Frankenstein obviously wasn't the look he went for, not that she could blame him.

Feeling more than a little deflated she wondered back out on deck but instead of finding Charlie swimming in the sea he was perched on the edge of the bathing platform staring into the distance. A couple of boats had sailed past but had moved out of sight so there was nothing to see except for the cloudless sky and the deep blue and green hues of the Mediterranean.

"Thank you Charlie."

"For what?"

"Persuading me to leave the villa." She meant it. The change of scenery made her feel good and without realising it, it was just what she needed.

"You're welcome darlin'."

"Can I ask you something?" She lowered herself down beside him, dangling her legs next to his in the sea. "Are we okay?"

"What do you mean?"

"You know what I mean, us...me and you. You've been really off with me all week, I feel like you've been avoiding me."

"You're imagining it," he said flatly.

It didn't feel like she was imagining it. In fact if felt as though he'd been deliberately going out of his way to prevent any contact between them. And although she knew she should leave the subject well alone, she just couldn't help herself.

"Do you blame me for what happened with Mickey?"

For a moment she didn't think he was going to respond and when he did he shook his head madly.

"*What*? How can you even think that?"

"Well it's obvious that something's bothering you, I just want to know what it is."

"You're way off beat darlin' so why don't you just drop it, yeah?"

The words were spoken with an unexpected harshness and she knew she'd upset him. She dropped her gaze and observed the foamy crescents as the waves broke against the hull of the boat.

"I'm sorry," she mumbled, wishing she'd just kept her big mouth shut. There was an awkward moment of silence between them that she found hard to cope with. Deciding to break it, she went to speak again but he huffed loudly.

"For fuck's sake, what do you want me to say?"

"I just want the truth."

"The truth?" He forced the words out with a sarcastic laugh and ran a hand through his hair. "Alright, if you want the truth then I'll bloody well give it to you. I'm angry darlin'. Actually if you must know I'm fucking furious because whilst Mickey was trying to rape you I was sitting in a strip club with some bird jangling her tits in my face. So no, I don't blame you for what happened with Mickey, I blame myself. And to be honest I'm pretty fucked off that you would even think it was your fault." He stood up and prepared to dive off the platform. "How's that for the truth?"

It took Charlie almost thirty minutes to swim to the shore and he stretched out on the sand, trying to get his breath back. There wasn't a soul on the beach. It was a secluded cove that could only be accessed by boat and lucky for him, today's travellers had passed it by. The water lapped at his feet and he was tempted to take a nap. He was tired, he hadn't had a decent night's sleep in a week. And now he was being forced to answer fucking ridiculous questions that had the potential to cause him a lot of fucking grief.

He looked up into the sky, squinting in the bright sun. Kate had been right of course. He *had* been avoiding her but it wasn't for the reason she thought it was. The guilt he felt over what happened with Mickey was understandable; the soppy feeling that washed over him every time he looked at her was not.

And that was how he knew he was in trouble.

Despite all his protestations to the contrary, he was in severe danger of becoming a sad infatuated bastard. Thoughts of holding hands and running off into the sunset had invaded his mind one too many times over the last week and he wasn't happy about it. He liked things easy; easy money, easy women and an easy life. That was it. There was no room for all this lovey-dovey bullshit. He'd tried it once years ago, failed miserably and as far as he was concerned, he was over it.

What he needed to do was man the fuck up.

He crossed his arms behind his head and closed his eyes, stifling a yawn. He hadn't even realised he'd fallen asleep until the sound of giggling voices brought him round. He glanced at his Rolex and realised that he'd been out for almost two hours. He stretched his muscles and sat up, craning his head behind him to find the reason for his impromptu alarm call. Two women, both Eastern European by the look of them, were sitting on the sand fifty metres behind him, pointing and laughing at him. He smiled and they smiled back.

"We thought you were dead," called out the dark haired one in broken English. "Washed up on the beach like a shipwreck."

Charlie laughed and checked out her tits. She was

topless and sported an even suntan. Thin, not bad looking, he'd had a lot worse.

"Where did you two come from?" He looked to see if there were any other boats anchored near the cove but The Lady Catherine was the only boat bobbing idly in the distance.

The girl pointed towards a rickety path that led down from the top of a jagged rock. "We came down from there. We've been exploring."

"Found anything interesting?"

The other girl smiled at him. "Maybe now we have. What's your name?"

"Charlie. Yours?"

"I am Yana and this is Viktoria. We are from the Ukraine."

"You're a long way from home girls."

"We are here for one week but have been in France for three weeks and Germany before that."

"You certainly get about."

The girls giggled. If he wasn't much mistaken he could be inside their knickers within fifteen minutes. A threesome on the beach was an appealing prospect and something he hadn't partaken in for a while. After the hellish week he'd had he certainly deserved it.

"May I?" He pointed to the bottle of water by their bags and the dark-haired girl held it out to him.

"Help yourself."

"Thanks," he said walking over. He took several huge gulps before handing it back.

The girls looked at each other and nodded, some

unspoken agreement between them he assumed. "You are... how you say in English...very handsome."

Charlie smiled. It was game on. He made himself comfortable on the sand next to them. "You looking for some R&R?"

"R&R?" the dark girl asked with a puzzled look on her face.

"Rest and relaxation," he said.

"Is that what they call it in Spain? In England they call it sex, no?"

He grinned. This pair definitely weren't backwards in coming forwards. Viktoria, the dark-haired one passed him a bottle of sun tan oil.

"Would you mind?" she asked rolling over onto her back. "The sun is very hot."

"Me too," said Yana and laid down next to her friend. "But I need it on my chest. I do not want my boobies to burn."

Charlie blew out a breath. It was just his luck to be propositioned by two raving nymphos on a deserted beach only to have him cast his gaze out at the Lady Catherine and think about Kate. He looked at the bottle of suntan oil, then back at the women who were lying in the sand waiting for him to rub his hands all over them.

It was no good, he couldn't do it.

Now he definitely knew he was turning into a sentimental douche bag.

"I'm sorry girls," he said tossing the bottle onto the sand. "Thanks for the offer. I know I'm seriously going to regret this but I've got to go."

Yana was disappointed. "No Charlie, where you go?"

"See that boat out there?" he said pointing into the distance. "That's where. And as lovely as it's been I'm leaving right now."

He didn't look back when the girls called his name. He just put one foot in front of the other until he cleared the sand and dived into the water. He only had one thing on his mind and that was to sort his bloody shit out and that included dealing with the woman currently residing on board his boat.

The wine that Charlie had loaded into the cooler was a crisp and zesty Rioja Blanco and Kate was already on her second glass. She'd prepared a prawn salad with the provisions that Charlie had brought on board but so far, only hers had been eaten. His she had wrapped and returned to the fridge. She'd made herself comfortable on the bow of the boat. There were two built in sun loungers so she was stretched out in her bikini enjoying the uninterrupted view of the sea to her right and to the left, the impressive sight of the jagged coastline. But she wasn't giving either view the attention they deserved. Her mind was solely occupied with the conundrum of what to do next.

It had been a hell of a few weeks; she had the bruises to prove it. What she needed to do now she realised was put an end to this charade. Declan believed the ruse that she and Charlie were married;

surely her work here was done?

Her only choice was to return home to England.

She had become far too comfortable being Charlie's wife and the only way it was going to end was when the whole sorry mess came crashing down around her. At least if she left now she could still escape with both her sanity *and* her dignity.

Footsteps on the deck caused her to swing round in surprise. She hadn't seen Charlie since he'd dived off the boat and that had been hours ago. Now he was standing before her dressed in shorts and a clean tee-shirt and was holding a bottle of beer in one hand and a jar of olives in the other. He nodded at the half empty bottle of wine on the floor.

"You started without me."

She shrugged. "I thought I'd be spending the evening by myself."

"Yeah, about that," he said, plonking himself down on the lounger next to her. "I shouldn't have lost it like that, I didn't mean to take it out on you. I'm sorry, I just needed to blow off some steam."

It was now her turn to blow off some steam. "I've been thinking Charlie," she said as she toyed with the stem of her glass. "Declan believes we're happily married and that you're not going to steal Francesca away from him, yes?"

"Yeah."

"And this deal you're working on with him is underway with no problems?"

"Yeah."

"So really then, as far as we're concerned, I've fulfilled my part of our deal."

He looked at her with wide eyes. "*You want to leave*?"

"Well I don't see much point in me hanging around, do you?"

He unscrewed the lid of the jar, went to take an olive but changed his mind. "Is this because of what I said earlier?"

"No, yes, well maybe…I don't know."

"You can't leave yet, it's too soon. I don't want to give Declan any reason to be suspicious."

"Why would he be suspicious? You could just say I've gone home to visit my family. He lives in Seville Charlie, how would he even know?"

"No," he said loudly and with more force than she was expecting. "You're not leaving. Besides, I've paid you for at least three more weeks."

"You can have a refund," she said and made the mistake of laughing.

"I don't want a bloody refund," he snapped angrily.

"Okay," she said, throwing her hands into the air. She misjudged how much wine was in her glass and it splashed over the rim and down onto her legs. "I was only joking. Jesus, you're still in a foul mood I see."

"I'm not in a fucking mood. I just want you to do the job I'm paying you to do."

"I *am* doing the job you paid me to do. I just thought you'd prefer it if I left that's all."

He stared at her blankly. "Where's all this coming from?"

Fuck it, she thought to herself. She'd been hoping she could avoid it but now she was going to have to spell it out to him.

"You've made your feelings pretty clear this week Charlie. You're bored and fed up and that's okay, I get it. It's not like I didn't know what I was getting myself into. Your deal with Declan is going as planned so I think the best thing now is for me to go home and leave you to get on with your life."

He ran a hand over his face and slowly rubbed the stubble on his chin. "That's what you think is it?"

"Well one minute we're okay and the next we're not. What else is there to think? I've actually got no idea what I'm still doing here."

He swung his feet round. At first she thought he was going to stand up and leave but he remained seated. "Has it ever occurred to you that I wanted to give you some space to come to terms with what happened with Mickey?"

As his words sunk in she felt the heat rise to her cheeks. "You thought I wanted to be alone?"

"Yes and to be honest darlin' I've found it really fucking difficult because being with you is all I seem to want to do these days. So the answer to your question is no, I wouldn't prefer it if you left so you can get that idea out of your head right now. It's the stupidest thing I've ever heard." He put the bottle of beer to his lips and took a swig. "And keep looking at me like that and I'm going to show you exactly what I'm talking about."

Kate felt her body tremble; despite everything that

had happened he still wanted her. She didn't need to think twice about what she was going to do next. She climbed onto his lap and straddled him. He didn't utter a word, not even when she tugged at his tee-shirt and yanked it over his head. She unclasped her bikini top and as her breasts fell loose Charlie lowered his head and kissed each one, sucking her nipples into his mouth then biting down gently, causing a cascade of pleasure to flow through her. He tugged her bottoms aside and slipped a finger inside her, then another. His cock was rigid so she undid his zip and slid her hand inside and ran her fingers over the tip and down the shaft. He groaned, dragged his shorts down and as she lowered herself onto him she threw her head back and let out a satisfied moan of pleasure.

They fell into an easy rhythm. It was slow and sensual; they were in no hurry.

"Harder darlin'," groaned Charlie as he grabbed her hips and ground her firmly against him. She obliged, gripping his shoulders to anchor herself to him. He urged her on, harder and harder and was moaning into her hair, breathless groans that were driving her crazy. She tried not to come but the sensation swept over her like a giant wave and she lost all control.

"I can feel you coming," he murmured as her body shuddered against his. He cupped her face in his hands and kissed her as the remaining throws of satisfaction slipped away. She was still gasping when he manoeuvred her down onto the lounger and flipped her over. On all fours now, he drove into her from behind. This time he was in charge and she surrendered to him, groaning so loudly she had to bury her head into the cushion.

"Don't," he said pulling her up gently. "I want to hear you."

His thrusts came harder and she felt his lips on her back, kissing her, running his tongue over her hot body. It was the combination of his hard pounding and his soft, wet mouth that made her cry out. She was on the brink of another orgasm. Suddenly he let out a deep guttural moan. He continued thrusting for a few minutes more then slowly his rhythm waned and he stopped. He kissed her between her shoulder blades then collapsed beside her, spooning against her.

"You've no idea what you're doing to me," he breathed into her ear. He pulled her hair to one side and buried his lips into her neck. "I'm enjoying this far more than I should be."

"I think we both are," she said honestly.

There was a rumble in the distance. A jet-ski was approaching their position and just behind it a speed boat surged into view. "I can't believe we just did that," she said, shaking her head. But being out in the open had added to the thrill, the chance of being seen making it all the more exciting. "That was reckless."

"But totally worth it," agreed Charlie. He stifled a yawn and tightened his arms around her. "Do me a favour will you? Wake me up in an hour."

Kate was having the most amazing dream. She was wrapped in Charlie's arms, her back was pressed against him and his hand was gently squeezing her breast. It felt so incredibly real that she could even feel his hot breath on her neck. His finger was circling her nipple and his lips were on her shoulders, planting little kisses, setting her skin on fire. And then she heard him utter her name.

She forced open her eyes; it wasn't a dream at all. They were spooning in the huge bed in the master cabin. It was dark, the middle of the night she figured, and she felt both sleepy and relaxed. She craned her head towards him and they kissed, slowly and leisurely; honestly, she could kiss him forever. And then, with an expert move, he gently eased her thighs apart and entered her from behind. She groaned into his mouth but he refused to let her leave their kiss. It was slow and sensual, their movements perfectly in sync with one another and when she came he followed, their gasps of pleasure filling the silent night air.

It was the second time they hadn't used a condom and Kate wracked her brain to remember if she'd taken her pill that morning. It wasn't like her to be so irresponsible but she'd lost the ability to think whenever Charlie was around. She must've taken it she reasoned, it was one of those automatic things she did without even thinking about it. She pushed the thought away, not wanting to dwell on it. Charlie passed her a bottle of water and she drank half of it down. All this sex was thirsty work. The boat was swaying gently on the water, creating a smooth rocking motion that was both comforting and relaxing. She closed her eyes knowing that sleep would soon overtake her but Charlie's voice roused her out of her slumber.

"I was an arsehole today."

She smiled at his confession; he wasn't great at apologising and she was astute enough to realise that this was the best she was going to get.

"It's okay, I'm getting used to it."

He gave her a dig in the ribs. "I'm being serious. You're not still thinking of leaving are you?"

She craned her head up to look at him. "Why? Will you miss me?"

"Not as much as you'll miss me darlin'."

"You're an arrogant bastard, do you know that?"

He laughed. "It's one of my many qualities. Goodnight, Lady Catherine," he said and kissed her on the top of her head.

Within a few minutes they were both asleep.

CHAPTER SIXTEEN

Kate crept out of the bed as silently as she could. Charlie was sleeping soundly next to her and she didn't want to wake him. Grabbing the first item of clothing within reach she pulled on a tee-shirt and headed to the galley. It was just after ten; she couldn't believe she'd slept in so late. The sun was shining and the sea was calm. Several boats were nearby, private charters hired for the day by tourists and a larger vessel, probably an organised day trip to Gibraltar or some other sunny destination.

She made a coffee and sat on the deck savouring both the view and the caffeine. She needed it; her body was aching in places she never knew existed. She thought of Charlie sleeping below deck and smiled. She loved being with him; he was exciting and the sex was incredible. But it wasn't just about the physical. Beneath his tough exterior he had a funny, softer side that made him impossible to resist and very easy to fall in love with. The reality of her situation was not lost on her; she was here to do a job and soon enough their time together would come to an end. If that meant that she was starring in her very own holiday romance then so be it; she was bloody well going to enjoy it while it lasted.

A hunger pang flashed across her stomach so deciding to scramble some eggs she headed for the galley. Clearly making more noise than she realised it wasn't long before Charlie emerged from the cabin. Wearing just a pair of boxers, his hair was tousled and his eyes were sleepy. She felt her cheeks go pink when he smiled at her, remembering vividly where that mouth had been just hours before. He wrapped his arms around her waist and planted a kiss in the crook of her neck. She was so distracted she almost forgot to stir the eggs.

"We need to head back," he said reluctantly. "Phil's just called, there's some trouble at the club."

Kate didn't like the sound of that. It was a gentle reminder that Charlie's business was still a mystery to her. There were things about him she didn't know, things she wasn't even sure she wanted to know but all the same, she hoped it was nothing serious.

"Have we got time for breakfast?"

He popped two pieces of bread into the toaster. "Too fucking right we have. My energy levels need replenishing, you've completely worn me out."

"*I've worn you out?*" she laughed, resisting the urge to slap him with the wooden spoon she was using to cook the eggs. "How dare you? You're a machine Charlie Mortimer."

"And I need to be permanently oiled," he breathed

into her ear. His lips found hers and his hand crept beneath her tee-shirt. "Tell you what? Let's go back to bed. We can eat on the way home."

The outside terrace was packed with people enjoying a leisurely afternoon drink. Wooden tables seated six with hexagonal canvas umbrellas sheltering its occupants from the sun's scorching rays. Large round pedestal fans were strategically positioned at the four corners of the rectangular decked terrace and were spraying a mist of water to offer some light relief from the heat. Not that they were doing much good today; the temperature was well over a hundred degrees and by the time Charlie made it inside he was already covered in a thin layer of sweat.

"Thank Christ you're back," said Phil from behind the bar. He was restocking the fridges and was surrounded by crates of wine and bottles of beer.

Charlie looked at his friend and sighed. Disappointed that his trip had been cut short he wasn't in the best of moods. He'd been looking forward to taking Kate to Gibraltar today and riding the cable car up the rock to show her the Barbary monkeys. "This had better be good Phil."

Phil rested the crate of bottles he was carrying on the top of the bar and held up a hand. "Before I tell you, you have to promise me you're not going to go ballistic."

"Well until I know what's going on I won't know, will I?"

Phil made his way out from behind the bar and beckoned for Charlie to follow him. "Let's go to your office."

"Just tell me here for fuck's sake. I'm already pissed off and all this cloak and dagger bullshit is giving me the right hump."

"I know mate but it's best you hear it from the horse's mouth."

Half-heartedly Charlie followed Phil to the office but as he turned the handle to enter, Phil put an uneasy hand on his shoulder.

"Whatever you do, don't overreact okay?"

Charlie was beginning to feel uneasy. Whatever was going on, he knew he wasn't going to like it and as he entered the room and gave his eyes a moment to adjust to the dim lighting he didn't know who to swing for first. His friend or the animal that stood before him.

Mickey, bearing the hideous scars of their previous encounter a week ago, was leaning against the desk like he owned the fucking place. Completely losing it, Charlie launched himself across the office with the intention of finishing him off once and for all. He was about to throw a punch when Phil suddenly leapt out and grabbed his arm.

"Before you go all John Wick you need to listen to what he's got to say."

Charlie's anger had gone from nought to one hundred in three seconds flat and he turned on Phil furiously. "I told you if I ever saw him again I'd rip his fucking head off. Now get the fuck off me."

"I don't like this anymore than you do," said Phil playing the role of devil's advocate. "But you need to hear him out, it's important. Please mate, do it for me, yeah?"

Charlie loved Phil like a brother. He had a lot of time and respect for him and it was only because of this that he relented. "Alright," he said shaking him off. "But he's got thirty seconds and it had better be good because I'm in no mood to listen to any of his bullshit."

Mickey, fully aware that he was at Charlie's mercy but still displaying his usual cocksure attitude, looked him squarely in the eye. "I need you to do something for me."

"Just spit it out Mickey for fuck's sake."

"I was with this bird, we were totally off our faces. She OD'd so I dumped her body in the quarry."

Charlie didn't know why he was so surprised. Mickey had set himself on a path of destruction a while ago now and it was inevitable that something like this was going to happen. His incessant drug use had finally robbed him of his scruples and had left him with no moral compass whatsoever. Charlie shook his head in frustration. He was trying to maintain some semblance of control but it was hard. His hands were shaking and his anger was bubbling away beneath the surface, threatening to boil over at any moment.

"Why didn't you just call the paramedics?" It would have been the obvious response from any normal person but Mickey was far from normal.

"I panicked, alright? I couldn't think straight. So I thought it'd be easier to dump her and be done with it."

Charlie was wondering exactly where he fitted into all of this. This was Mickey's mess and for once he could bloody well deal with it himself. "And the reason you're telling me is?"

Mickey shrugged coolly. "Someone saw me and reported it to the Policia. They came sniffing around this morning asking where I'd been all night. I didn't know what to say so I told them I was with you."

Charlie, out of sheer amazement, laughed. "Are you for real? What the fuck did you tell them that for?"

"It's no big deal mate. All you need to do is confirm my story, that's all."

"That's all, is it? You're fucking unbelievable, do you know that? I can't confirm your story you dickhead because I wasn't even here. I was out on the boat all night with Kate."

Mickey, realising that his alibi was shot to bits, began to pace the room. His bravado had slipped and he finally resembled exactly what he was; a desperate man who had lost his grip on reality. His eyes were bleary, his clothes filthy and he physically stank. He had addict written all over him. Charlie wanted to feel sorry for him but after everything Mickey had done, he just didn't have it in him.

Mickey swore under his breath and lashed out, kicking a cardboard box on the floor. The bottles inside it rattled but remained intact, much to Charlie's relief. There was a big enough mess to clean up as it was.

"If the Policia start digging into this they'll realise I'm here on a fake passport. I'll be extradited back to the UK where they'll bang me up for good. I need you mate, you have to make this go away."

"And just what is it that you think I can do?"

"I need an alibi."

"You need a stint in rehab. You're a fucking addict Mickey, you need help.

"I'm not a fucking addict, I can stop anytime I want. At least I haven't had my head turned by some old slapper who let's face it, is only interested in one thing and that's your wallet. She's out for all she can get mate. You should've seen her at your party, she was all over me. I practically had to drag her off, she was so up for it."

Charlie was under no illusion that he'd make the silent count to ten in his head but he was impressed that he at least made it to number three before he lost it. He picked up the nearest object, a bar stool with a broken wheel, and hurled it in Mickey's direction. It missed him and hit the wall.

"Say one more word Mickey, I fucking dare you."

Mickey held his hands up. He realised he'd gone too far but wasn't going to admit it. Instead he sidled up to Charlie and offered him a deal. "Give me an alibi and I'll fuck off for good. I'll go somewhere in Europe, you'll never have to see me again."

Charlie was also aware that he'd never have to see him again if he buried him face down in a shallow grave somewhere in the hills of the Costa Del Sol. And the way he was feeling right now, that was alright with him. He bunched his fist and took a step forward but Mickey backed out of his way.

"Come on mate, think about it. You know this isn't what Jamie would've wanted."

The mere mention of Jamie's name propelled Charlie back to the night his friend had died and the almighty guilt he felt washed over him, just as Mickey had known it would. He clung onto the edge of the desk to steady himself. He was shaking, from rage or guilt, he wasn't sure. He could never atone for what happened to Jaime and Mickey knew it as much as he did which is why he was able to play him like a fiddle. Awash with remorse, Charlie hung his head in shame.

"It won't work Mickey, I can't lie to the police for you."

"Course you can," said Mickey confidently.

"I'm telling you, I can't. If I say you were with me Kate will have to collaborate the story and I won't have her lying for you, not after what you did to her."

"Well tell her to put up or shut up. She fucking married you, didn't she?"

"Easy Mickey," said Phil, intervening before Charlie lost his rag again. "Why don't you just tell the police what happened? It was an overdose, pure and simple. Unless there's something you're not telling us."

"That *is* what happened. She was popping pills like Smarties all night, the stupid bitch. So are you gonna give me an alibi or what coz I'm thinking that maybe you've lost your bottle?"

In a fit of rage Charlie grabbed an empty glass from his desk and threw it at him. Mickey jumped to the left and the glass only narrowly missed him. It smashed against a cabinet and shattered into a thousand tiny pieces. Charlie knew he didn't have a choice; the guilt he felt over Jamie's death would make him agree to anything.

"You want an alibi, fine, I'll give you one. But shut the fuck up or so help me God I'll kill you with my bare hands and throw *you* in the fucking quarry. And just so we're clear, I'm doing this for Jamie, not for you."

Mickey allowed himself a triumphant smile; he knew he'd won. He controlled Charlie like a puppet. One mention of his brother's name and it had gotten him exactly what he wanted. He walked from the room, leaving Charlie in one hell of a predicament.

What the hell was he going to say to Kate?

After surviving on takeout for the past few weeks, Kate was desperate for some home cooked food so she decided to whip up a Spaghetti Bolognese for dinner. Pushing a shopping trolley around the Mercadona she was genuinely bewildered by the fact that a bottle of gin cost only eight euros but a packet of English custard creams and a bag of frozen sausages cost ten. She supposed she could understand it, there were shipping costs to consider after all but it just seemed odd to her that it was far cheaper to get drunk in Spain than it was to actually eat. She selected some onions, carrots and celery and added them to her trolley, practically salivating at the thought of consuming a vegetable for a change. She was oblivious to the strange looks from the other shoppers as she negotiated the aisle in her extra-large brimmed sunhat and dark sunglasses. Not exactly the attire for supermarket shopping but it was far easier to look like a diva than have to explain the bruises on her face.

After she'd packed the shopping away she took a swim, had a little splash about and sat on the steps of the pool idly waiting for Charlie to return. After an hour with no sight nor sound of him she laid on a lounger and dozed off. By seven o'clock he still wasn't home. Deciding to start preparing dinner anyway she was halfway through chopping the celery when she finally heard his key in the door. The urge to leap into his arms was overwhelming but she played it cool, not wanting to come across like an over clingy girlfriend.

"What was the urgent problem that nobody could deal with then?" she asked as he sauntered into the kitchen.

He grabbed a beer from the fridge, pulled off the top and took a mouthful. He looked really agitated and she could tell that something was wrong.

"What is it?" she asked as she put the knife down on the chopping board. "Are you okay?"

"Not really darlin'. Let's go and sit down."

She followed him into the lounge. He indicated for her to take a seat so she perched precariously on the arm of the sofa. Wracking her brain, she tried to come up with an explanation as to why Charlie looked so tense. Maybe somebody had discovered the truth about their relationship and the deal with Declan had been called off. She panicked as she realised that her entire reason for being here was about to vanish into thin air. Her hands felt clammy and her mouth felt dry. She hoped to God that wasn't it; she wasn't ready to say goodbye to Charlie just yet.

"There's no easy way to tell you this so I'm just going to say it. I have to tell the police that Mickey was with me on the boat last night."

The relief of not having to leave was short lived because the mere mention of Mickey's name caused panic to grip her throat. She opened her mouth but when she spoke the word came out more like a cry. "Why?"

"He was with some girl, she died of an overdose so he dumped her body in the quarry."

Kate's hand flew to her mouth in horror. She was both stunned and disgusted at the same time. "And you have to give him an alibi because?"

"Trust me I feel as bad about this as you do and I wouldn't be doing it if I had any other choice."

"You do have a choice Charlie. How the hell can you defend him after what he's done?"

"It's complicated," he said staring down at the floor.

"Not to me it's not. In fact it seems pretty bloody simple from where I'm standing."

"You don't understand."

"You've got that right. And if you expect me to lie to the police for that bastard you're going to have to give me a bloody good reason."

Charlie frowned at her. "You won't be lying to the police. This is my mess, I'll sort it out."

"And how are you going to do that? You do realise there will be CCTV footage from the marina which will clearly show me getting on and off that boat. Whichever way you look at it Charlie I'm involved in this too."

"Don't get yourself at it darlin', the police aren't even going to want to talk to you."

"And what if they do?" She took a deep breath to steady her nerves. She couldn't believe this was happening, let alone the fact that Charlie was allowing them both to be dragged into it. There had to be something more going on here, something he wasn't telling her and she was determined to find out what it was. "What's this really about Charlie?"

Without warning he slammed his fist down onto the mantelpiece causing a framed picture to crash to the ground. The wooden frame fell away and the glass cracked.

"For fuck's sake, just leave this for me to deal with."

"In case you haven't noticed we're not really married so you can't tell me to do anything." She stood up to leave. He obviously wasn't going to tell her so let him keep his bloody secrets, she was better off not knowing anyway. She needed to get some air. Getting to her feet she was about to walk out of the room when he spoke.

"It happened five years ago, in a pub in South London."

She stopped dead in her tracks. "*What* happened five years ago?"

"It was a typical lad's night out. We'd been on it all day, drinking, fucking, fighting. We ended up in our local pub, about eight of us in all. Phil was there, so was Jason." He paused and took a swig of his beer. "I've never told anyone this before," he said and she thought he wasn't going to continue. "Anyway, this group came in all mouthing off and getting rowdy. They were making a fucking nuisance of themselves and started getting handsy with one of the barmaids. I lost it and cracked one of them. He went down hard; I wasn't fucking about. And then it all kicked off. They all weighed in and there was a hell of a fight, chairs were smashed, tables broken, we totally trashed the place. It was only when they all legged it that I saw Jamie lying on the floor. One of them had taken a blade to him, slashed his face and stabbed him in the stomach. I'd been too busy throwing punches to notice and when I did, it was too late to do anything. As he bled out in my arms he made me promise to take care of his brother. And that's what I've been doing."

"Mickey," said Kate, at last understanding the hold Mickey had over him.

"Mickey," confirmed Charlie.

"But it wasn't your fault…."

"Of course it was. If it wasn't for me Jamie would still be alive and that's something I have to live with, every single day. And that's why I'll lie to the police for Mickey. I'll do whatever it takes because I owe it to Jamie."

Kate remained silent, digesting his words. She got it, she really did. Charlie was atoning for the death of his friend. He believed he was responsible for Jamie's death and nothing she could say would change that. She felt tears sting her eyes but they weren't tears for Jamie. They were tears for Charlie and the burden he had placed upon himself.

And now it was time for her to do the same. The second she'd agreed to be Charlie's wife she'd been walking a thin line. And now the time had come for her to step over it.

"Okay," she said after thinking it through in her head. "So the way I see it is that you need to tell the police we were all on the boat together."

"No, I already told you, I don't want you involved in this. I'll find another way."

"There is no other way. You'll have to say we picked Mickey up from the beach and that he was with us the entire night. It won't matter that he wasn't seen boarding the boat at the marina but the story won't hold any credibility unless I confirm it too."

Charlie vehemently shook his head. "You're not doing it, not after what he did to you."

"For fuck's sake Charlie I'm not doing it for him," she snapped, annoyed that he hadn't worked that out already. "I'm doing it for you."

He stared at her, his eyes wide in surprise. "Why would you do that?"

Surely he knew she was in love with him.

And if he didn't know what was the point in explaining it to him now? She just prayed she knew what she was doing because now she'd crossed that line, there was no hope of ever turning back.

CHAPTER SEVENTEEN

Kate woke with a start. There was a loud buzzing sound coming from the control panel on the wall. Charlie was snoring softly next to her so she rolled over and gave him a gentle nudge.

"What the fuck?" he groaned sleepily, peering an eye out from under the duvet.

"Someone's at the door."

"At this time of day? Don't people know what a lie-in is anymore?"

He threw back the covers, padded naked into the bathroom and promptly slammed the door. After a few minutes passed it was clear he wasn't coming out so cursing under her breath, Kate retrieved yesterday's shorts and vest top from the floor, hastily pulled them on and made her way downstairs. Mickey's attack was still reminiscent in her mind so she checked the newly installed monitor and looked at the two men standing at the gate. Even though neither of them wore a uniform she instinctively knew that they were police. She panicked; she hadn't expected them to arrive so soon. Waiting for Charlie to emerge was clearly not an option so she pushed the button to allow them entry. Taking a deep breath to steady her nerves she resigned herself to the fact that she was now about to break the law and she opened the door thinking it was just best to get it over and done with.

"Mrs Mortimer, I am Detective Fernandez and this is my colleague Detective Vargas. Please may we come in and ask you some questions?"

ID badges were flashed along with tight smiles but Kate barely took any of it in as she motioned for them to step inside. Detective Fernandez was tall and gracefully thin with high cheekbones and walked with a swagger that suggested he fancied himself a little bit too much.

"What's this about?" she asked, successfully managing to hide the quivering in her voice.

"Is your husband home?" asked Detective Vargas. He was the polar opposite of his partner; his shirt was creased and there were two dark circles under his arms from the heat. Older than Fernandez, he had a friendlier face and offered her a lopsided smile. Kate daren't look him in the eye for fear that he would see straight through her.

"He'll be down in a moment. Can I offer you some tea?"

She had the feeling that Vargas was about to say yes but Fernandez shot him a warning look. "No thank you, we're not here on a social call."

Not in the mood for their good cop bad cop routine she led them through to the dining area where they all took a seat at the table. Fernandez made a show of looking around; whether he approved or not of the luxurious surroundings was hard to tell because his face remained impassive. He was weighing her up, deciding whether to slide in gently or go for the full-on approach. She hoped he'd go for the former but that theory went up in flames the moment Charlie stomped nosily down the stairs.

"What the fuck is this? Who the hell are you and what are you doing in my house?"

Fernandez stood and flashed his identification. "Mister Mortimer, I am Detective Fernandez and this is Detective Vargas. We are here to ask you some questions about Mickey Davis."

Charlie crossed his arms and stared stonily ahead. "What about him?"

"Would you like to sit down?" Fernandez pointed to the chair next to him.

"No." Charlie's voice was edged with sarcasm and Kate shrunk back in her chair. This wasn't going to go well. Vargas clearly agreed.

"You have a lovely home Mr Mortimer," he said in a vague attempt to dampen Charlie's hostility. But Charlie was having none of it.

"I haven't got all day mate, is there something you want to say?"

"Are you familiar with Estelle Garcia Ramirez?" asked Fernandez. "I believe that she frequented your bar." He pulled a photograph from a manilla envelope and showed it first to Kate, then to Charlie. It was of a young, raven-haired beauty with sparkling eyes and a magnetic smile. Kate shook her head. She'd never seen her before.

Charlie shook his head also. "What does this have to do with Mickey?" he said handing back the photograph.

"Her body was discovered in a quarry in Benalmadena two days ago. Mickey Davis was seen in the area."

Vargas pulled another photograph from the envelope and placed it onto the table. It was also of Estelle Garcia Ramirez but in this picture she was lying on a mortuary slab. Her face, what was left of it, had at least half a dozen slash wounds, her right eye was completely blackened and swollen to ten times its normal size. Her neck was black and bruised and bore ligature marks, suggesting that she had been strangled. Vargas retrieved another photograph from the envelope. This image showed her whole body and clearly visible on her pubic area was a series of purple bruises and scratches. There was also bite marks on her genitalia.

"Miss Ramirez was subjected to a lengthy sexual assault and a severe beating before being strangled to death. We have questioned Mister Davis in relation to this and he states he was with you at the time the murder took place."

"And when was that?" asked Charlie tonelessly.

"The autopsy puts the time of death around ten

o'clock to midnight on Thursday. A witness has placed Mister Davis at the scene but he has claimed he was with you at that time."

Kate was fighting the urge to vomit. That could have been her lying on that slab. If Charlie hadn't come home when he did, she could have been raped and murdered too. And now she was going to have to cover for a sick twisted bastard who got his kicks from raping and torturing women. The alternative was just as unthinkable; if Charlie was caught in a lie there was a good chance he'd be arrested. And she wasn't prepared for that to happen either.

"Thursday night, you said?" Charlie put his hand to his head as if in deep thought and Kate braced herself for the story he was about to spin. "Nah, he wasn't with me. We'd taken the boat out, ey darlin'? Went for a cruise along the coast. We left Thursday morning and didn't get home until nearly lunchtime on Friday."

Detective Fernandez seemed surprised by the omission. "Are you quite sure?"

Charlie looked at him as if he was stupid. "I know the fucking days of the week, mate."

Fernandez gathered the photographs and stuffed them back into the envelope. "Thank you Mister Mortimer, we won't take up any more of your time."

Charlie led them to the door but just as he opened it to allow them to leave, Fernandez turned to him. "I understand that Mister Davis is an associate of yours. I'm sorry if the photographs were disturbing and upsetting for your wife but in my experience, I find it better not to waste time. It helps to clear matters up more expediently."

"I know what you did detective and I know why. And just so that *you* know, Mickey isn't and never will be, an associate of mine." He slammed the door so hard it almost came off its hinges.

"Fuck!" he muttered as he stormed into the kitchen. Kate, who was leaning up against the worktop, didn't know what to say. Charlie's truthful version of events was completely unexpected and she couldn't have been more pleased; Mickey would at last get what he deserved.

"What?" snapped Charlie angrily when he saw her looking at him. "You saw the state of that girl. What was I supposed to say?"

He thumped his fist down onto the granite worktop causing her to jump. He was angry and in a move that she never saw coming, he picked up a decorative glass vase from the worktop and lobbed it across the room. It crashed against the wall, tiny shards of clear glass flying everywhere. And then in a mad rampage he proceeded to tear the place apart. Anything he could get his hands on went hurtling through the air. The kettle was ripped from its socket and thrown at the wall, followed by the toaster. And when he finished throwing things he swooped his arm across the worktop and everything in his path clattered nosily to the floor. He was in a rage, destroying everything in sight. Kate had never seen him like this before and logic told her not to interfere. Her phone was in her bedroom so she took the stairs two at a time, almost losing her breath in the process. With shaking hands she pulled out the charging lead and called Phil's number. He answered on the fifth ring.

"What's up, love? A bit early isn't it?"

"It's Charlie, I don't know what to do."

"Alright, calm down and tell me what's happened."

"The police have been here. They said that Mickey's killed some girl. They had photos Phil, it was awful. Charlie's gone crazy, he's tearing the place apart."

"Shit," shouted Phil so loudly that she held the phone away from her ear. "Give me a few minutes, I'll be there as soon as I can. Don't worry love, everything'll be alright, just stay out of his way and leave him to it."

"That's easy for you to say," she muttered as the call disconnected. She sank down onto the bed, her legs shaking all over the place. There was another loud bang from downstairs and she jumped; there would be nothing left of the kitchen at this rate. She wasn't stupid enough to go down there so she just sat and chewed on her fingernails until the intercom buzzed from the control panel on the wall.

"Let me in love," came Phil's voice so she pressed the button quickly. A second buzzer announced that he was at the front door so Kate opened that too, thanking God for the sophisticated security system that had been installed.

She lost all track of time as she sat there; she couldn't be sure if it had been ten minutes or two hours before the noise finally subsided. Gingerly she crept downstairs but not wanting to interfere, she bypassed the kitchen and went and sat beneath the naya. The oppressive heat didn't bother her, her mind was on other things and she was so relieved when Phil finally stepped outside that she jumped up and threw her arms around him.

"Thank God you're here, I didn't know what else to do."

He sat down on the wicker sofa and ran a hand over his face. There were dark circles beneath his eyes and his beard needed a good trim. She'd clearly woken him up.

"I'm so sorry," she said and meant it.

He waved away her apology. "Don't worry about it. You did the right thing calling me. It's not the first time I've had to sort him out and I dare say it'll be the last but the show's over love. He's calmed down and gone to take a shower. I guess you've never seen him like that before? You know he wouldn't have hurt you?"

"If I thought that I wouldn't be sitting here." She leant her head back and sighed. "I was just worried he was going to hurt himself."

"Well the kitchen's taken a hell of a battering, that's for sure." Phil grinned and once again, she felt so relieved that he was here.

"Thank you Phil."

"You don't need to thank me, love. To be honest, I should've seen this coming. Charlie's spent too many years trying to protect Mickey but I guess there was only so much he could take. Discovering what he'd done to that girl tipped him over the edge. He blames himself of course, as he always does."

"He told me about Jamie."

"To this day it still haunts him. It wasn't his fault, we were all to blame but he shouldered the burden of responsibility and as usual where Charlie's concerned, there was fuck all anyone could do about it. But we all have our crosses to bear. Speaking of which, I guess now would be a good time to tell you that I know about this deal he's made with Declan and your part in the arrangement."

Kate cringed. Caught barefaced in a lie she felt her cheeks burn.

"It's not a problem love," reassured Phil as he patted her knee. "I've lost count of all the crazy shit he's pulled over the years. There's one thing I've got to ask though as it's been bugging the hell out of me. What's the score with you and him?"

"What do you mean?"

"Well I don't want to state the obvious but it's clear you two have feelings for each other. I've known him for a lot of years and trust me, I've never seen him like this before."

"It's all part of the game Phil," sighed Kate, wishing there was more to it. "Besides it's not like I didn't know what I was getting myself into."

Phil was about to add something but Charlie chose that moment to appear. Wearing a pair of jeans and a blue tee-shirt he walked around the back of her chair and rested his hands on her shoulders.

"I'm sorry darlin'," he said and kissed the top of her

head. "But I just saw those photos and lost it. I didn't mean to scare you."

She covered his hand with her own and gave it a squeeze. "It's okay."

"It's not though, is it? That girl lying in the morgue could have been you. I should have finished him when I had the chance."

Phil was watching intently, scrutinising their every move. If he was waiting for a sign that Charlie had fallen head over heels in love with her he was going to be sorely disappointed. And deep-down Kate knew he wasn't the only one.

"I think it would be a good idea for both of you to lie low until Mickey's been arrested," said Phil wisely. "God knows what he might do when he finds out you've blown his alibi."

"I wish I could get my bloody hands on him." Charlie sat down on the sofa next to Phil and pinched the bridge of his nose with his thumb and forefinger.

"Leave it to the police, mate. They can place him at the scene and from what you said about the girl's injuries, there's bound to be DNA evidence. You don't inflict that kind of damage without leaving a trace. They'll catch up with him and when they do he'll spend the rest of his life rotting in a prison cell."

"Amen to that," said Charlie.

"Do you want a hand clearing up?" Phil asked but Charlie shook his head.

"Nah mate, my mess, I'll sort it."

Phil stood up to leave.

"Thank you," said Kate earnestly. She didn't know

what she would have done without him.

"No problem, anytime love." Phil gave her a kiss on the cheek and headed into the villa, Charlie following close on his heels.

Charlie was fully aware that his temper was going to be the death of him. All the calming techniques he'd learnt over the years had evaporated the second he'd seen the photographs of that girl. The very real knowledge that it could've been Kate lying dead on that slab had tipped him over the edge and he hadn't been able to control himself. He wasn't proud of what he'd done; he'd always been a hothead and at the age of thirty-seven, he knew it was unlikely he'd ever change.

As irrational as it was, he felt responsible for Mickey's behaviour. He'd been far too soft on him over the years and had let him get away with too much. And the shocking result was a brutal death that Charlie felt he could have prevented if he had only kicked Mickey into touch years ago. Encumbered by his promise to Jamie, he had let Mickey run wild. Now however, Charlie knew for a fact that Jamie would turn in his grave if he knew what Mickey had done.

Charlie wasn't by nature a downer. It simply wasn't in his genetic make-up so he knew he needed to snap out of his self-reproach and pull himself together. He made a call to Isaura with the assurance of a hefty bonus if she returned the kitchen to a more liveable condition and then he told Kate to go and get changed. They were getting the hell out of the villa and wouldn't be returning until long after the sun went down.

He drove them to Ronda, a city renowned for being one of the most beautiful in Andalucía and a popular tourist location for people holidaying on the Costa Del Sol. They visited the legendary Plaza De Toros, home to one of Spain's famous schools of bullfighting and spent an hour wondering around the museum. Charlie only found it interesting due to the bloodthirsty stories of matadors being slain by vicious seven hundred kilo fighting bulls. As he expected, Kate was more interested in the architecture of the bullring; he was just happy that she was thinking about something else for a while. After the dusty bullring, they visited the Puento Viejo, the old bridge that was constructed in the 1400s. Being the older of two bridges, it was significantly less crowded with tourists but the views were astounding and looked across the gorge which divided the town.

The oppressive afternoon sun drove them inside an air-conditioned bar where Kate ordered a glass of wine and Charlie an ice-cold beer. He ordered them a selection of Tapas and spent a good ten minutes trying to entice her into tasting a marinated sardine and Gilda, a mini sized kebab with pickles, olives and anchovies skewered onto a cocktail stick. He couldn't stop laughing when she proclaimed it 'too fishy' and almost spat it out at him.

They walked around some shops but Charlie found it boring; his interest level had plummeted and he couldn't muster up any more enthusiasm for tacky gift shops with their endless selection of overpriced tat. Eventually he steered Kate back to the car. He drove them up into the mountains and with the roof down and the music on full blast, they covered another hundred or so kilometres and as the sun finally started its descent in the sky, they arrived at a small village that was nestled in the hills.

Whitewashed houses lined cobbled streets and at the centre of the main square was an ancient fountain carved out of stone with water cascading down into a large circular font. He parked the car and led them inside a small restaurant. It was filled with locals conversing over glasses of red wine and enjoying the flavours of their favourite Tapas dishes. The owner, a short, round man with a heavy moustache and wispy grey hair made a beeline for them.

"Charlie it has been too long my friend," he said in heavily accented English.

"Antonio, it's great to see you mate."

"What brings you all the way up here? One of my steaks, si? And who is this?"

Charlie looked at Kate and smiled. She had caught the sun on her nose and looked both fresh faced and beautiful. "This is my wife, Kate," he said, the lie coming so naturally to him now it was frightening.

"Your wife!" Antonio clapped his hands together and muttered something in Spanish that neither of them understood. "We must celebrate. Come, I have a special table for you."

Leading them past the dozen or so people, Antonio took them through a door which led to a small open-air courtyard. There were half a dozen tables, all of them occupied except for a table beneath a criss-crossed pergola that was adorned with purple trailing bougainvillea.

Antonio seated them and a waiter arrived with a bottle of champagne and two glasses. "With my compliments, congratulations to you both. You do not need this," he said taking the menu out of Kate's hands. "I have the perfect dish for you." The waiter poured the champagne and disappeared with Antonio leaving the two of them alone. The soft strum of a Spanish guitar played in the background and the smell of garlic wafted through the air.

"This place is amazing," said Kate wistfully.

"Antonio is a cousin of Maria's. I came with Phil a while ago and once I'd tasted his steaks I was hooked. I like it up here, I like the peace and quiet."

"And there I was thinking it was all about the partying with you."

"What can I say?" said Charlie, shrugging his shoulders. "The late nights and the drinking eventually take it out of me, I am nearly forty you know."

"No way!" she blurted out loudly.

"How old did you think I was?" he asked, intrigued.

"Not that old. You look way too fit to be forty." She blushed, her cheeks turning a bright rosy red. He liked it; it made her look sexy and demure at the same time.

They enjoyed the most delicious meal; fillet steak served medium rare with a creamy peppercorn sauce with sautéed potatoes and roasted vegetables. It was simple, yet the flavour of the meat was extraordinary. Kate chose crème brulee for dessert, Charlie settled for a brandy and by the time they finished eating it was almost eleven o'clock. Antonio joined them shortly afterwards and they chatted away easily until nearly midnight.

"Are we stopping at the bar?" Kate asked when they were almost home.

Charlie thought about it but in all honesty, he didn't want to. He just wanted to take her to bed and forget about everything that had happened.

"It's up to you," he said, leaving her to decide. "What do you want to do?"

She put a hand on his thigh. "It's been a really long day. I just want to go to bed."

He smiled and covered her hand with his own. "Your wish is my command, Lady Catherine."

CHAPTER EIGHTEEN

Rain had fallen overnight. The potted plants that had been wilting from the heat had been instantly revived and the garden was restored to its natural glory. Blue sky was in residence and the heat of the early morning sun was already evaporating the droplets of water that had soaked the patio furniture. Charlie finished his length of the pool, dried himself off then went downstairs into the basement to his newly finished home gymnasium. He ran for five miles on the treadmill and despite the air conditioning he started sweating profusely after only a few minutes. He was out of shape. The lack of exercise over the last few weeks was having a profound effect on his body. Although he wasn't particularly vain he did enjoy a certain sense of satisfaction when he looked in the mirror and if he wasn't careful he was going to end up with a gut on him. He took a five-minute breather, did some stretches then settled down for twenty minutes on the bench press.

The endorphins his body was releasing were helping him clear his head. He had some serious thinking to do. The deal with Declan was causing him a lot of worry and he was battling with his conscience over what the job entailed. Granted, he didn't have many scruples but holding hostage the innocent family of the security manager was low, even for him. Declan had made it clear that it was only a back-up plan but what if something went wrong and he was expected to harm them? He was no angel but this went against every principle he had and he knew he wouldn't be able to do it. He wiped his forehead, the sweat was now dripping off him and he threw the towel across his shoulder. He had a very big decision to make.

Kate was sound asleep when he walked into his bedroom. Her dark hair was fanned out across the pillow and she was clutching the sheet over her body, leaving her long brown legs stretched out bare on the mattress. He'd be lying to himself if he didn't acknowledge the warm feeling that swept over him when he looked at her. They'd made love twice in the night and all he wanted to do right now was climb back on top of her. Instead he headed for the bathroom. He stripped out of his clothes and stepped inside the walk-in shower. As he turned the dial water shot out of the rainfall shower head and he stood beneath it letting the pounding jets refresh his aching body.

He wasn't entirely sure when the fucking had become love making. There was no doubt in his mind that it had happened and the reality was, it scared the shit out of him. He took the bottle of shampoo and squeezed an amount the size of a golf ball into his hand. As he washed his hair he wondered how he'd let things get this far. His intentions had been crystal clear from the beginning. He definitely wasn't looking for a relationship, it was just meant to be sex, no complications and no commitment. But now they were sharing lingering glances and he had this ridiculous fuzzy feeling in the pit of his stomach whenever they were together. He put his hands on the wall and leant forward, allowing the powerful jets to pummel his back. This situation was spiralling out of control. He needed to cool it down, take a step back and remind himself that Kate was only here to facilitate his deal with Declan. In a few weeks' time she would be gone and this whole episode would come to its natural end. And his life would regain some semblance of normality again.

His mind suddenly feeling clearer, he was determined to take charge and if that meant putting some distance between the two of them then that's what he would do. But then two arms wrapped themselves around his waist and he felt the warmth of a body as Kate pressed herself against him.

"Morning," she murmured softly as she placed a kiss between his shoulder blades.

He melted at her touch and everything he had just told himself was washed down the plughole with the deluge of soapy water. Maybe it wouldn't matter if their affair lasted a little bit longer. They were both having a good time, after all. He sought out her mouth and as they kissed he realised that whichever way he looked at it, he was completely fucked.

The walk to the bar that evening was a quiet one. They were holding hands. Kate wasn't sure how it had happened but they'd fallen into a steady rhythm the moment they'd left the villa. As a newly married couple it was a perfectly normal thing to do. As a fraud being paid ten thousand pounds to pretend she was in love with him it shouldn't have felt so natural, or so good. But it just did.

The heavy-duty foundation she'd applied to her fading bruises had hidden the lingering traces of Mickey's attack. It was hard to tell now that it had ever taken place. She only wished she could wipe the memory as easily. Mickey still haunted her dreams and there were times when she woke in the night having dreamt that he was not only trying to rape her but strangle her as well and leave her for dead in some Godforsaken place. She gripped Charlie's hand tighter, comforted by his presence. She felt safe knowing that as long as he was by her side, Mickey would never hurt her again.

The sun was setting to the west and as they made their way along the promenade the sight was spectacular. The sun, reminiscent of an enormous fiery orange ball, looked as if it were bobbing on the surface of the Mediterranean Sea just waiting to be pulled under. A crowd had gathered to witness it and they had to side-step a couple taking a selfie, the glowing fireball the perfect backdrop. They looked so in love and the scene couldn't have been more romantic. The girl was gazing tenderly at her man and his giddy eyes were staring back at her. Kate imagined for one wistful moment that it was her and Charlie posing for the camera but she brushed the idea away with a shake of her head; she was getting herself at it now.

The atmosphere when they arrived at the bar was electric, a combination of the salty sea air infused with the hedonistic lifestyle of a wealthy society where the sole purpose was enjoyment. These people didn't have a care in the world. Kate breathed in the feeling and tucked it away to the back of her mind so she could retrieve the memory when she was feeling lonely on the long days ahead of her back in England. As much as she hated to think about it this charade would soon be over and Charlie would be free to do as he pleased. The thought bothered her far more than it should have but at the end of the day her unrequited love was her problem, not his, and she had no option but to deal with it.

Charlie checked-in with the doormen and after being assured that there'd been no trouble they continued inside. The music was loud enough to create ambiance without inhibiting conversation. Charlie wasn't the type of person who could slip in anywhere unnoticed and as such, he was accosted several times as they crossed the room. As the women fluttered their eyes at him Kate couldn't help but feel the smug sense of satisfaction of being by his side. They might be lusting after him but she was the one he'd be taking to bed tonight.

She made herself comfortable on a bar stool whilst Charlie and Phil talked business. She didn't mind, she had developed the art of people watching and took the opportunity to have a good look around. The air conditioning ensured the inside of the bar was as appealing as the outside and almost every table was occupied by groups of well-dressed individuals who flashed their wallets as easily as they flashed their designer white veneers. It was a world away from reality but one that fascinated her; there was nothing as exciting as witnessing someone waving their American Express Gold Card in the air and ordering six bottles of Dom Perignon champagne at four hundred and fifty euros a throw.

Charlie placed a gin and tonic on the bar in front of her and she took a much-needed sip. Despite there being an empty stool by her side he remained standing, surveying the room and everyone in it. He was uncharacteristically quiet; he had many traits but silence wasn't one of them.

"Are you okay?"

"Why d'you ask?"

"It looks like you've got something on your mind."

He stroked her bare thigh. "You. You're on my mind."

Unconsciously she reached for him and their fingers entwined, fusing together in mutual agreement. His stare made her pulse race; the emotion in his eyes looked real and tangible and could in no way be mistaken as part of any pretence. She had the full focus of his attention and felt as if she was the only woman in the world. But that was his speciality she reminded herself.

Until he got bored and moved on of course.

A sudden push from behind startled her and the glass she was holding lurched forward, its contents sloshing over the rim. She shouted a loud 'fuck' as the clear liquid sprayed over her legs and frantically she tried to wipe it away. It was a group of rowdy lads vying for a space at the bar, all shoving each other forward and having no spatial awareness whatsoever. Charlie was not impressed and reared up instantly. He made a move towards them but Kate put a hand on his arm to stop him.

"Don't bother. It'll dry, it's no big deal."

For a moment she wasn't sure he was going to let it go. He kept his eyes fixed on them, waiting for an excuse to wade in but when none came he re-took his place beside her.

"Fucking pricks," he mumbled under his breath.

Kate dabbed her legs with a serviette. "They're just pissed, forget it." A loud jeer came from behind and she grinned as if emphasising her point. "See?"

"Come on, let's move."

He led her to the VIP section where they had the pick of the booths. The area was unusually quiet and they settled into a seat undisturbed. Their bodies were closer than necessary, after all there was nobody there to witness their deception, but Charlie snaked his arm around her shoulders and pulled her close anyway. And when he kissed her she responded, their lips meeting in total surrender. He coiled his hand around her neck and she pressed herself against him, leaving him in no doubt about how she was feeling. He planted a series of soft kisses on her face, her nose and her chin and she countered this by raking her hands through his hair and gently nuzzling her lips into his neck. But just as the world started to evaporate around them he unexpectedly pulled away.

"Jesus fucking Christ," he said forging a gap between them the size of the Grand Canyon. "I need a minute."

"What is it? What's wrong?"

"This is wrong darlin'." He straightened his shirt and ran his hands through his hair. "This has gone far enough. You need to pull your head out of the clouds and realise that whatever you think is going on here, me and you just ain't gonna happen."

His words were hurtful and unnecessary. They'd been sleeping together for weeks now and she was well aware that it wasn't headed anywhere. But something had changed between them and if he was too stubborn to acknowledge it then he was just deluding himself.

"What's the matter Charlie?" she taunted. "Like it a bit too much, do you?"

"Don't be fucking stupid. You're confusing yourself darlin'."

"If anyone's confused it's you."

"You need to quit with all this lovey-dovey bullshit and face the facts. You're here to do a job, one that

I've paid you a lot of fucking money to do so if you don't think you can handle it anymore then now's the time to fuck off."

Her mouth fell open in amazement. "I can't believe you've just said that to me." She stood up and grabbed her bag from the table. She had to leave or else she was going to thump him. "You've got some bloody nerve Charlie Mortimer. Have you ever considered that maybe it's you that can't handle it? You carry on using people if that makes you feel better. Me, I'm going home. And I'll be thinking very hard about whether I'm still gonna be here tomorrow."

"Well that suits me fine coz I need some space, you're doing my fucking head in."

"Good." She walked away huffing under her breath.

"Good," she heard him shout back at her.

Not good she thought when she reached the entrance of the bar. Not good at all. She held a hand to her forehead in despair.

What the hell had just happened?

Charlie folded his arms tightly across his chest and leant against the wall. He'd left the bar via the rear entrance and was standing in the area that passed as a delivery bay. There were two enormous grey wheelie bins crammed with empty bottles waiting to be collected and four rubbish bins stacked with waste, kicking up an awful smell in the heat. Why he'd chosen to come out here and not gone down to the beach he had no idea. But then again he wasn't thinking straight right now. Not that that was anything new. He kicked the wall with his boot. Instead of simply admitting that he was in love with Kate he'd freaked out and made a right cunt of himself in the process.

He was pacing up and down now with his hands in his pockets. It would serve him right if she never spoke to him again. There was a bottle on the floor, a reject from the overflowing wheelie bin, and in a rage he booted it and watched it skid across the tarmac.

"Idiot," he shouted loudly. A stray cat hissed beneath a lavender bush where it was lying in wait for an unsuspecting mouse to appear. Charlie rolled his eyes; even the fucking cat hated him. He had two options that he could see; one, go after her and pour his heart out like a sad pathetic bastard or two, retrieve the bottle of Jack Daniels from his office drawer and get totally fucking wasted. His decision made he went back inside the building and headed down the dimly lit corridor to his office. As he entered the room however there was someone sitting in his chair with his legs stretched out on the desk in front of him.

And that someone was Mickey.

"What the fuck?"

His mind started to race. Mickey was the last person he'd expected to see. Why the hell wasn't he locked up in prison by now? And how had he managed to sneak into the bar without being seen?

In his peripheral Charlie caught a flicker of movement and turned to see two men standing either side of the door. Both were broad-shouldered with tattooed arms and hair that suggested it had suffered a near death experience with a pair of clippers. He didn't recognise either of them and didn't like the way they were staring at him.

"Who the fuck are dumb and dumber over there?" he asked as Mickey rose from the desk and came towards him. "Do you want to tell me what the fuck is going on?"

"I'd have thought that was obvious. You fucked me over Charlie."

Charlie wasn't even going to bother denying it; he *had* fucked him over and with good reason. "Did you honestly think I'd give you an alibi after what you did to that girl?" He wasn't scared of Mickey but the look in his eyes had him worried; they were bloodshot and watery and his pupils were dilated. Mickey was volatile at the best of times but off his head on smack meant there would be no rationalising with him.

"You had one job, mate, one fucking job. All you had to do was tell the Policia I was with you but you couldn't even manage that. Big shot fucking bar owner, you really think you're something don't you?"

"I don't rape women Mickey so yeah, compared to you that does make me something. Now get the fuck out of here and take these clowns with you."

Charlie was weighing up his options in his head. Mickey was an easy target. He was pretty sure he could take him down with one punch but that left the two heavies he'd brought with him. Charlie was no mug, he knew he couldn't take them both out but if he could catch them off guard he could at least take one of them down. That would leave a much fairer fight and he'd take those odds any day.

Leaving no time for indecision he drew his arm back and in a move that Mickey never saw coming he flexed his wrist and jabbed upwards, hard into his face. Mickey recoiled and as he staggered back Charlie punched him in the side of the head. As Mickey hit the floor Charlie swung round in time to see the two men coming for him. The taller of the two reached him first but he landed a blow on his solar plexus. The man bent forward as his diaphragm spasmed, his breath coming in gasps, preventing him from moving. Charlie knew it wouldn't keep him at bay for long. The second man moved towards him then. A punch caught Charlie on the cheek but he managed to keep his balance. He responded with a sharp elbow strike, hitting him on the jaw. But the man was clearly a tough guy and he barely flinched. Charlie attempted to throw another punch but the man blocked it and shoved him so hard in the chest he went spiralling through the air, landing awkwardly on the floor. He scrambled to his feet but a blow to the head sent him hurtling backwards against the wall. The room started to spin as he kicked out, his boot brutally connecting with the man's knee and as he crumpled and yelled out in pain, Charlie took the opportunity to grab a bottle from a nearby crate and smash it over his head. Miraculously the bottle remained intact but the man slumped to the floor, groaning in agony. Charlie could feel blood trickling in his mouth but ignored it; adrenaline had kicked in and whilst he knew he would hurt like a bitch later, for now it was blocking the pain. As Mickey struggled to his feet Charlie knew his only chance was to take one of them out as fast as possible. Two against one was not going to end well.

The first attacker was back on his feet and coming at him. Charlie fisted both hands, ready to strike. What he hadn't counted on was the baseball bat that came out of nowhere and smashed him hard across his lower back and straight into his kidneys. The pain ripped through him and he slumped to the floor on his knees, fighting for breath. Mickey pitched the bat high over his head and took another swing, this time hitting Charlie's upper back, causing a ripple of agony that he felt all the way down his legs.

The pain was excruciating and he fell forward onto the floor. He tried to move, to defend himself but was unable to make his limbs respond. Mickey's face was the last thing he saw before a foot kicked him in the head and sent him into oblivion.

CHAPTER NINETEEN

When it became clear that Charlie wasn't going to come after her, Kate returned to the bar with the intention of having it out with him. But when she peered up into the VIP section he wasn't there. Feeling disheartened that he'd left already she propped herself up on a bar stool and decided to get completely drunk. She sacked the gin and tonic and moved onto wine in the hope that it would go to her head a lot faster. Dulling the pain was her only option now but when Phil poured her second glass he finally gave in to his curiosity and asked her why she was drinking alone.

"Let's just say the divorce is likely to go through sooner rather than later."

"That can't be true."

Tears stung Kate's eyes. Charlie's outburst had affected her far more than it should have and she was really upset. "I don't know what happened Phil. One minute everything was fine, the next he told me I was doing his head in."

Phil flashed her a sympathetic smile. "Listen love

and believe me when I say this because I know what I'm talking about. He might come across all brusque and self-assured but the moment he starts to feel any kind of real emotion he can't handle it so he backs away. He's been the same all his life."

"Huh," she snorted. "What emotion?"

"The feelings he has for you."

"He doesn't have any feelings for me, Phil. He's made that perfectly clear."

"You shouldn't believe everything he tells you, love."

Kate was starting to feel angry. She took a massive gulp of wine as she tried to make sense of it all. "I just don't understand."

"I've known him a long time and I still don't understand why he does half of the things he does. What I can tell you is this. He made the biggest mistake of his life when he married Francesca and after their divorce he made himself a promise never to go through that again. So women come and go but none of them ever hang around for long, his choice not theirs. He leaves a trail of broken hearts everywhere he goes."

"Great," said Kate sarcastically. "That makes me feel so much better."

Phil patted her hand gently. "And then you came along."

"You think he's in love with me?" laughed Kate as she knocked back the last of her wine. "I know you're trying to make me feel better but come on, you couldn't be more wrong."

He leant across the bar and kissed her on the cheek. "You're a smart girl, you work it out. I've got to go, someone's got to take care of this place while that idiot husband of yours is having a mid-life crisis. I saw him go into his office earlier, he's probably still there. Why don't you go and talk to him? I'll bet money you'll find him sitting at his desk with a glass of Jack Daniels in his hand waiting for you."

Reaching Charlie's office, Kate paused and took a deep breath. You can do this, she told herself firmly. All you have to do is open the door and talk to him. What's the worst that can happen?

Finding courage from the wine she'd drunk, she turned the handle and walked into the room. Charlie was sitting on a chair in the centre with three men standing beside him. Thinking she had interrupted a business meeting she was about to apologise and leave when all three men suddenly turned towards her. Recognition hit her fast and the urge to flee came too late. She spun around to retreat but a sweaty hand clamped down on her mouth and she was strongarmed into the room.

Charlie didn't react at all; his head was slumped forward onto his chest and his eyes were closed. And that's when she realised he was either unconscious or he was dead. Her whole body started to shake and fear made her voice tremble.

"Oh my God, what have you done to him?"

"I'd be more worried about what I'm going to do to you, sweetheart," said Mickey with a smirk on his face. He nodded at the man standing beside him. He was huge with muscles like a body-builder and a thick, bull-like neck. His empty black eyes stared back at her as with one hand he shoved her into a chair. Seated opposite Charlie now Kate could clearly see the injuries on his face. Blood was oozing out of his ear, his nose and from a cut on his cheek.

"Charlie's gonna be psyched to see you sweetheart," said Mickey excitedly. "Why don't we wake him up, ey?"

Kate had no choice but watch as Mickey pulled back his hand and struck Charlie hard across the face. There was no reaction so he hit him again, much harder this time.

Charlie groaned and shook his head, trying to orientate himself. As his eyelids fluttered open he couldn't remember where he was. The pounding in his head was making it impossible to think and he couldn't see properly, there was just a cluster of shapes flashing in front of his eyes. As his vision cleared he made out the silhouette of a man standing in front of him and in that second it all came flooding back. He was in his office and Mickey had taken him down with a thump to the head.

"Welcome back," said Mickey. "I have a surprise for you."

And that's when he saw her. Sitting in a chair in front of him, her face contorted with fear, was Kate. She was frantic; her chest was rising up and down rapidly and she looked as if she was struggling to breathe. Their eyes met and she attempted to move towards him, but Mickey's other henchman yanked her head back viciously by her hair. She let out an anguished cry and Charlie leapt to his feet; he was fucked if he was going to let anything happen to her. But as he put one foot in front of the other he barely managed to take a step before dizziness overtook him. He faltered, thinking he was about to fall and two hands suddenly wrenched him back down into the chair. Not giving up, he instantly rose again but the glint of something sharp hovering beneath Kate's chin stopped him dead in his tracks.

"Sit the fuck down or watch your woman die," growled the man holding the knife at Kate's throat. He also happened to be the man Charlie had smashed over the head with the champagne bottle and judging by the line of blood oozing from a gash just beneath his hair line, he wasn't fucking happy about it.

Charlie surveyed the blade; it was a curved trailing point knife used for slashing and slicing. One cut and it would rip her throat out. This was no bluff, one move and it would all be over. He remained still, trying to calm the fury burning inside of him. There was no way counting to ten in his head was going to work. The sweat was dripping down his forehead and his core temperature had rocketed another few degrees. His brain was running through every possibility of how this scenario was likely to end.

One thing he knew for sure; if anything happened to Kate he was going to kill every last motherfucking one of them.

Kate's white hands gripped the tattooed arm that was wound around her neck. Charlie knew she'd never escape, she didn't stand a chance, but he needed to get her attention before she did something stupid and got herself hurt.

"Look at me," he said in as forceful a tone as he could muster, but she couldn't meet his eye. She was in shock; her face was pale and her eyes were darting all over the place.

"Look at me," he said again and this time her eyes connected with his. He wanted nothing more than to take her in his arms and comfort her. There was a real possibility that this situation was going to go tits-up right before his eyes and if that was the case, the least she deserved was to know the truth about how he felt. They weren't words that came easy to him but he was going to say them anyway. He figured he owed her that much.

"It's gonna be alright darlin', I promise." He gave her his best attempt of a smile which under the circumstances took a lot of doing. "About earlier," he whispered to her softly, "about what I said. I didn't mean it. I didn't mean any of it. I've been in love with you the whole time."

Mickey was shaking his head; he didn't get it. But Kate did and that's all that mattered to him.

"That's enough of this bullshit," shouted Mickey angrily. "There's no need to worry mate, you can have her back when I'm finished with her."

Charlie looked him squarely in the eye. "I swear to

God Mickey if you touch her, I'm going to rip your fucking heart out. This is between you and me, it's got nothing to do with her."

"Course it has, she's the reason you've gone soft, mate. Now sit the fuck down, it's time for us to have a chat."

Charlie resigned himself to the fact that Mickey had gone completely nuts. There was going to be no talking him out of whatever he had planned so Charlie thought it best to try and humour him. "Alright then, I'll start shall I? Let's talk about what a sick deranged fuck you are."

"We could talk about that or we could talk about Declan Connors."

So Mickey had found out about his deal with Declan. That in itself didn't bother him. What concerned him more was that Kate didn't have a fucking clue and after admitting he was in love with her, he wasn't sure she could handle any more of his confessions. Reluctantly he resigned himself to the fact that all his dirty little secrets were about to come spilling out of Mickey's mouth and there was absolutely nothing he could do about it.

"What's this really about Mickey? If you're just pissed because you're not part of the deal with Declan then maybe you should ask yourself why? Look at the fucking state of you, you can't even tie your shoelaces together."

The punch hit him on the nose, not hard enough to break it but it hurt like a bastard nonetheless. He shook away the pain. He wasn't bothered; if Mickey was hitting him it meant he was staying away from Kate.

"This isn't about me Charlie it's about you and I'm going to ruin your life the way you ruined mine. And I'm gonna start by telling your little whore wife all about the man she married."

"Don't call her that," spat Charlie angrily.

Mickey gestured to Kate who was sitting with her dress bunched up in her lap and her thighs on full show. "What else would you call her, then? She's just another slag in a long line of slags that you fuck and throw away."

Charlie took a deep breath. "I'm going to kill you Mickey."

"Yeah, course you are mate. But not until I've had my fun."

Charlie watched in horror as Mickey ran his thumb across Kate's lips. Then he stuck out his tongue and proceeded to lick the side of her face, the trail of wet saliva glistening in the dim light. She gagged and tried to shake him off but she couldn't move. Her head was being held in place by her hair and the knife was still at her throat, ensuring that any sudden movement would result in it puncturing her skin.

Charlie didn't know how he was still sitting there; it was the hardest thing he'd ever done. Mickey was really enjoying himself and when he finished licking her face he squeezed her cheeks together with his thumb and forefinger.

"Did you know that Charlie's responsible for killing

my brother?"

Kate managed a weak nod.

"What you won't know is that after Charlie tracked down the gang involved he left a trail of bodies from one end of London to the other."

Charlie was barely holding it together now and vowed that as soon as he got his hands on Mickey he was going to kill him. "Shut the fuck up," he growled, trying to keep his voice calm but Mickey was determined to make the most of his revelation.

"I can tell by the look on your face sweetheart that you're not phased so why don't I fill you in on a few more details. As well as your loving husband being a murderer, did you know he's also a liar and a thief. How else do you think he affords this place?" Mickey swung his arms wide to encompass everything in the room. "He and Rick had an enterprise robbing Post Offices up and down the country. If violence is your thing then you'd have been proud. Armed raiders frightening little old ladies out of their pension books takes a special kind of man, doesn't it? And then there was the extortion. I mean who wouldn't hand over their cash rather than risk having both their kneecaps blown apart with a sawn-off shotgun? Then they brought young Jack into the fold, that's Charlie's nephew in case you don't know. Quite the fucking genius is Jack and between them they fleeced millions out of Fortune 500 companies holding their computer systems to ransom. Fucking clever really, but of course Jack was the brains behind that little project. Charlie's always been the muscle which leads us on nicely to the deal he's made with Declan. Whilst Jack is fucking about tapping on his keyboard, Charlie here will be holding a couple and their two kids at gunpoint waiting for the nod from Declan to put a bullet in their heads." Mickey tutted and looked at Charlie who was now holding his head in his hands in shame. "And you think I'm a fucking low-life? Take a look in the mirror, mate."

"You're lying."

But even as Kate spoke the words Charlie knew she didn't believe them. Mickey had just spilled the beans on his life and whilst he had exaggerated a lot of it for effect, in essence it was the truth. And he'd never been ashamed of any of it, not until now, not until he looked into Kate's eyes and saw the utter revulsion that lie there. Leaping out of his chair in undisguised anger he launched himself at Mickey, his fist catching him on the side of his head and dropping him to the floor with one single punch.

He didn't give a thought to the repercussions of his actions, he was being driven by the need to shut Mickey the fuck up. Realising too late the consequences he turned, expecting to find Kate bleeding out before him. The relief he felt at seeing her unharmed was overwhelming and he saw an opening; maybe this situation was going to go his way after all.

"Come on then," he said as the other man, the one who'd been holding him in the chair, moved towards him. "If you think you're hard enough."

Angered by the jibe the man ran at him, his right fist poised to deliver a blow. Charlie dodged it and landed an elbow strike against the man's chin, forcing his head to snap back. The blow might have knocked out a weaker man but not this one. Taller than Charlie and the larger of the two of them by far, he simply rotated his shoulders and shifted his balance from one foot to the other.

"You're a tough guy, huh?" The man spat on the ground and gestured at Kate's captor to throw him the knife. He tossed it and it came hurling through the air, landing handle up in the man's hand. He waved it menacingly then advanced, ripping the blade across Charlie's forearm. It stung like fuck and immediately blood began to seep from the wound and drip onto the floor. The man lunged again but Charlie grabbed him by the arm and pulled him downwards. He kicked out a leg to trip him and they both went hurtling to the floor, the knife skidding across the room. Charlie was in position behind him now so he wrapped his arm around the man's neck, keeping his elbow beneath his chin, and put him in a choke hold. He squeezed, grunting with exertion as the man struggled to break free. But Charlie was strong and wouldn't let go. The man kicked his legs out wildly in front of him as he gasped for air. Charlie's muscles bulged as he gave it everything he had; he was literally forcing the life from him. As the man fought for breath his momentum slowed, the oxygen no longer able to reach his lungs. Finally, after what seemed like forever, the man stilled and

Charlie threw his head back onto the floor in sheer exhaustion. His body was crying out in pain but he didn't waste time thinking about it; he had to get to his feet.

A scream pierced the air. Kate was being dragged across the room, her captor propelling her towards the desk with a vicious shove. She fell into it and without managing to hold her hands out to soften the blow she bounced off it and crumpled to the floor, cracking her head on the tiles. If Charlie had a gun he would have put a bullet in the bastard's head. What he did have however was the blade that he'd picked up from the floor. He considered throwing it but didn't trust his aim. What if he missed and hit Kate? He couldn't risk it. He made a run for them instead and the man, in a last-ditch attempt to inflict some pain, crouched down and thumped her in the stomach.

Charlie drew the knife from left to right, catching him across the abdomen. He retaliated with a crack to the jaw that took Charlie by surprise and he floundered, trying to stop himself from falling down. But Charlie had the advantage, he had the knife and with a loud grunt he drove it into the man's chest with such a force that the man stumbled backwards, his legs collapsing beneath him. As he slumped to the ground, his cold dark eyes stared out lifelessly.

A loud groan emerged from Mickey as he struggled to his feet, coming round after the blow to his head. As he registered his accomplices lying motionless on the floor he quickly came to the conclusion that without his muscle men, he was in deep shit. He looked at Charlie, an unexpected flash of fear on his face.

"Come on mate," he said nervously, backing up against a stack of boxes that were lining the wall. "You know I was never going to hurt her, right?"

Charlie shook his head madly. "What do you take me for? You were going to rape and kill her right in front of me, just like you did that other girl. I might be a thief and a liar Mickey but I'm not a sick perverted bastard like you. You came here to my bar with your two fucking goons thinking you could get one over on me. And then you touched my wife Mickey, *my fucking wife*. You were right when you said I'd gone soft because I should never have let you walk away the first time. So now I'm gonna finish what I started and just so you know, there's no fucking way you're gonna be breathing by the end of it."

Killing in self-defence was one thing; Charlie had had no choice but without his two accomplices, Mickey was no longer a threat to him. Killing him in cold blood, no matter how much he deserved it, was murder. And Charlie knew it.

But he didn't give a fuck. He was going to do it anyway.

Psyched up on adrenaline he swung a punch so hard that it knocked Mickey off his feet. There was a loud thud as he crash landed and a stack of boxes tumbled down on top of him. Preparing for the assault he knew was coming, Mickey rolled into a foetal position in an effort to protect himself but Charlie had no intention of going easy on him. He rained down blow after blow until his fists were numb and bleeding, not stopping until Mickey slipped into unconsciousness. Then he booted him in the head several times for good measure and threw in a series of kicks to his groin. If by some miracle he survived he sure as hell wouldn't be raping anyone again.

Physically and mentally exhausted, Charlie slumped to the ground next to Mickey's lifeless body and brought his knees up to his chest. His hands were covered in blood and were shaking uncontrollably. He was finished. Kate would never be able to look him in the eye again, not after this. She knew exactly who and what he was now and wouldn't want any part of it. Not that he could blame her. But he at least gained some satisfaction from knowing that Mickey would never hurt her again and to him, it was worth it.

"Is it true?"

Her words rang in his ears and he looked up, surprised to find her kneeling beside him. She was deathly pale and there was a trickle of blood oozing down her neck from where the knife had nicked her skin. It was only a tiny cut and he was certain he felt the pain way more than she did. He stopped himself reaching out to her, after what she'd just witnessed she wouldn't want him to anyway so he decided to save them both the heartache.

"Yes it's true," he admitted, fighting to keep the remorse out of his voice. "Mickey twisted some of it for entertainment value but the facts remain the same. This is my life darlin' and there's nothing I can do to change it so do me a favour and spare me the lecture, yeah? I don't need your judgement or disapproval or whatever the fuck it is you're feeling right now, I've had more than enough for one night." He daren't look at her, instead he took his phone out of his pocket and fired off a text to Phil; he was going to need some help cleaning this mess up.

"That's not what I meant Charlie," she said, her voice almost breaking. "You said you loved me. Did you mean it?"

Fuck.

He took a deep breath in, holding it a few moments longer than necessary to allow himself time to think. Yes he loved her but admitting it right now wasn't going to do either of them any good. The last thing he wanted was for her to be embroiled any further in his train wreck of a life so he put on a brave smile and shrugged like he didn't give a shit.

"Seriously? What do you think, darlin'? You were gonna get us both killed and I said what I needed to in order to make you calm the fuck down. If you want an apology that's too bad because I'm not giving you one."

The hurt on her face tore him apart.

"You lied to me. About everything."

"So what if I did? I'm a bastard darlin'. I know it and now you know it too."

A tear escaped from her eye and at that moment his heart broke, he literally felt it ripping in two.

But there was nothing he could do about that now. The timing perfect, there was a loud noise as the door crashed open and Rick and Phil rushed into the room.

"Jesus Charlie, what the actual fuck?" Rick's eyes were wide as he inspected the carnage. It was quite a mess, the centrepiece being the three dead bodies on the floor.

"Looks like we've missed the party," said Phil. "Are you both okay?"

"We're fine," said Charlie getting to his feet, gritting his teeth as the adrenaline finally started to wear off and the pain began to set in. He held out a hand to Kate; at first he wasn't sure if she was going to take it but she put her shaking hand in his and let him pull her up.

"We should've been here," said Phil sadly. "I had no idea what was going on."

"Don't worry about it," said Charlie putting his hand on Phil's shoulder. He gestured towards Mickey who was lying motionless on the floor, his head a bloody mess. "Is he dead?"

Rick felt for a pulse. "No, the fucker's still breathing. Leave him to me, I'll finish it."

Charlie shook his head. "I can't ask you to do that, mate."

"You're not asking me. Now fuck off and take her with you. I mean it," he said, when Charlie didn't move. "I'll sort this out."

"I'll take you home," said Phil. "Then I'll come back and clean this up. Are you alright to walk?"

"Yeah," nodded Charlie, then turned to Kate. "You?"

She nodded too. Good; he wanted to get out of here as fast as possible. The whole evening had been a fucking disaster and the sooner he could drink himself into oblivion the better.

CHAPTER TWENTY

Arriving back at the villa Kate immediately went to her room and slammed the door. Charlie contemplated going after her but quite honestly he didn't know what to say. She hadn't uttered a single word to him during the very short ride home in Phil's car and secretly he was relieved. He was afraid that if she pushed him, he'd open his mouth and all manner of deep and meaningful shite would come tumbling out of it. And that wasn't the best thing for her right now.

Phil helped him to his bedroom and he collapsed onto the bed in a sweaty and bloody heap. After peeling off his clothes he took the ice packs that Phil had left him, wrapped them in a towel and packed them against his body. The coldness took his breath away but it would help the almighty purple bruises that were already forming. The pain was excruciating. He also had a fucker of a headache, courtesy of Mickey's boot in his head and knew it was likely that he had a concussion.

His phone beeped. It was a message from Rick to

say that the bar was clean. He didn't provide any details but Charlie suspected he'd dumped the bodies in the deep dark waters of the Mediterranean. He dreaded to think how many other men had suffered the same fate but if anyone deserved it, Mickey did. Now all he had to worry about was his broken body and how he was going to deal with the woman downstairs.

He drifted off into a drug induced sleep but awoke groggy from too many pills and an awful feeling of nausea. A slow and incredibly painful walk to the bathroom meant he only just made it in time. He threw up in the sink, twice. The reflection in the mirror was grim; he looked a fucking mess. A black eye, an inch-long gash on his right upper cheek bone and a fat lip didn't do much for his looks. He inspected the bruising on his back; purple splodges in a long line, courtesy of the wooden baseball bat that had struck him. The cut on his arm was superficial and would barely leave a scar but he was more concerned with any damage to his kidneys. At least he wasn't pissing any blood, not yet anyway. He shuffled into the shower and let the water wash away the dried blood that had congealed on his skin then he hobbled back into the bedroom and pulled on a pair of cotton pyjama bottoms and a tee-shirt. The last thing he wanted was to have his injuries on display for Kate to see; she was traumatised enough already.

He couldn't avoid her any longer. He wasn't expecting much in the way of conversation but they needed to talk nonetheless. He just hoped she wasn't going to fall to pieces because the way he was feeling right now, he'd pull her straight into his arms and never let her go.

Kate watched the sun as it rose above the mountains to the east, it's streaking hues of orange and red lighting up the sky. It was breath-taking and she was really going to miss it when she left for England. She pulled a blanket over her knees, more for comfort than for warmth. It was just before seven in the morning and the temperature was set to soar above one hundred degrees by the afternoon. It was inside that she felt cold and empty. She'd made a huge mistake. She'd played a part in a deception she hadn't fully understood and for what? Ten thousand pounds and a holiday in Marbella? And as if she hadn't sunk low enough, she'd fallen for Charlie so hard that she was now in a worse emotional state than she'd been in when she'd arrived.

Not surprisingly sleep hadn't come easy last night and after hours of staring at the ceiling she'd finally climbed out of bed and made her way downstairs. Three cups of coffee hadn't given her the answers she was looking for nor had they helped unravel the muddled mess of her mind. She was floating somewhere between the state of fantasy and reality.

Mickey's words kept playing over and over in her head. She knew Charlie was no angel, he'd told her as much himself but she could forgive him for that. Everyone was entitled to their past. The most important thing was that he'd left that life behind. But clearly he hadn't. The idea that he could be involved in something so heinous as kidnapping women and children was causing her to re-evaluate everything she thought she knew about him. How could he, the man she had fallen in love with, be capable of such cruelty?

She curled her legs up beneath her and readjusted the blanket. The only clear thought in her head right now was that she had to leave and it had to be today. She needed to go home, if only for her own sanity. She'd already booked her ticket and all that remained was for her to pack her things. There was no point in staying here now. It wasn't the fact that Charlie didn't love her, that she could handle. It was everything else that came with it.

A sound from the doorway made her jump and she looked up, surprised to see Charlie standing there. His appearance shocked her; he was battered and bruised and looked as though he'd gone three rounds with Mike Tyson.

"We should talk."

The three words should have represented a lifeline but instead they felt like a death sentence. There was no hope in his voice, no expectation, just the finality of the awful situation they were in.

"Can I sit down?"

"It's your house," she shrugged. "You can do what you want."

He manoeuvred into the armchair opposite her. The slow and deliberate way he moved told her that he was in agony and it took everything she had not to leap to her feet and help him. She wanted to comfort him, to nurse his wounds and take away his pain but she was torn by the love she felt for him and the disgust over his immoral association with Declan Connors.

"I never wanted you to see me like that," said Charlie, his voice low and husky. "I can't even imagine what you must be thinking."

"I'm thinking that if it wasn't for you we'd probably both be dead," she admitted truthfully. "You had no choice, you did what you had to do."

"I never intended for any of this to happen."

"I know you didn't." She took a deep breath and sighed. "But you do realise that I have to leave now?"

He nodded as though he expected it. "For what it's worth, I really am sorry. I should've been upfront with you from the start."

"Yes you should have," she agreed. "But it doesn't matter now, what's done is done." She felt the tears bubble up in her eyes but held them back. She didn't want him to see her cry. "I need to go and pack, my flight's at six o'clock. I'll book a taxi to take me to the airport."

"No you won't, I'll drive you."

"You don't look like you're in a fit state to do anything. I can make my own way."

"It's not up for discussion," he said flatly. "We'll leave at four."

The drive to Malaga was fraught with tension.

Charlie was driving like a madman. He'd already ploughed through two sets of red lights without stopping and had almost collided with a coach coming from the opposite direction. On top of that he seemed to have forgotten what the indicator was for. They were careening around corners at the last minute and pulling out of junctions with no consideration for any other vehicle on the road. It was a relief when they finally arrived at the airport as Kate couldn't wait to get out of the car. They fought their way through the swarm of holidaymakers, Charlie not caring who he wheeled her cases into in the process, much to the annoyance of the other travellers. Thankfully nobody dared confront him; one look at his angry battered face was enough to deter anyone from approaching him.

At check-in they joined the queue of people in line for the 1815 to London Gatwick. They stood behind the family from hell and were forced to watch as the children beat the crap out of each other whilst their parents were busy unloading items from their suitcases and redistributing them into their hand luggage. The bored check in assistant didn't give a shit that they were only half a kilo over the weight limit. Rules were rules.

When it was finally her turn Kate approached the desk and handed over her passport. Her luggage was whisked away into the bowels of the airport leaving her ready to take the short walk to the security gate. Charlie was still by her side but he'd barely said a word to her the whole time. She had no idea what he was thinking, she only knew that he must be relieved she was finally leaving.

A large group of giggling girls wearing matching tee-shirts and pink cowboy hats pushed their way past them and Kate caught her foot on the wheel of one of their suitcases. She went crashing into Charlie who automatically put his arms around her but the mere touch of him caused a red-hot jolt to burn right through her skin. She leapt away in a panic.

"Jesus darlin', take it easy will you? I know you can't wait to get away from me but you don't have to make it so obvious."

She tutted, annoyed by his presumption. If only he knew how difficult this was for her, that all she really wanted to do was to forget the last twenty-four hours had ever happened. That everything was as it had been before Mickey, before she'd found out the truth.

"What?" he said deliberately bating her. "Is there something you want to say to me?"

"Like what?"

"How the hell should I know darlin'? You're the one treating me like a leper."

His shitty attitude didn't make leaving any easier. There were fifty metres between her and Passport Control so she turned and started walking. After everything they'd been through it broke her heart that it was ending like this but there was nothing she could do about that now. She took her place in the line, retrieved her passport and boarding pass from her bag and awaited her turn. The elderly couple in front shuffled forward. She went to follow them but her arm was grabbed and she was swung around so fast she landed straight in Charlie's arms.

"Don't go," he said, his voice almost a whisper. There was a sincerity in his eyes and for a moment she didn't understand what he was asking her.

"What?"

"Stay here, with me."

She considered it for the longest moment. And then she remembered that he didn't love her. And even if he did, she couldn't stay. Not now she was aware of what his deal with Declan entailed.

"I can't. I need to go."

She pulled away from him and holding back the tears, headed for the security gate. Moments later she stole a look behind her. Her heart sank.

He was already gone.

CHAPTER
TWENTY-ONE

D own on her knees in front of him, sucking his cock like her life depended on it, was a young blonde called Nicky. At least that's what Charlie thought she was called. Three quarters of a bottle of Jack Daniels and half a dozen beers hadn't prevented him from getting a hard-on but it was sure playing havoc with his memory. She'd been flirting with him all night and whilst he hadn't been interested in the chit-chat, (her Geordie accent was really annoying and she was actually boring the tits off him), he had graciously accepted her offer of a blow job. So now his trousers were round his ankles and her head was bobbing up and down in his lap like the proverbial fiddler's elbow.

He'd been into it at first. After two weeks without so much as a single knee trembler the prospect of getting his rocks off really appealed to him. A few minutes into it however and he realised that she wasn't doing anything for him. Ordinarily, the way she was running her tongue along the shaft and cupping his balls would have been enough but as he looked down at her, he was sad to realise that he felt absolutely nothing.

He put his hands on her head and urged her on. She continued, sucking and licking enthusiastically, trying her best to bring him to a thundering climax but after a few more minutes he could feel his erection slowly dying.

"Stop, for fuck's sake stop," he muttered awkwardly.

She slid him out of her mouth, her heavily made-up eyes peering up at him. "You want me to go slower, honey?"

"No," he said, grabbing his trousers and pulling them up. He shoved his cock away, fastening the zip swiftly. "I want you to go full stop."

"Would it help if I got my tits out?"

"No, I don't want you to do that."

She rose to her feet and wiped her mouth with the back of her hand. "Shall I give you a moment? It's okay you know, it happens to a lot of guys."

"No, I don't need a moment," said Charlie embarrassed. "I just need you to leave."

She was disappointed, he could tell. But fuck it, so was he. This had never happened to him before and he was just as frustrated as she was. He took a bottle of champagne from the crate behind his desk and thrust it into her hands.

"Have this, it's on the house. Now fuck off and enjoy the rest of your night."

She took the bottle and shrugged as if realising it was better than nothing. "Call me when you're ready to continue."

He waved her away and slumped into his chair. What a great evening this had turned out to be. He was going to be the talk of the bar and could almost hear the words 'erectile disfunction' on the tip of everybody's tongue.

"Fuck," he groaned as he dropped his head in his hands. Talk about use it or lose it. Then he laughed out loud, what else could he do?

He knew what the problem was and it was simple; she wasn't Kate.

He woke just before noon the next day with a major hangover. This had pretty much been the standard over the past two weeks. Long nights at the bar throwing absurd amounts of alcohol down his neck followed by long days in bed, sleeping it off. He liked it; it made him incapable of thinking and that suited him just fine. But it was proving impossible to shut Kate out of his head completely and his mind constantly drifted to her, reliving the time they'd spent together. More often than not this left him feeling empty and alone but occasionally he'd be consumed with anger and frustration and when that happened he just wanted to drink himself into oblivion.

He sank down into his hot tub and appreciated the warm bubbles on his body. He was still sore and the bruises still visible but on the whole he was okay. Thankfully the doctor confirmed there was no long-term damage to his kidneys but he'd taken a good kicking and had cracked a few ribs. Being no spring chicken, the healing was taking that much longer. He was just grateful that he wasn't dead.

Phil was holding a meeting when Charlie arrived at the bar just before seven. Two barmen had left to join the party scene in Ibiza so Phil had employed two more to fill their places. Both starting tonight, Phil was giving them the rundown of the place. Luckily they were both experienced in preparing drinks and making cocktails so there shouldn't be any problems; slow service was not something Charlie would tolerate.

He shook the hands of both new lads. Angel was a smooth-talking Spaniard employed as a deck hand on a visiting super yacht but had been fired when the yacht's owner, a Russian billionaire, had discovered him in the master cabin playing strip poker with his wife. And there was John, a Brit studying to be an engineer who was taking a gap year from university to backpack around Europe with his girlfriend. Neither would last beyond the season but Charlie wasn't worried; there were plenty more where they came from.

Rick was sitting in the VIP section so Charlie grabbed a Jack Daniels and coke from the bar and made his way over. Jamal, his head of security, was in his usual position at the edge of the cordon and gave him the nod as he walked through. Rick put his phone away and gestured for him to sit down.

"So, when's the missus coming back? No offence mate, but you've been a right miserable cunt since she left."

Charlie laughed. "Yeah, I have, haven't I? But fuck knows, she said she needed some space."

He hated lying to Rick but the incident with Mickey had provided him with the perfect cover story to explain her absence. Of course he'd leave it a while before announcing it was over between them and that she was never coming back.

"Yeah well I can't say I blame her," said Rick as he sipped his pint. "It couldn't have been much fun watching you go psycho on those two fucking clowns."

"Cheers for the reminder mate."

"Ah come on, you know I'm only messing with you. Women love all that macho bullshit. Take my Sharon. She saw me beat the living crap out of some dipshit who thought he could touch her up in a pub car park. After that she was all over me like a cheap suit. Once you've got them hooked, that's it." He winked at Charlie and grinned. "Bit like a Golden Retriever really, loyal for life. Doesn't matter how much crap you give them they always come back for more."

"Have you heard yourself, mate? Comparing your old lady to a dog. I'm sure she'd fucking love that."

They both chuckled. Charlie's phone vibrated in his pocket and he took it out, hoping for one mad minute that it might be a message from Kate. But it was only Maria inviting him to dinner tomorrow night. He shot back a quick reply to accept and stuffed his phone back into his jacket.

"D'you fancy coming down the strip club? Sharon's out with the girls and I could really get off on some bird flashing her fanny in my face."

Charlie downed the rest of his drink. "Let's go," he said, setting the glass down onto the table. "I think a lap dance might be exactly what the doctor ordered."

An invitation to Phil and Maria's for dinner was an event not to be missed. Maria had a book of family recipes that had been passed down from generation to generation and her Paella was one of the best Charlie had ever tasted. He was feeling a little fragile as he rocked up at the door holding a bottle of Rioja in one hand and a bouquet of flowers for Maria in the other. Having been out on the town the previous night with Rick he was still hanging badly. It had been a laugh though. They'd stopped for drinks at a couple of the bars in Puerto Banus before heading to the strip club. Watching naked girls strut their stuff on the stage had certainly been entertaining but in the end, he'd passed on the offer of a lap dance. His total lack of interest in having his cock sucked the other night was still bothering him and he found the same lack of enthusiasm in the idea of some exotic dancer grinding her pussy all over him.

Rick, however, showed no such restraint. He'd taken the hand of a lively Asian girl and had disappeared for twenty minutes, leaving Charlie in the booth, watching the show alone like some sad and lonely pervert. When it became clear that Rick was otherwise engaged, he'd downed his drink and fucked off.

Whilst Maria worked her magic in the kitchen, Charlie and Phil sat by the pool with a cold beer. They talked shop for a bit but inevitably Phil got round to asking about the deal with Declan. Charlie was out, he'd made up his mind and wasn't going to change it. Not because of Kate but because in his heart of hearts, he just couldn't do it. Despite Mickey's reminder of his crooked and corrupt ways, he'd never actually hurt anybody who hadn't deserved it and kidnapping a woman and her two young children was beyond even his penchant for violence.

Declan however wasn't aware of Charlie's decision yet because he hadn't informed him. He knew to leave it much longer would become an issue but he was still trying to work out how to tell him. The job was scheduled to take place in a week's time and he was meant to be heading back to the UK in a few days to put the final touches in place. He wasn't going to pull the plug on Jack, he was a grown man and could make his own decisions and there was such an exorbitant amount of money to be made that Charlie figured Jack would still want to push ahead regardless.

"Here we go," said Maria clutching a huge round metallic pan with handles. She positioned it in the middle of the table and took a step back to admire it. The paella was pretty impressive; stuffed full of chicken and prawns, it was large enough to feed half the starving children in Africa. Maria, red-faced from her efforts in the kitchen, sat down and fanned herself with her hand.

"It looks gorgeous, darlin'," said Charlie enthusiastically as he poured her a glass of wine. He quickly got stuck in and piled his plate high. After a squeeze of lemon he shovelled a forkful into his mouth and savoured the taste.

"Oh my God," he said between mouthfuls. "This is like sex on a plate."

Maria laughed. "I'm glad you like it. Now can you please tell me what the hell is going on with you and Kate."

Charlie froze, the question totally unexpected. "What do you mean what's going on?"

"You know what I mean Charlie, I want to know why she left. And I don't want to hear any of the crap you've been telling Phil."

"Ah come on, babe," said Phil shaking his head. "I told you not to mention it."

"Don't you babe me. You shouldn't have told me if you didn't want me to say anything."

Phil looked across the table at Charlie and shrugged apologetically. "I'm sorry mate."

"Brilliant," said Charlie, putting his fork down with a crash. "That's what this is all about, isn't it? Butter me up with paella and listen to me spill my guts out? Well I'm sorry to disappoint you but there's nothing going on."

"That's just it, Charlie, there's nothing going on," Maria repeated. "Phil told me about your deal with

Declan and your fake marriage." She motioned speech marks with her fingers to emphasise the word 'fake' and when she saw the surprise on Charlie's face, she smiled. "Relax, you know I'd never tell a soul, you're like family to me. But it's obvious that you two have feelings for each other so what I want to know is, what are you going to do about it?"

Charlie let out a breath. He didn't need this right now, his head already hurt. "I'm gonna carry on doing what I usually do."

"And what's that? Bury your head in the nearest vagina?"

Phil smashed his palm against his forehead and rolled his eyes. He wished he'd never told Maria a damn thing.

"What's wrong with that?" asked Charlie.

"Nothing, if you want to spend the rest of your life giving head to a string of dumb blondes."

Charlie laughed. "How do you know that's not what I'm doing anyway?"

"Okay then, how women have you slept with since Kate's been gone?"

"Who are you? My doctor?"

"Answer the question please."

He chewed on a mouthful of chorizo while he did the sum in his head. It was an easy one. "If you must know, none."

"Huh! I knew it." Maria sat back and folded her arms across her chest. "You're in love with her."

Charlie squirmed in his seat. She was using some kind of Jedi mind trick on him and it was seriously fucking him up. "Jesus, you should work for MI5. What do you want me to say, Maria?"

"I want you to admit that you're in love with her."

"I don't want to talk about it. Just drop it, yeah? You're putting me off my dinner."

Maria pointed an accusing finger at him. "This is so typical of you. You build up these walls and won't let anyone in."

"Don't psycho-analyse me, you're not my shrink."

"I'm just trying to get to the truth."

"I hate to tell you darlin' but the Spanish Inquisition was over a long time ago." Charlie ripped apart a chunk of crusty bread with his teeth but seeing the sad look on Maria's face he relented. "Okay, if you want the truth I'll give it to you. I killed two men, right in front of her eyes. I strangled one and stabbed the other one in the heart. Then I battered the fuck out of Mickey. So it doesn't really matter how I feel does it, it's about how *she* feels and she doesn't want anything to do with me now."

Maria shrugged. "It was self-defence."

"It was murder." He picked up his wine glass and twiddled the stem in his fingers. "Would you want to be involved in *that*?"

"Isn't that her decision to make?"

"She already made it. I asked her to stay, she left. That's the end of it."

"You actually told her you were in love with her?" asked Maria, surprised.

"Not in so many words, no." He had told her he loved her in his office though, whilst she had a knife against her throat. But to make things easier for the both of them he'd just as quickly denied it. But he wasn't going to tell Maria that, she was already chewing his ear off.

"Did you tell her you were finished with Declan?" asked Phil, finally joining the conversation.

Charlie shook his head. "What was the point?"

"I don't fucking believe you," said Phil in frustration. "You're an absolute tosser."

"What difference would it have made?" asked Charlie, genuinely perplexed. "She either loves me or she doesn't. And I think we've established that she doesn't."

"I've known you for a long time Charlie and there've been a lot of women. A lot," he repeated with an eye roll. "And you've never looked at any of them the way you look at her. You're perfect for each other and if you had any brains in that head of yours, you'd get down on your knees and beg her to come back."

Charlie brandished his fork at him. "You're giving me the right hump now. This is the last time I'm coming to dinner here."

"Good because you're a miserable bastard anyway."

"Oh for fuck's sake," groaned Charlie. "If it's gonna shut the two of you up I'll think about it, alright? Now, if you don't mind, I'm going to finish my food before it gets cold. I just hope you've made those frita things for dessert Maria or I won't be fucking happy. You need to seriously sweeten me up after all this earache."

CHAPTER
TWENTY-TWO

Kate held the key in her hand and stared at the house she'd once shared with Mark. A two up, two down brick mid-terrace with a shiny white front door and neatly trimmed lawn to the front, it had been her first home and she'd been happy there. She glanced up at the 'For Sale' board attached to the gate post. She wasn't sad about her break-up with Mark, just the finality it represented. At twenty-nine years old she was back to being single again with no job and until the sale of the house went through, no bloody money either.

She'd put the remaining seven thousand pounds that Charlie had paid her into a separate bank account and one day she would return it to him. She hadn't summoned the courage to speak to him since she'd returned home almost three weeks ago but she would once she felt a little stronger. She'd stared at his name on her phone at least a million times, her finger hovering over the screen, daring her to press the call button. But she couldn't do it. She had absolutely no idea what she would say to him.

She swung open the wrought iron gate and proceeded down the concrete path. Mark had assured her that he would be out. He hadn't been happy when she'd informed him that she was coming to pack the rest of her stuff, she knew he still harboured the crazy illusion that the two of them would get back together. Not that there was a hope in hell of that happening.

She turned the key in the lock and gingerly pushed open the door. She didn't know why she expected it to look any different. The duck egg blue sofa they'd chosen together still dominated the living room and the canvases they'd picked out from Ikea still hung on the walls. She made her way through to the kitchen; it was small but she'd liked the layout and the glossy white cupboards. She popped the kettle on to make herself a drink when her phone beeped. She grabbed it, hoping by some miracle that it would be Charlie, but it was only Mark, reminding her that he would be leaving work at four o'clock and to ensure that she was gone by the time he got home. She poured the hot water into her mug and stirred her coffee then took the wrapper off an energy bar she'd found in her handbag. She needed the extra calories to keep her strength up as she was about to undertake the mammoth task of packing her things. She'd borrowed Jason's car for the occasion and it was parked outside the front of the house, its boot empty and waiting to be filled.

She was surprised by how calm she felt. When she'd first discovered that Mark had been cheating on her she'd wanted to burn the house down. With him in it. But now, as she opened cupboards and drawers and collected the things she wanted, not once did she feel the urge to break down and cry. Maybe she was just a cold, heartless bitch? Maybe she hadn't really loved Mark at all? She felt more cut-up over her break-up with Charlie than she had ever been about Mark.

If that made her some kind of fruitcake then so be it.

She filled two suitcases and stuffed her clothes into black bin liners which she stacked neatly by the front door. There were a few photos she wanted to keep, none of which included Mark so she popped them on top of a cardboard box that she'd loaded with her shoes; Imelda Marcus eat your heart out, she had over twenty-five pairs. Then there were the Le Creuset saucepans her parents had gifted them when they'd moved in; she was fucked if Mark was keeping them. He never liked cooking anyway. And just because she felt like it, she threw in the toaster and the almost brand-new coffee maker. Fuck him and his frothy cappuccinos, she thought with a smile on her face, he'll have to make do with instant. She took a few of Mark's DVDs just to piss him off and satisfied that she'd taken everything she wanted, she loaded up the car and headed back to Clare's.

There was a large glass of wine waiting for her on her return which she appreciated; unloading the car had been thirsty work. Clare's spare room now resembled a charity shop with piles of stuff everywhere. She needed to find her own place to rent but that involved getting a job. She had an interview lined up next week for a finance assistant at a local manufacturing company but didn't hold out much hope. For every vacancy there were about a hundred applicants and so many people were out of work that the odds were stacked against her. Still, she'd give it her best shot.

Clare came into the room and topped up her wine. They were having pre-drinks; they were heading to Coco's later and Kate was looking forward to it. She was going to spend the evening enjoying herself rather than thinking about Charlie and recalling the horror of their last night together. People being beaten and murdered before your eyes tended to leave its mark and she hadn't had one decent night's sleep since she'd been home. Being hopelessly in love with him didn't help either and she lay in bed every night wishing he was lying next to her.

She thought back to their final moments at the airport, when he'd asked her to stay. He'd already told her he didn't love her so she hadn't understood what he'd meant. Now however, she'd reached that crazy point where if she saw him again, despite everything he'd done in the past and all that he was planning to do in the future, she knew she would melt into his arms and stay there forever. Whoever said that love was blind was definitely onto something.

Clare was less enthused. After hearing the whole story she was fuming and whilst there was no question of shopping Charlie to the police, she'd made it clear that she was going to give him a very large piece of her mind.

Three weeks on that still hadn't happened.

"What shall we drink to?" asked Clare as she held up her glass.

"To my divorce," said Kate. She looked down at her ring finger and saw the stretch of white skin that signified the removal of her wedding band.

"Cheers," they said in unison. "What a pity the settlement didn't include the boat," added Clare with a grin. "You could've sold it and bought a nice little apartment in town."

Kate clocked Mark the minute she walked into Coco's. He was standing at the bar with a crowd of his friends and by the looks of it, they were well into a heavy drinking session.

"Do you want to go somewhere else?" asked Clare, seeing the apprehensive look on Kate's face. But Kate shook her head. After everything she'd been through she was tough enough to look her ex-boyfriend in the eye and front it out. They did however move to the opposite end of the bar where Jason met them with a look of thunder on his face.

"Do you want me to throw him out? Honestly, it would be my absolute pleasure."

"Nah," said Kate, touched by his concern. "Don't

worry about it, he's not worth the effort."

"Well in that case, let me get you both a very large drink." Jason busied himself behind the bar creating a cocktail that was heavy on the vodka and light on the fruit juice and presented two glasses onto the bar with a flourish. "Porn star martinis for my two favourite girls."

After her second one, Kate was really feeling up for it. They relocated to a side table along with two exotic looking Pina Coladas for company. Kate knew the night would end with her head down the toilet but she didn't care, it just felt good to be out. The music was thumping and it wasn't long before they were dancing. The Weeknd's Blinding Light was blasting out of the speakers, the strobe lights were flashing and the heavy base was pulsating through the sweaty bodies on the dancefloor. Kate let the rhythm take her away but just as she reached the point of no inhibition she felt a heavy tap on her shoulder. She spun round and came face to face with Mark.

"Why did you take the coffee maker? That was well out of order."

Kate looked him squarely in the eye and smirked. "You're lucky I didn't empty the whole fucking house."

"I want it back."

"Tough. Now fuck off, I'm busy." She turned her back to him and carried on dancing. She was irritated that he'd disturbed her; she was supposed to be having fun.

"Can we go somewhere to talk?"

She moved out of the way of another dancer who had decided to strut his John Travolta Staying Alive dance moves and was threatening to poke her in the eye with his fingers.

"Please."

He looked so pathetic; maybe if she humoured him he'd go away. "Okay. You've got five minutes. I won't be long," she said to Clare as she let Mark lead her off the dancefloor. She followed him out of the back of the club to the covered smoking area. It was, as she'd suspected it would be, cold and dark with a blanket of smoke curling in the air. He took her arm and ushered her to a corner that was devoid of people but where the smell of cigarettes made her eyes sting.

"You look fantastic," he said as he looked her up and down.

She supposed she did; her tan was holding thanks to the vast amount of moisturiser she was applying to her skin daily and she'd lost a few pounds in the last week. Stress related of course. But she hadn't agreed to meet him so that he could admire her summer holiday body.

"What do you want, Mark?"

"I've accepted that we're not getting back together and I wanted you to know that."

"You've accepted it have you?" she mouthed incredulously. "Is that it? Can I go now?"

"I think it would be nice if we could stay friends."

She could smell the alcohol on his breath and turned up her nose. "Why would we do that?"

"I just thought we could stay in touch, that's all."

"In case you feel a booty call coming on? Like you did with Tina?"

He spluttered a bit at that point, unable to think of a comeback quick enough.

"I don't want to be your friend Mark, I've got enough friends. I'll be in touch to sort out the selling of the house but that's it. There's no reason for either of us to see each other again."

"What about my Band of Brothers DVD? Are you going to give it back?"

"I've already thrown it away."

"That was my favourite."

"I know," she said with a grin. "Why do you think I binned it?"

She walked off then and didn't look back. Clare was waiting for her with a Margarita which she downed in three gulps. "Come on then," she said dragging her back to the dancefloor. "Let's get this party started."

Hangovers were not Kate's friend. She should've been used to them by now but this one seemed to be the mother of them all. It was the mixing of the drinks that had done it. Her father's words rang in her head; don't mix the grape and the grain. Last night, not only had she mixed the grape and the grain but she'd done it with cream in the Pina Colada, orange juice in the Tequila Sunrise and with ginger beer in the Moscow Mule. This morning, her stomach was feeling the effects. She was sure she was being sick not from the alcohol, but from the array of mixers that had diluted it. One day, when she was a proper grown up, she'd learn. But not today.

She ran an anti-bacterial wipe around the toilet bowl. At least there were no lumps anymore. She was tempted to take a shower but the idea of getting back into bed won and she stayed there all day, not even getting up for anything to eat. It felt comforting to be wrapped up in the duvet and she drifted in and out of sleep all day. There was nothing to get up for anyway.

The next day dawned and she'd forgotten it was Monday until Clare banged on her door to remind her that she had an interview to get to. An hour later she was sitting cross legged in the waiting area of Carbonflex Limited along with six other women who had all applied for the same position.

Kate hated group interviews and remembered the last one she'd attended. *Imagine you're shipwrecked on a desert island and can only take three things with you. What would they be?* And then there would be a list of random items like a lipstick, a sat phone and a box of matches. She stifled a yawn then noticed the red-hot death glare from the woman sitting next to her.

"Sorry," she mumbled apologetically. "I just find these things so boring."

It didn't get much better. After the initial group interview which had been exactly as she'd expected, right down to the stranded on a desert island part, each girl had been interviewed separately. After sitting patiently in the waiting area for over an hour Kate was the last one to be summoned to the office. She knocked on the door and when she entered she saw a big, burly man in a bad fitting suit motioning for her to take the seat in front of his desk. He was about fifty Kate guessed, and had an enormous pot belly that hung over the waistband of his trousers and stretched the buttons of his blue gingham checked shirt to near breaking point.

"So Miss…" He checked the sheet of paper in front of him. "Newman. Tell me why I should employ you."

Kate launched into her pre-rehearsed spiel of how talented and amazing she was, what an asset she'd be to his company, how her time-keeping was exemplary and basically all of the bullshit she knew he wanted to hear. He took her on a quick tour of the facility; a large warehouse where they manufactured high performance composite solutions, whatever that meant, and a row of offices on a mezzanine floor where the sales, purchasing and accounts departments were situated. It was noisy and dull. She couldn't imagine working here every day from nine to five but she desperately needed the money.

She was introduced to the Payroll Manager, a woman in her forties with curly brown hair that looked as if it hadn't seen a comb in weeks. The woman took one look at Kate's brown legs and short skirt and Kate realised right there and then that she wasn't going to get the job. Not if this old bag had anything to do with it. Still, she smiled politely and let Mr Walker continue with the tour. She left with the promise of a call by the end of the day but she really didn't care one way or the other.

She met Megan for lunch in a pub in town. They hadn't seen each other for a while and had to lot to catch up on. One glass of wine turned into two but Kate drew the line at a third; there was no way she could cope with another hangover so soon after the last one. They went on to do some shopping and it was almost half past six by the time she arrived home.

The moment she turned her key in the lock Clare appeared in the entrance hall and hovered in front of her suspiciously.

"Have you seen the news?"

"No, I've been shopping with Meg." Kate dropped her shopping bags to the floor and shouldered off her denim jacket. "Why?"

"I don't want you to panic, okay?"

A tingling sensation shot through her body, like liquid ice flowing through her veins. "What is it, what's wrong?"

Jason appeared in the hallway, his arms folded across his chest, a serious expression on his face. "It's Charlie."

Kate's hand shot to her mouth. "Oh God, what?"

"You'd better come in here."

Jason retreated back to the living room leaving both Kate and Clare to follow. The news was on the television, the newsreader mumbling on about the growth of the economy. Kate tried to tune it out.

"Tell me what's happened. Is he alright?"

Jason picked up the remote control and suddenly the picture on the television was in rewind.

"For fuck's sake leave the bloody telly alone and tell me what's going on."

Jason pressed the pause button. "You need to see this, you might want to sit down though."

Kate sat on the sofa as Jason resumed playback and the newsreader announced the headlines in her no-nonsense factual tone:

'More than forty-three million pounds in used banknotes has been stolen from a depot in Brighton after its security manager and his family were kidnapped by armed robbers posing as police. The assailants were armed with AK-47s and forced their way into the home of Michael Feldman who has been the manager of Select Security Services for three years. His wife and their twelve-year-old twin boys were held at gunpoint whilst Mr Feldman was forced to give them access to the facility where the cash was stored. Eight members of staff were also held at gunpoint whilst the raid took place but police were alerted when a silent alarm was triggered. An armed response unit arrived at the scene and it is understood that two of the assailants were detained and a third was shot attempting to evade capture. The other six assailants are still at large and forensic teams are currently searching the surround-

ing area looking for a white Ford Transit van which has been reported by police as the get-away vehicle. Anybody with any information should call the number at the bottom of the screen."

The newsreader continued with a description of the men wanted for questioning but Kate begged Jason to turn it off. She didn't want to hear anymore. She felt physically sick. Despite the horror of what had just been reported there was only one thing on her mind.

"Who was shot?" she asked Jason, expecting him to know the answer. "Was it Charlie?"

But Jason shook his head. "I don't know, love. All I can tell you is that I've tried calling him and he's not answering his phone."

Kate rubbed her forehead and tried to think logically. Charlie was meant to be the one holding the family hostage so he couldn't have been at the depot. Unless for some reason the plan had changed. She cursed under her breath, not knowing whether to be relieved or outraged. The man she was in love with was leading a double life. He was involved in some heavy criminal activity that if caught, could see him in prison for the rest of his life. But worse, if shot, he could be lying dead in a hospital morgue somewhere.

She started to hyperventilate and sank to the sofa. Her legs were shaking and she didn't think they would hold her up.

"Just take it easy," said Jason sensibly. "We don't even know he was involved."

"Seriously? Weren't you listening? This is what this whole bloody mess has been about. I can't believe he's putting us through this. If he was here right now I think I would bloody well kill him."

Suddenly Jason's phone rang. All three of them froze. Jason checked the caller id and looked over at Kate apprehensively. "It's him, it's Charlie. Be quiet both of you," he said and put the phone to his ear.

"Charlie? Yeah, it's just been on. Okay mate, yeah, right. Okay, no worries."

Kate had no idea what was being said. There was just a string of one-word replies and a lot of nodding. She fought the urge to grab the phone from Jason's hand but just like that, the call was over.

"He's on his way here."

"He's coming here?" echoed Kate in astonishment. "Is he hurt?"

"No, he's fine."

The relief was instant but now she had another matter to contend with.

Was she ready to see him?

Panic started to build in her chest. How would she be able to look him in the eye after the hell he'd put that family through?

"What are you doing?" asked Jason as she leapt from the sofa and hurried towards the front door.

"I can't do it." She was mixed up and confused and just couldn't face him. "I'm out of here."

Jason called after her but she slammed the door.

She hurried down the stairs, not stopping until she was outside. Then she put one foot in front of the other and started walking.

Charlie stepped out of the taxi and paid the driver in cash, bunging him a huge tip. He'd been a friendly bloke and they'd spent the entire ride from the airport chatting. He looked up at the modern purpose-built apartment block where Jason lived and tried to calm the somersaults that were performing in his chest.

He realised he should've called much earlier but his flight from Malaga had been delayed and he'd been held up at Customs by some dickhead who thought it was okay to smuggle a Chihuahua in his suitcase. If he'd arrived hours ago as he'd intended, he would've spared Kate the trauma of watching the entire robbery fiasco play out on the television. He couldn't even imagine what she must be thinking.

He pressed the buzzer for Jason's flat and waited impatiently for it to be answered. He was really anxious about seeing Kate again. Whilst she had never actually said the words, he could only hope that she felt the same way about him as he felt about her. He'd wasted time, spending the last three weeks fighting his feelings for all they were worth. But all he'd accomplished was to put off the inevitable. It was almost as if he enjoyed being bloody miserable.

Phil was right; he was an absolute tosser. And that's why he was here, to put things right and tell her how he felt. For real this time. He only hoped he wasn't too late.

There was a loud buzzing sound as the door opened and he marched in, taking the stairs two at a time until he reached the top floor. He rapped his knuckles on the door and gave it a good hammering. The door swung open and he was greeted by Clare, the slap around the face the last thing he was expecting.

"Fuck me!" he groaned as she hit him hard across the cheek. It wasn't the first time a woman had slapped him and he daren't say it would be the last, but he had forgotten what a sting it created. "What was that for?"

"Don't act like you don't know Charlie. I entrusted my sister to you and look what you did to her."

Charlie held his hands up in defeat; he definitely deserved that one.

"Get in here," she snapped opening the door wide enough for him to enter. "You've got some bloody explaining to do."

Jason met him in the hallway and both men embraced. "She took off mate, the minute she found out you were coming. I didn't even have a chance to tell her what you told me on the phone."

"It's my own fault, I should've called her. In fact I should never have let her leave in the first place. Just goes to prove what a fucking idiot I am."

Jason grinned. "Tell me something I don't know. What's the deal then? What the bloody hell's going on?"

Clare discretely disappeared leaving the two of

them alone. Charlie followed Jason into the lounge and they sat down on the sofa.

"It's a mess," said Charlie shaking his head. "Declan's fucked up big time. I told him I was out and seeing as Kate saved his kid from drowning he knew he owed me one so as far as I was concerned, the job was over. But then he decided to go ahead regardless and recruited some blagger at the last minute."

"Who got shot?"

"Fuck knows," said Charlie with a shrug.

"I wish you'd have told me what was going on. It would've saved a lot of worry."

"I know mate but I haven't exactly been thinking straight lately. My whole bloody world's been turned upside down. I've never been into theatrics but I reckon I'm gonna end up on my fucking knees this time begging for forgiveness."

"Whilst making a prick of yourself in the process?"

"Probably," smirked Charlie. "So where is she then?"

"I dunno mate, but I think Clare might have an idea."

It was a chilly night. Despite it being August the weather was still so unpredictable. The sun that had been shining all day was now setting and dark clouds were rumbling overhead; it looked like it was about to pour down. Kate wished she'd grabbed her jacket on her way out because now she was freezing. She was sitting on a park bench like a wino without the wine. Luckily there was nobody around to witness her poor choice of clothing; she was still wearing the short black skirt and thin white blouse she had worn for her interview this morning. It may have been acceptable as prospective-employee attire but it wasn't the eight o'clock in the evening, the sun has gone down and it's going to rain look. The goosebumps on her arms and legs could testify to this and she suppressed a shiver.

She'd been sitting there for ages now, her mind consumed with thoughts of Charlie. They hadn't parted well, they'd had no contact whatsoever since she'd been home and she didn't know what she was going to say to him when she saw him again. And why, if the job had gone as badly as it had been reported, would he risk coming to the flat? Surely he would be better off lying low somewhere until it all blew over?

She saw a man enter the park but didn't pay him any attention. A spit of rain bounced onto her legs and caused her to shiver. The man drew closer, probably thinking she was a homeless person. She stood up, intending to leave rather than explain herself, but as she turned something about the man caused her to take a closer look. Checking him out from top to bottom she ran her eyes over the tan boots, the dark jeans and the navy jumper. Her heart was beating frantically in her chest before she even allowed herself to look at his face. The designer stubble, tousled dark hair and those gorgeous chocolate brown eyes made her swoon. Never mind the fact that he had been involved in an armed robbery, the relief of seeing Charlie again was just too much. She launched herself at him and clung onto him for dear life. He swung her around in his arms and their lips met in a long, frenzied kiss.

"God darlin', I've missed you so much," he breathed as they parted. "There's some stuff I need to tell you. Things I should've told you before."

"If you're about to tell me the police are on their way I don't care."

He laughed, a deep throaty sound that made her toes curl. "What do you think I am? Some kind of fucking amateur? Come on, let's sit down."

They walked to the bench and he pulled her down onto his lap. Although her legs were covered in goosebumps she wasn't feeling the cold anymore. Her senses were dominated by the touch of him and the spicy, woody smell of his aftershave.

"Tonight, on the news, it wasn't me."

"What do you mean it wasn't you?"

"After you left I told Declan I was out. I just couldn't go through with it. I know I should've told you before and I'm sorry."

"You called the whole thing off? Because of me?"

"Not just because of you. I did it for me too. I real-ised I had a choice to make. It took me a while but the truth is darlin', I've been fucking miserable without you. I'm not proud of the things I've done, the things you saw me do…"

"Don't," she said cutting him off. "You had no choice Charlie. I was there, remember?"

"When I said I didn't love you I didn't mean it. I just

thought that you deserved so much better."

The rain was really coming down now. Kate shivered so Charlie pulled her closer and she buried her head against his chest.

"I love you," she whispered and had never meant anything more in her life.

"I love you too, darlin. Come home with me, I'm lost without you."

She looked up at the grey sky as the rain pelted down onto her face. "Give up all this you mean? For a life in sunny Spain with you?"

"How about I make you an offer you can't refuse?" He knelt down onto the sodden ground, his knee squelching in the mud. "Marry me. For real this time. No fucking about, we go to the registry office tomorrow and make it official."

Kate couldn't help but laugh. As proposals went it was hardly the most romantic, not that there was a chance in hell she was going to say no.

"Well seeing as you put it so delicately, how can I refuse? I do have just one condition though."

"You name it darlin'."

"This time you choose the ring."

He nodded. "I can do that."

"Oh and one more thing."

"What now?" he snapped, feigning annoyance.

She grinned. "This time I'll do it for free."

EPILOGUE

K ate stared at her reflection in the mirror and admired her hair. A sophisticated updo, the intricate silk petals of the flower crown were entwined in her curls at the back of her neck and she looked chic and classy. She mentally congratulated the hairdresser for such an incredible job. Her newly applied make up gave her a fresh faced and pretty look and with just one more layer of pink lip gloss she would finally be ready.

The Honeymoon Suite at the Burgess Hotel was a hive of activity. Hairdressers, beauticians and three young bridesmaids had been in and out of the room all morning, all preparing for the ceremony that was about to take place in the Wedding Room on the ground floor where a hundred guests were already sat waiting in anticipation along with one very nervous bridegroom.

Clare was sitting patiently on the elegant four-poster bed sipping champagne and munching her way through the box of complimentary Godiva chocolates. Their mum Rose was standing by the window staring out at the three acres of perfectly landscaped lawn thinking what a perfect day it was for a wedding. It might be a cold Friday in February but the sun was shining and the sky was blue. And it wasn't as if they had to go anywhere. The ceremony and the reception were both being held at the hotel so there would be no complaints from guests who had to endure sitting in a cold and draughty two-hundred-year-old church.

"Are you ready yet?" asked Clare as she popped another chocolate into her mouth.

Kate nodded, wishing she had half of her sister's composure. Clare may be calm but Kate's tummy was doing somersaults. "Yes I'm ready."

"Good, because if you don't hurry up we're going to be late."

"I thought it was tradition for the bride to be late."

Kate's phone beeped. It was a text from Charlie. *Where r u? I'm going out of my mind here*

She typed a quick reply. *We're just coming – patience is a virtue*

Don't give me that crap darlin now hurry the fuck up so we can get this thing over with

Kate grinned; Charlie had a way with words that never failed to make her smile. She couldn't wait to see him. They'd been apart for two days whilst she had spent girlie time with Clare and their mum indulging in pre-wedding rituals such as bottomless Prosecco lunches and spa treatments. The knock at the door made Kate jump.

"That'll be your dad and the bridesmaids," said

Rose as she strode across the room. She adjusted her incredibly large fuchsia coloured hat in the mirror on the way; it was a statement piece she'd told them when she'd brought it. Kate hadn't dared to comment that the huge brim dwarfed her tiny face and she looked absolutely ridiculous.

John Newman entered the room and held out his arms to his two daughters. "You both look beautiful."

"Thanks dad," they echoed in unison. He looked incredibly dapper himself; at fifty-eight he was still a handsome man. His hair was grey but he pulled it off in a sexy Richard Gere kind of way. His grey morning suit made him look even more distinguished and the obvious pride he felt for his girls was reflected in his smile.

"Right you two, let's get this show on the road. We don't want to give the poor man an excuse to change his mind."

Kate peered into the crowded room. The chattering was purposely low and muffled but the anticipation was building. She could feel waves of electricity radiating through the guests as they waited patiently for their bride. There was only one person Kate wanted to see however and he was standing beside Jason at the front of the room engaged in an in-depth conversation with the Registrar. He looked as gorgeous as she'd expected him to in his grey morning suit and her heart fluttered in her chest. After spending forty-eight hours without him she couldn't wait to be by his side again.

Clare looked radiant, not a nervous bone in her body. Kate wished she felt as calm; it was a big day and she didn't want to mess it up. Suddenly the pre-recorded wedding march boomed through the stereo system and resonated around the room, causing a shiver to run down her spine. Both girls looked at each other and smiled; this is it thought Kate.

It's time.

Holding the bouquet of red roses in front of her, Kate put one foot in front of the other and began a deliberately slow walk down the aisle. Charlie observed her every step and had a smile on his face that beamed from ear to ear. She actually went weak at the knees when he winked at her. She moved into position and turned to watch Clare, the blushing bride, glide down the aisle with their dad. Kate had never felt so proud. Clare looked stunning, her white gown sparkling as it caught the light but it was her smile that lit up the room. Jason was looking at his future wife with a smug look on his face, egged on by an elbow from Charlie, his Best Man. Clare handed Kate her bouquet when she reached the front and as the Registrar began the ceremony, she took Jason's hand and smiled.

Kate let out a breath. Everything was going to be okay..

The guests spilled out of the ceremony room into the function room next door. It was presented in a typical wedding style; round tables that seated ten with satin bows adorning the backs of the chairs, champagne glasses twinkling on the tables and the traditional top table overlooking it all. It was romantic and Kate was starry-eyed as she gazed at it. The atmosphere was jolly and there were loud voices and laughter everywhere. The bar that ran along the back wall was already knee deep in wedding guests, all looking smart and stylish in their three-piece suits and pretty dresses. Kate spied Charlie amongst the other groomsmen, centre of attention as always, with a glass in his hand, roaring with laughter. She couldn't wait to hear his Best Man speech; she somehow knew that Jason wasn't going to be disappointed. Their eyes met and he excused himself and made his way over to her.

"You look gorgeous darlin'," he said, running his eyes over her. The long dusky pink gown hit her curves in all the right places and she had to admit, she did feel pretty gorgeous. He pulled her towards him and they kissed. They'd just spent the longest time apart in almost seven months and she couldn't wait to get her hands on him. Charlie took a glass of champagne from the tray of a passing waitress and handed it to her.

"Cheers," she said, taking a sip.

"Don't drink too much," he warned. "I've got plans for you later."

"I hope they include a hot bath and a foot massage, my feet are killing me."

Charlie ran his hand over her huge swollen belly and grinned. "Maybe, maybe not."

By Kate's calculations she'd fallen pregnant on board the Lady Catherine but it was hard to say for sure. "I'm serious," she said as she placed her hand over his. "You've got no idea what having your baby is doing to my body."

"You've got no idea what *I'm* gonna do to your body," he whispered into her ear. "Let's nip to our room, I'll make it quick. Nobody will even know we're gone."

She rolled her eyes, feigning surprise. "And who said romance is dead?"

"I can't help it if I find my pregnant wife really fucking hot."

It had been three months since their own wedding, a very small affair that had taken place in a Registry Office with only Kate's family present and Phil and Maria who had flown over from Spain. Not a grand wedding on this scale, but it had been perfect just the same. He kissed her again and slipped his tongue into her mouth.

"Ten minutes you say?"

He arched an eyebrow. "Fifteen tops."

She grabbed hold of his hand. "You've got five."

"That'll do darlin."

He ushered her towards the elevator, almost as if he was worried she was going to change her mind.

Not there was any chance of that happening.

Now that she had him, she was never going to let him go.

The End

ACKNOWLEDGEMENT

This story has been a long time coming. I first began writing it in 2008 and it's true what they say - love never dies. So basically, I've been in love with Charlie for 13 years! I have to give credit where its due so thank you to my husband Andy for putting up with me whilst I was daydreaming.

There are lots of people I'd like to mention in the writing of this story but I'll make it short:

My sisters and my mum for their utter belief in me.

Nicky; long time no see but I can still remember our nights together over a decade ago proof reading and rearranging sentences.

And finally to my friends and family - your encouragement has made this happen.

ABOUT THE AUTHOR

Angie Bayliss

The Price of Passion is her debut novel.

Angie lives in Portsmouth with her husband and two grown-up children and works full-time at her local primary school.

BOOKS BY THIS AUTHOR

The Trouble With Izzy

Coming soon

Printed in Great Britain
by Amazon